WHISPERS OF INNOCENCE

a novel

NATASHA SIMMONS

Whispers of Innocence
Red Adept Publishing, LLC
104 Bugenfield Court
Garner, NC 27529
https://RedAdeptPublishing.com/

Cover Art by Streetlight Graphics[1]

---

1. http://StreetlightGraphics.com

In memory of Tyler. Love you always.

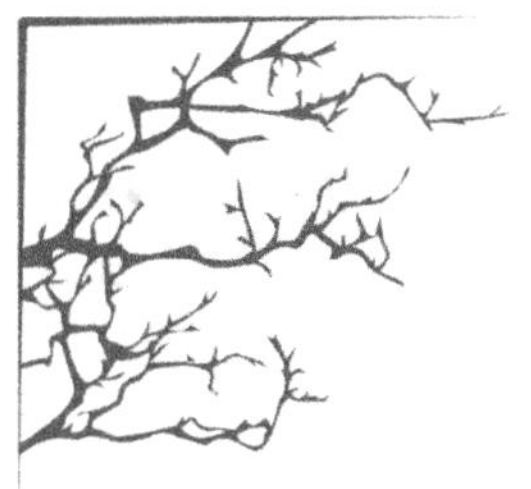

Part I
Madeline

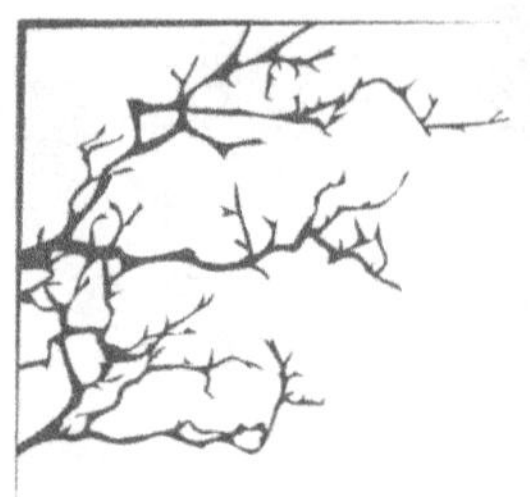

Chapter 1

She was quiet. For the first time since we'd brought her home, Abigail had gone more than an hour into the night without battering the walls with incessant cries. I leaned against the doorway and closed my eyes, almost crying with relief. It had been the best night's sleep, and it wasn't even morning yet. She wasn't even screaming yet. I opened my eyes.

The moon reached through the window to baptize my little night owl with light. I'd heard artsy folks like to stay up all sorts of odd hours. Maybe we were raising the next great musician, painter, poet. I was just thankful for the little victories, the quiet assurances that I could make it through this. Perhaps one day I would miss these moments, but right then I looked forward to escaping the trying times. *Things had to get better, right?*

Pink shadows followed me across the room. I tiptoed so carefully. I couldn't wake her, but I needed that moment to remember why the hardship was worth it. I took a moment to appreciate my angel, so peaceful like that. Her baby blues were closed. I kissed the top of her head, touched the fine blond hairs starting to cover it, breathed in that baby scent. Paused.

Something was wrong. I listened for that noise—so faint, I could simply be missing it. Except, when I put my hand over her little chest, it didn't move. And she was so quiet.

"Brian!" I screamed. Tears blurred her perfection, too perfect. "Oh my god, Brian!" My words disintegrated into sobs. Maybe it was all a dream, a nightmare. I didn't feel fully awake. Footsteps sounded too clear, too real.

"What's wrong?" he asked as I collapsed in his arms.

"It's Abigail," I sobbed.

He held me close with one arm as he looked into the crib. He let me fall to the floor with a hard thud as he reached for our daughter and started doing the special baby CPR we'd learned in parenting class.

"Call 911!" Brian demanded.

I couldn't move.

"Dammit, Maddy! Abigail isn't breathing! You need to call 911!"

His sharp words stitched me together just enough to get me off the floor. No time to panic. Our baby needed us. I couldn't breathe as I tripped over my feet in a desperate race to the phone.

"It's too late. Too late." The words clung to my skin as I stumbled into our bedroom. I tried to stay with it long enough to dial those three numbers. My hands shook so badly it took me four tries to dial the numbers in the proper order.

"911. What's your emergency?"

The voice on the phone was so distant from my reality that I almost hung up. They couldn't help. Only Brian and I were there now. We were the only ones wrapped up in the nightmare, the only people who could do anything in that space.

"My baby's not breathing!"

The world blurred.

"Where are you located?"

An alternate reality, in a place where children died and I could do nothing to save them. A nightmare. A horror movie.

"Ma'am? I need your address so we can help your baby."

Darkness drowned me. Guilt, a noose around my throat. It was my fault. Abigail was dead. If only I were a better mother. I tried and tried and couldn't get another breath. The phone fell as I collapsed onto the bed.

"Madeline!" Brian bellowed, bringing the world back into focus, fear fueling my clarity. "Call 911! What the fuck are you doing?"

"I called them." The words were too small for him to hear, so I forced myself up. I just wanted to sleep until it was all over—restart that whole night, wake up to a better reality. I walked to the nursery like it was haunted. Now, it would be haunted. "I called them."

"And?" His eyes raged red as he looked up from our daughter, laid on the bedroom floor.

Her eyes remained unopened, chest still not moving.

"And..." I dropped the phone. *Stupid.* I didn't hear their reply, any instructions. "And they said they'd be here as quickly as they can. In the meantime, just continue with the CPR."

"It's not working!" His attention fell back to Abigail. He pumped her tiny chest with two fingers, breathed into her mouth. Again. And again.

And what if they aren't coming? It was too late to save Abigail. Brian would be furious regardless. I never confirmed they were coming. *What if they don't know where we live?* Maybe he would finally kill me. Then I wouldn't have to face it all, wouldn't have to accept that my angel...

Sirens screeched onto our street, echoing the ones going off in my brain.

"Go wave them down," Brian commanded, "so they don't get the wrong house!"

I'd heard horror stories about that happening before. I ran down the stairs, finally in control of something. That was a disaster I could prevent. If I could prevent that—and I could—maybe I could save Abigail.

Hope pushed me through the front door. Neighbors peered out of their homes that kept them safe from our nightmare. *Don't they know they might confuse the ambulance? Selfish.*

To stand out among them, I moved to the very edge of the street and waved my arms like a madwoman, desperate to get their attention. Maybe they could save her. Maybe it wasn't too late, my redemption not quite out of reach.

The sirens grew closer, louder. I drew them toward me. Lights splashed through the darkness and reassured me I wasn't alone. The situation was out of my hands. Someone more capable would take care of it. I wasn't a good enough mother to save Abigail, but maybe someone else could. They would. They had to.

"She's upstairs!" I screamed to any heroes who would listen. "My baby! She stopped breathing! She's upstairs!"

They leaped out of the ambulance and ran past me like I wasn't there. I wished I weren't. Now that they had arrived, my last ounce of strength seeped into the grass. My bruised knees cried out as they hit the ground. I sobbed as if I could cry all the pain out and bring my baby back, a trade I desperately wanted to make.

A tall man in uniform walked up to me like he had full control over the situation, like it was just another day on the job. A ginger—he probably had no soul. I glared through my tears as he approached.

"Are you okay, ma'am?" A young lady stepped past the male officer, blanket in hand. She, too, wore a uniform with her blond hair pulled back, ready for business. Except her eyes held kindness.

"How could I be?" I asked.

She knelt on the ground next to me, wrapped the blanket around me, and helped me up.

A gurney surrounded by nameless faces burst out of my house. I sensed Abigail in the middle of the mess, so young, too little.

"My baby," I sobbed. "She stopped breathing."

"These medics will do everything they can to help her," the officer assured me. "It can be difficult riding in the ambulance with them, so would you like me to—"

"I'm going with her!"

The officer steadied me as I joined Brian in the back of the ambulance. So much noise. So much white. So much work to be done, so we were pushed to the side to make way for the professionals holding Abigail's life in their hands. The ambulance barreled down the street, never quick enough.

Everything needed to slow down. Brian and I were being shoved into a terrible space of parenting, and we weren't prepared for it. We couldn't even comfort our baby, though we cared more about her than those people ever could. She wouldn't be aware of our presence anyway.

And if she is? If she saw how much we failed her? "My baby," I sobbed.

Brian held me as if by keeping me together, he could keep our family from being torn apart.

"Abigail. She's gone, she's gone, she's—"

"Don't say that."

I was so used to listening to him that I stopped. The pain didn't stop, the guilt. If only I were a better mother. If only. If only. Maybe then they could save her.

Everything moved so quickly as the world came to an end. The ambulance stopped after two seconds—after an eternity. Brian and I ran after the medics, but we were stopped outside the swinging doors, a portal to a world where Abigail survived. Those cruel keepers wouldn't let us in.

"We're her parents!" Brian protested.

Will he actually punch the nurse? He usually kept that side locked behind closed doors.

"We need to be with our daughter!" he said.

"The doctor needs to do anything he can to save her," the nurse explained. Calmly. Like she had done it all before. Impossible. No one else could've experienced exactly what we were going through right then. "He needs space. He needs room to focus, and he'll be better able to do that without outside distractions. Don't you want what's best for your daughter?"

"What if she dies?" Brian whispered, as if saying the words too loud would make them come true. "She must be so frightened already, without us there. What if she dies and we aren't there with her?"

If she died, then it was already too late. She was already dead. That was what the nurse couldn't say. And if Abigail was to have her best chance, the doctor couldn't be tripping over her panicking parents. I wanted to be with her, but I understood. I hoped Brian would understand, hoped his anger wouldn't put our daughter's life in danger.

"I promise we'll do everything we can for her," she assured us. "To give her the best shot, the doctor's attention needs to be fully focused on her. If you'll just wait over here—"

"I don't want to wait!" The mask slipped so the whole room could see a glimpse of the anger I lived with, the danger. "I don't want to just sit and wait for my daughter to die!"

Anger dissolved in a hurricane of tears as we were escorted to the waiting room, whitewashed in devastation. We confined all our grief and worry to our bruise-colored plastic chairs, under the heat of everyone's stares. They were all grateful they weren't us. I desperately wanted to be them. I needed to escape my tragedy, to take back everything, rewind to the beginning of the night, and find a new future. I knew I could do better if I just had a second chance.

All I could really do was cry. And wait. Cry. And wait.

Each second was prolonged agony. The unknown, the known, tore through me. Until finally a doctor came out. *The doctor who saved our daughter?* I couldn't face him, didn't want to know if he was a hero, because that might mean finding out he wasn't.

Brian had always been braver than I was. He stopped pacing and turned to the doctor, suspicious of him, afraid—as if he'd killed our daughter. "Is she okay?" Desperate eyes begged her to be okay.

I begged her to be okay. She had to be. This couldn't be happening. I joined him slowly. We had been fighting so much lately, but in that moment, we presented a united front.

"Our daughter? Abigail? Do you know about her? Is she... is she okay?"

The doctor's expression was replaced by sorrow, regret, helplessness. I wanted to walk away before he could speak, to spend a little more time unknowing, still warmed by a bit of hope. I knew his words would change our lives forever.

"I'm sorry," he said. And he should be because he was supposed to save her. "We did everything we could, but she was gone before she reached the hospital. Abigail died tonight."

My heart shattered, and I bled to death on the hospital floor.

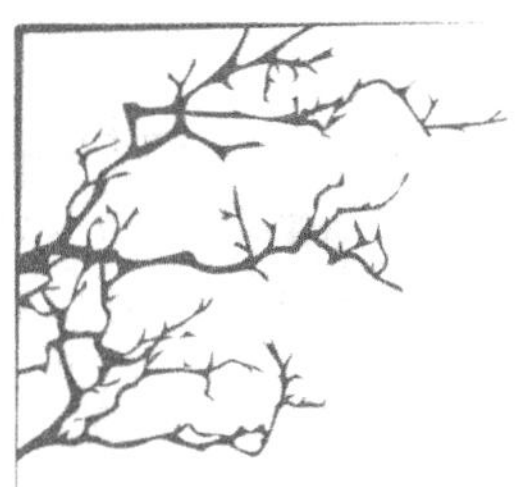

Chapter 2

Brian's sister, Allison, and her wife, Cassandra, waited patiently as we clung to our daughter, holding her for the last time. We rocked her, ignoring how cold her body was, how still, how rigid she was getting.

I never wanted to leave her. *How could life go on without her?* No life existed beyond that horrible moment anyway.

I held her and held her. And wept and held her. I leaned into Brian just to have someone. He was the only person who could understand. Pain brought us together, knitted a space for us to exist with each other in a way we hadn't in a very long time. Just the three of us. Just Brian, Abigail, and me. Until hours went by. Seconds.

Allison and Cassandra brought us home with a lock of Abigail's hair, a footprint, a handprint, a picture of what once was. The life we loved, created, and were forced to leave behind. They brought us home without our daughter.

"Can we do anything for you?" Allison asked as we walked into our empty, lifeless house.

The sun left dirty streaks across our floor as it rose. The moon didn't want to see what lay before us. It couldn't bear to say goodbye to my daughter of the night.

"We'll make you breakfast, tea. Anything I—"

"Thank you for all you've done, Alli." Brian touched his sister's shoulder.

They looked so much alike, dark-brown hair, tall, ice eyes, though hers were melted into droplets. I forgave her because she was always so kind.

"You, too, Cassandra."

Cassandra helped offset the uncanny resemblance with her black hair, petite physique, and green eyes that were the plant Allison watered. Together, they tried to nurture us. They didn't understand that nothing could help. Nothing could grow here. Nothing could live here ever again.

"You've been amazing," Brian said. "But I think what we need most right now is a little time to ourselves. To try to process everything."

"Of course," Allison said. "Can I call you this evening? I just want to make sure you're both doing okay."

We would never be doing okay. Never again. We would be forced to say it eventually, but it would never be true. Brian agreed and walked them out. I watched the door, on guard for any intruders until he came back.

We stared at each other, lost. *What do we do now? What is one supposed to do after losing their child? I thought I was unprepared for motherhood, but this... this is something else entirely. How does life go on after something so horrible demolishes everything? Why was life still going on? How could I let this happen again?*

"Madeline," Brian said formally, as if we were meeting for the first time, seeing each other for the first time. He sighed as his hands fell to his sides. "Why don't you get some rest? I'll bring you some tea. Maybe breakfast?"

I wasn't hungry. I would never be hungry again. But his absence would give me some much-needed peace—time to process, mourn by myself—so I nodded, a motion that sucked up all my energy. I couldn't make the trek up the stairs, where her empty room waited next to our room, which held its own share of bad memories.

The living room was closer, so I shuffled to it. I covered my eyes—a vampire threatened by the morning light. Everything was pristine. White carpet remained unmarked with crumbs, though

Abigail had tried her best to ruin it. Pictures of the perfect family hung on light-blue walls, poses that took us hours to perfect. Shiny black surfaces without fingerprints alongside leather furniture made living with a child bearable.

And her little rocker in the middle of the room. I had been too tired last night to take care of it. I always took care of it. She had left me too exhausted to keep up with everything like I used to, and it was only getting worse by the day. I looked away and made my way across the room, careful not to touch it. Dark curtains were my heroes.

I only turned back once it was safe to do so. With shadows settled across the room and if I squinted just right, the rocker could be anything. And maybe we hadn't had a baby yet. Maybe I hadn't given birth to a child, just for the world to steal her.

Or maybe we still had our child—sleeping upstairs, as she was far more prone to do during the day. Maybe I was just exhausted after a long night of staying up with her. I sank onto the couch and grabbed the blanket my mother had made for me. I couldn't bear to be around her, but once upon a time, it had made me think she loved me. Even though I knew better, wrapping myself up in it gave me the comfort I needed.

I closed my eyes. Maybe I had nothing to feel guilty for. Maybe I was the perfect mother, the perfect wife with a perfect husband. I dove into my dream world until the sweet scent of tea and honey coaxed me out of it, sizzling, salty bacon in the background. I opened my eyes.

Brian set a steaming mug on the coffee table, no coaster under it. I would have to clean that once he left. If I did so in front of him, he would think me ungrateful.

"I hope it's how you like it." He put his hands in his pockets like he was a kid again, unsure, clinging to something to do because he didn't know how else he was supposed to deal with it.

I sipped the tea. It was a little too sweet, especially for a morning like that, but I liked being taken care of because I didn't know how else I was supposed to deal with our situation.

"It's perfect. Thank you."

"I'm cooking breakfast. You're probably not hungry. I don't even know if I can eat. But I don't know what else to do." He looked at me, his muscles tense. His dark hair fell over his forehead, just a little messy like when we first met. His everything begged me to be hungry, to guide him through by leaning on him.

"I understand." I was the only other person who could possibly understand. "It'll be good for us to eat something."

He nodded, relieved. "That's what I thought. It'll be good to eat something. I..." He looked over at the kitchen—an open concept house, no place to hide secrets. "I should get back to cooking. Are you... will you be...?"

Okay? He knew I wasn't okay. He was just as not okay as I was.

Speaking became difficult when all the right things to say sounded wrong, the polite things, naive. No one really taught people what to say to someone during times of such intense grief. Or at least, no one taught the smart things to say, the helpful things. Maybe because no one really knew.

"Can I get you anything?" He needed to be useful when everything went wrong.

I needed to be cared for. The perfect fit. Maybe that was the core of what held us together when everything else was falling apart. "No, thank you."

He nodded then returned to the kitchen. If we didn't see each other, didn't talk to each other, we could pretend that nothing bad had happened. We could hold off facing it until maybe we could learn how. *How do you deal with losing a child?* I'd been on the earth for twenty-eight years, and I still didn't have the answers. Perhaps I never would.

I closed my eyes and tried not to think about it, but Brian's presence had broken the veil. I wouldn't have time to reconstruct it before breakfast, so I drank my tea. I stayed alive by the warmth of my mug, stayed alive by not thinking about Abigail.

My fault. If only I were a better mother. If only. If only.

Brian set a plate in front of me: toast, bacon, and chocolate chip pancakes with maple syrup dripping over them. A bit of syrup oozed toward the edge of the plate. Syrup would probably be on the bottom of it, too—grease, dough, getting on the coffee table.

We never ate in the living room. Well, Brian ate snacks in there sometimes. He claimed it was a space for living, so we should be able to enjoy it. But I'd broken that habit in him a while ago. Mostly. Or so I'd thought. *Would it be inappropriate to bring it up now? Is he being obnoxious by testing the boundaries?*

It didn't even seem to cross his mind as he sat on the other side of the couch. He usually sat on his chair. It was like he wanted to be close to me but not too close. Unsure, he watched me as he sipped his coffee.

My stomach was so twisted. Surely, I would throw up anything I ate. The pancakes mocked me. A fun food Abigail would never eat. The thought of trying to choke down anything was daunting. Not as awful as the prospect of talking to my husband though.

He looked at me, waiting to see if that was what we should be doing. *Should I scold him for serving breakfast in the living room?*

I tasted the pancakes and hated myself because, not only did I not throw them up, but my stomach actually demanded more. I was starving. I shouldn't be hungry, not with Abigail gone. The grief shouldn't have left any room to eat, or I must not be grieving enough.

Brian looked just as guilty as he took his first bite. We'd gone through so much, used up all our energy. *But could we really eat? Ever sleep? People weren't supposed to be able to do those things when they lost a child, were they?*

Yet it was easier to tiptoe around things, to eat instead of talk. So, I tried to ignore the guilt. I ate slowly, savored the quiet moment.

Halfway through my plate, it became difficult to swallow. A lump in my throat reminded me that my daughter wasn't upstairs sleeping. That she was—I stopped. Silent tears did their best not to interrupt Brian's breakfast. My baby was gone. Dead. And we would have to learn how to live without her. The last seven months had been all about her.

Brian stopped and looked at me. Now he had a real job. I needed his help. He put his plate down, wrapped his arms around me, and pulled me close. Lying next to him like that destroyed all my defenses. The well that held the blood from my ruined heart broke, splashed over the couch. I broke for him—broke for us. But I couldn't cry enough to drown out that incredible pain.

Eventually, the tears ran out, my energy depleted. There was nothing left of me. My eyes fluttered. Plates strewn with food lay on the coffee table along with mugs that needed to be taken care of, dishes to clean—and a house. A home without a baby.

I closed my eyes and fell asleep. I hoped that when I woke up, everything would be back to how it should be.

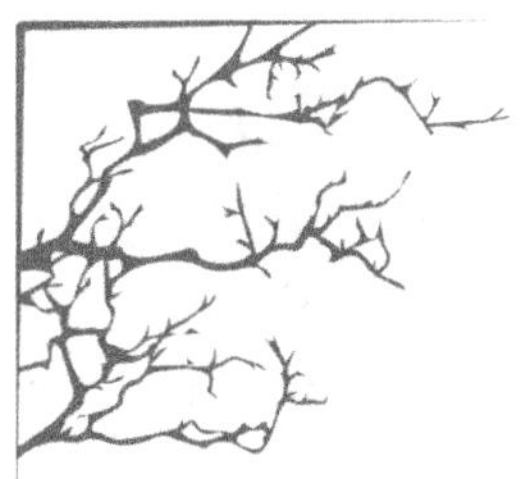

Chapter 3

I leaned over the crib and tucked her favorite pink blanket around her. She was quiet. She had been for months. She started sleeping through the night pretty quickly and never fussed too much. Everyone always asked how I got so lucky. I still didn't have an answer.

An angel, she was so pretty, her gray eyes warming to brown. Born with a full head of hair, her mocha locks began to curl just like mine. For that, I could forgive her for not having blond hair like me. She would have my eyes, my face shape, my everything.

Except, she was so still, too still. I leaned down, searching for a noise so faint that the whispering stars could overpower it. I listened, but there was nothing to hear. Her heart had stopped beating.

"Abigail!" I cried out, waking myself.

Brian stirred then sat up on the couch, dazed. For a moment he enjoyed the bliss of not remembering as it all hit me. "What's...?" He stopped, remembered.

Our baby. A lock of hair. A handprint. A footprint. A million pictures. That was all we had left of her. Really nothing at all.

He looked at me as if waiting for me to cry so he could save me—a distraction from his pain, which I would pay the true price for. I was surprised I didn't cry. I was too thirsty, parched really. I looked at the time. I'd been sleeping for two hours. I guessed that was all I needed to gain some self-control.

"I'm going to take a shower," I said. Like I might be able to wash the memory off. Mostly, I wanted to avoid this, avoid him.

"Okay."

We untangled ourselves from each other, awkwardly. Because it was—so strange and awkward. It was all new, and instead of having time to get used to it, like we had for all our previous life changes, it was sudden, and no one had taught us how to deal with something like it. We had become strangers living in the same home, thrown into a situation we had no skills for, no preparation.

I escaped into the warm water and steamed up the bathroom, attempting to purge the pain from my pores. Swirls of soapy bubbles comforted me as I sobbed at the bottom of the bathtub. It was better to cry there, alone, safe. I could be honest about my grief there. I could make headway in the battle I would be fighting for the rest of my life.

Once I cried as much as I needed to, I stood. I was reborn under the water, transformed by heat. A mother without a child—my new role.

My warm robe welcomed me back into the life I was still trying to make sense of. I brushed through the tangles in my hair, brushed my teeth. I thought about putting on makeup, but I couldn't quite make it that far. I got dressed in pajamas. It was a start.

A knock at the door drew me back downstairs. The sizzle of the pan answered it. Brian didn't. Somewhere in the kitchen, the phone rang. After two chimes, it shattered and died.

The knocking stopped. Pieces of our home phone colored our kitchen floor black. Brian looked up from the stove. *Cooking lunch? Dinner?* I couldn't keep track anymore.

"That was the third person who's come over since we woke up." He shook his head. "Like ten phone calls. I shut off the cell phones, so they resorted to the house phone. I didn't think you'd want guests. I don't."

"Me neither," I admitted, grateful for his commitment to being my buffer from the rest of the world. "I'm not quite ready for that."

"I won't ever be." He closed his eyes.

Is he going to break? Would I care if he did?

He opened them. "We should probably talk. About everything."

"First lunch."

"Dinner," he corrected me. "First dinner."

First dinner. Then the impossible conversation.

As I set the table, I tried to figure out what to say. To somehow prepare myself for the next steps. *Should we talk about our feelings? About what happened? What we're to do now? The funeral? How we'll deal with worried family members, friends?* We couldn't ignore their calls forever.

Unless we just left, started over somewhere new. *Would Brian be okay with that? Do we have any other choice? Could I leave him behind if he won't go? Could I just... leave him behind?* The thought was a burst of hope almost bright enough to melt some of the pain. I looked up. He didn't seem to notice the new glow. I couldn't leave him. I needed him. For the time being. *But later...*

I sat at the table while Brian served the food. Our old routine had disappeared since we'd brought Abigail home. Quiet, uninterrupted dinners were rare, granted only when Allison and Cassandra took the baby for the night. The silence was unsettling. The routine was all wrong.

Brian's chewing grated on my nerves, how he gulped his drink an offense to my senses. And I didn't want to talk about it, but I couldn't go on like that. Despite him saying that we must, my husband seemed quite reluctant to venture a single word.

"We're supposed to call Allison tonight," I said.

Brian chewed his bread, followed it with wine.

"She'll be worried if we don't."

"What happened last night?" He wouldn't meet my eyes.

"What do you mean?" My fingers clenched around my knife. I put it down, steak forgotten. *Is he accusing me?*

"You know what I mean." He looked up, his red eyes streaked with pain, maybe fury. "You're the one who found her. What happened?"

"I don't know. I woke up. I had to go to the bathroom. Abigail had been abnormally quiet all night, so I decided to check on her on my way back. Then... then I noticed..."

Brian took my hand. Tragedy brought out a kindness I hadn't received from him in so long. I still expected his touches to go back to painful at any time.

"I'm sorry," he said. "I'm just trying to make sense of this. I... I can't believe she's gone. It doesn't seem possible for her to just... die like that."

His mask cracked, revealing tears. My strong husband was brought to his knees, and I didn't know what to do, how to react. It wasn't my part to play.

"It's horrifying," I whispered. "But I guess sometimes these things just happen to babies. Sometimes they just—"

"She's seven months old." He paused. "Was seven months old. I thought we were well past that point where things could just happen. I thought we didn't have to worry about that anymore."

I thought so too. No one had ever given us an exact day, but secretly I'd worried—for the first few weeks at the very least—that something would happen. Somewhere along the way, I had thought we were out of the danger zone. Too soon.

A knock broke the silence that followed. I moved instinctively.

"Just ignore them," Brian said. "They'll go away eventually."

I ate a piece of steak and remembered I was starving. They knocked again, louder that time.

"Mr. Miller?" someone with a familiar voice called out, a woman.

I recognized her from somewhere but couldn't remember exactly.

"Madeline? It's Officer Moore. We'd really like to speak with you."

The woman from that night, last night. *Was it really only last night?* It had to be much longer ago. Brian and I exchanged a look. *What are they doing here? Will they tell us what to do next?*

"Just a moment." Brian stood.

I followed him and waited just behind him as he opened the door. The young officer stood there, warmth in her brown eyes, next to that soulless ginger.

"We're sorry to interrupt you," the ginger said. "But we were hoping to speak to you both."

"We're actually in the middle of dinner," Brian said.

I loved him more at that moment than I had in a long time. My hero.

"Can't it wait?" Brian asked.

"Actually, we've received news from—"

"It sure can," the woman cut off the ginger police officer then smiled at us. "After all you've been through, we'd be more than happy to give you some time. How about you stop by the station once you're finished eating?"

She could be playing the good cop to his bad cop. It could be a setup. I appreciated it regardless.

Brian's muscles lost some of their tension. "Thank you. We'll be there as soon as we finish."

We did leave as soon as we finished, but we took our time eating. We didn't discuss what had happened any further. We couldn't after that. It made us lose our nerve, and it had been nearly impossible to attempt the conversation to begin with.

We ate dinner slowly, talked a little bit. We didn't need to talk though. We knew the nightmare we were in, and we were content in the knowing, in just being around each other. We followed it up with dessert then took our time getting ready to go.

"What do you think they want to talk to us about?" Brian asked as we neared the station. "I mean, I'm sure it has to do with... you know. But why would the police want to talk to us about that?"

"I don't know." My mind ran wild with all the possibilities, but surely Brain was thinking the same things, so I didn't say them out loud. "They probably just want to talk to us about what comes next."

"Shouldn't someone from the hospital explain all that?"

"I don't know."

We parked in front of the police station. A few other cars were there, but it didn't look too intimidating. We didn't talk, didn't get out. *Why do they want us to come here?* Brian got out of the car. I followed him in silence.

"Thank you for coming in," the woman said as she approached us. "You remember my partner—"

"Grady," Brian interrupted.

I was a little impressed. I hadn't remembered any names from that night.

"Grady and Felicia. We talked to you both last night. What's this about?" Brian asked.

Felicia looked momentarily dismayed then pulled herself together. "We'd like to speak with you both about what happened yesterday," she explained. "Separately."

"Why?" Brian crossed his arms over his chest. "Anything I have to say to you can be said in front of my wife. We're in this together. Shouldn't we be discussing it together?"

He made me feel safer just by being there. A familiar face, and I didn't want him to leave. I needed his strength, even if he was as lost as I was.

"We will," she promised. "We'll go over the next steps with you, connect you with some helpful resources. We're not here to make things more difficult. But right now, we have some important questions that need answering. And it'd be best if we spoke with you privately. Then we'll all talk together."

And really, what could he say to that? He didn't have power there, no matter how he faked it. It was odd to see him like that.

Brian kissed my hand. "I guess it's best we get this over with." He took a step toward Grady.

"Actually, you'll be coming with me," Felicia said.

How could she abandon me like that? Take Brian away and cast me off to a stranger? She must have known I didn't like Grady. And I had thought she was nice, considerate. Yet I was in a police station, so I didn't bother to protest.

Voiceless, as always, I followed him into a small room with a desk, threadbare gray carpet, off-white walls, and a bright light that was far from inviting. *An interrogation room? Why would he lead me into an interrogation room? Am I being interrogated?*

"Please." Grady motioned to one of the seats like it was his living room. "Have a seat. Can I get you anything? A drink? Something to eat?"

He could get me out of there.

"We won't be here for long, will we?" I smiled as sweetly as I could. I wanted to scratch out his eyes, run back home with Brian, never come out of my house again.

"No." He smiled, too, just as fake as mine, as he sat. "I don't suppose we will be. I'd like to start off by saying how sorry I am for your loss."

It sounded a little less genuine coming from someone who was keeping me in an interrogation room.

"I can't imagine what it's like to lose a child and—"

"No." I wasn't in the habit of interrupting people, but this was torturous. "You can't."

He shifted in his seat as his cheeks reddened. He looked down at some papers in front of him. "I'm sorry," he repeated. "If we can do anything for you, please let us know. We really are here to help people." He waited. "I don't want to make this more difficult on you than it already is, but I do need to ask you a few questions."

A few questions. *Why?* People didn't normally get thrown into an interrogation room after a loved one's death. I never had before. *Are they suspicious? Why?*

"Mrs. Miller, I'd like you to tell me exactly what happened last night. In your own words. I want every single detail, even if it doesn't seem important."

And of course, there wasn't much to tell, not much to remember. Not a night I could ever forget. But with him staring at me like that, making little notes, it felt like everything I said was wrong. I questioned myself. *Am I explaining things right? Am I missing something? What exactly happened in that moment of time?*

He was quiet as I talked and for a few minutes after I was done speaking. A few eternities. *To make me sweat?* I wouldn't, not under his gaze. I'd faced much worse—a man who could actually hurt me. Then, the questions started.

"Did you get up at any time during the night prior to when you found Abigail unconscious? Were you concerned when she didn't cry throughout the night? Were these late nights starting to stress you out, causing feelings of anger, resentment? Is Abigail your only child? How is the relationship between you and your husband? Mrs. Miller, have you ever thought of harming your child?"

"What?" The questions had been grating on my nerves since he started firing them off, but that—that was too much.

"You must understand that I am required to ask these questions. I'm just trying to get an idea of what may have happened last night."

"You already know what happened," I hissed, trying to keep the tears at bay. I needed to gain control of the situation. Tears would ensure I never could. "I told you everything. We fell asleep. Sometime in the night, Abigail stopped breathing."

"But why did she stop breathing?" he pressed.

"I don't know! Shouldn't the doctors tell you that?"

"I want to hear it from you." He sat back in his chair with a smug look on his face. Very punchable. "What do you think happened to your daughter, Madeline? I suspect you know a lot more than you're sharing."

Fury and shock fought for control of my mind. I wanted to scream at him. *How dare he make such accusations?* I wanted to cry. *Could someone really think I killed my own daughter?* It was all a mess, so I held it together. I weighed my next words very carefully. They were my only defense, my only weapon.

"Do you know what it's like to feel a little human growing inside you?" I asked, leveling my gaze at him. "To know that everything you eat nourishes that tiny body? Everything you do now affects another life? Do you know what it's like to hold your child for the first time? To share that precious soul that was once yours alone to cherish?"

I scoffed as his cheeks turned red. That big, tall man didn't look so tough anymore.

"Of course you don't. If you did, you wouldn't be asking me these awful questions. You would know that I would've done anything to keep my daughter safe. Babies are so vulnerable, so fragile, precious. I did all I could, but sometimes even a mother's love isn't enough protection."

Lies! I could've done more, been better. I let a few tears escape to add emotion to my words, but I wouldn't let him see my guilt.

He tried to keep a mask of indifference, but it slipped, revealing a glimpse of the human behind it. "I'm just trying to do my job," he said, his cheeks turning red as he caved in on himself a little. "It's nothing personal."

"Nothing personal?" The metal chair creaked as I leaned toward him. I was small, trapped. Yet in that moment, I overpowered him. I was in control, and he got a taste of the way he had made me feel since he'd led me into that room. "Do you question all grieving mothers, Officer?"

He shrugged. "You had an insurance policy on the child. She was only seven months old."

I tripped over his findings. *How could they know that?* They must have really done some investigating. *Why?*

"We did everything we were supposed to when I got pregnant with Abigail. We went to parenting classes, decorated the nursery, babyproofed everything. When we took her home, we brought her to all the doctor's appointments, got health insurance, life insurance. It was just another thing on the list. We were diligent about checking all the boxes. Like I said, babies are fragile, and we can't afford the unexpected expense of a funeral right now."

"You seem to be pretty well-off financially, and the policy covers far more than a funeral." His nerve was coming back. An unsupervised smile wandered onto his face, as he seemed well aware of my struggle. "Most parents don't get out a two hundred thousand dollar life insurance policy on an infant."

They'd really gone through everything. Perhaps the amount was excessive, but we did everything in excess when it came to our first child. "Brian and I have a life insurance policy out on each other," I explained. "We each have five hundred thousand dollars, and though we know how important it is to be prepared, it's not something anyone really likes to think about. So, we just bought a policy that was about half of our own."

"Two hundred thousand dollars is a lot of money, no matter how you spin it. It's a pretty big motivator in my eyes."

"A motivator for what?" I demanded.

He shrugged.

"For murder? I did not murder my daughter!"

"Then who did?"

"What?" My head spun. *Why is this happening? People die of natural causes all the time.* "No one murdered her. Abigail was only seven months old. Don't these things just happen to babies sometimes?"

"Sometimes," he admitted. "But bruises around a child's neck don't just happen."

"Bruises? I didn't notice any bruises when I... when I found her." More tears escaped as I pictured her perfect skin colored with bruises, tainted. The moon would always protect my child of the night. There was no way.

"Sometimes they take a while to show," he explained.

"Oh."

I felt diffused, defeated. The tiny room was silent as the walls moved closer, attempting to hear all the juicy secrets. An inner war raged. *Should I share what I know?* Grady waited. *Does he know I harbor a secret?* Surely. *Would he believe me?* Certainly not. *Would anyone believe that our perfect life isn't quite so perfect?*

"It... it might've been Brian."

"Brian?" he asked, eyes narrowing. "Your husband?"

"Yes," I whispered. He would be so angry—furious. He would kill me, hopefully.

"What makes you think your husband killed your daughter?"

His tone told me everything. He really thought that I killed my baby. That I was trying to turn his attention to Brian just to take the heat off myself. He wouldn't believe me. It was a waste of time to even try to explain. That was why I never tried to explain.

I hesitated, debating. *Could I really share this now?* A horror that had been kept behind closed doors for so long. Our little secret. A decision. I pushed up the light-pink sleeves of my cardigan to reveal my own collection of bruises.

Grady cringed even as he leaned closer. Even though I hated him, I couldn't blame him for that. *We're all drawn in by horror, by tragedy.*

Drawn in and trapped. Perhaps that's why I always stayed. I could never find a way to escape.

"There's more," I confessed. "I know it was wrong to stay. It's just... I got pregnant, and I didn't think I could make it on my own. He was always so good with Abigail, the perfect father. I never imagined he'd harm our daughter."

"This changes things." Grady sat back in his chair, dumbfounded. "This changes things."

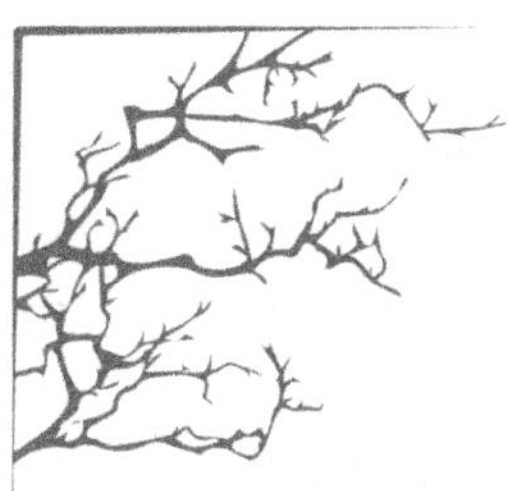

Chapter 4

If I had any doubt that Felicia was playing the good cop to Grady's bad cop, it was killed when she entered the room after I told Grady my secret. Perhaps Brian refused to budge. Perhaps that was why they turned their focus on me, just waiting for the perfect moment. Felicia and Grady thought they had their interrogation tactics all planned out. She wasn't expecting that though. Neither was I.

I still couldn't believe I'd actually said the words out loud, long after they had left my mouth. I'd kept the secret for so long. I was exposed, vulnerable without the darkness there to cover me, protect us.

What will happen to Brian now? I hated him for all he'd done to me, how much he'd hurt me physically, emotionally, mentally. I hated him for the loss of Abigail. *But I still loved him? Maybe.*

What will happen to me now? Will they believe me? Will Brian be out of my life for good? When will all this end?

"Grady, why don't you get us some tea?" Felicia sat across from me. "Maybe a snack?"

Grady nodded. He looked relieved to leave the room. Felicia touched my arm gently, so kind I almost forgot she was playing a part.

"I'd like to talk to you more about what happened," she said.

"I already told him everything I know." My voice wavered. With Grady gone, I didn't feel like I had to try so hard to keep it together. Felicia wasn't a bully. She could be trusted. Even though she'd left me before, she was there now. She cared.

"You told him what happened last night. I want to know more about what happened before then. I want to know what it was like living with Brian."

"I mean..." I looked down at my hands. After showing them the bruises, I needed to elaborate. I would have to explain everything. I wasn't ready for that, but I had no time to get ready. "Living with Brian has been... well, it's been a maze. I thought it was going to be a fun one at first. I thought I liked the challenge. I thought he'd always be there to guide me through it. But I realized it's like one of those they make you walk through when you go to haunted houses, only scarier. Some days are wonderful. He helps me around the house, supports us, brings me flowers, gifts, and special treats when I'm having a tough day. He plays..." I paused. "Played with Abigail, took care of her in the most loving way. It's a fairy tale, truly. Then, other days... other days we get into these awful fights that seem to spring out of nowhere and grow out of our control. I always tell myself not to feed into it, that if I can just keep my cool, it won't be so bad. But it's like he thrives off my anger, so he pushes me until I snap."

I paused as I flashed back to different fights, different times when I'd acted like the kind of person I had never wanted to become, different times when I'd looked at my husband and hadn't recognized the man in front of me.

"When I snap, he seems to think it gives him reason to escalate. It started with just yelling, but then things got more violent—a push at first. He grabbed my wrists one time, punched a hole in the wall, broke things. Then one day he... he..." The taste of iron and fear fluttered over my tongue. "One day he hit me. All boundaries crumbled after that, never to be rebuilt."

Screams echoed through my brain. Pain. Emotional. Mental. Physical. Our marriage had taken everything from me. Everything. *So, what will I have left after all this? Do I even exist beyond this?*

Perhaps that was why I never left. *Because something is better than nothing, right?* And I knew I would be nothing after. He stole my soul so he could live.

But since I'd let a little out, the rest was unstoppable. She made it so easy, just by listening. She threw in an empathetic statement now and then, but mostly just by being there she made me feel like it was okay to tell her my secrets, that somehow, everything would be okay if I trusted her to help me.

"Where do we go from here?" I asked once I told her everything. *She has to have the answers, right?* Our tea was long gone, the cheap cookies eaten. We'd been there for hours. *Can I finally go home? Is it finally over yet?*

"Well, we still need to gather more information," she explained. "My partner is talking with Brian right now, and I'll join him soon. We can press charges against your husband for abusing you, but we'll have to wait a little longer to charge him for Abigail's murder. We need to ensure we have a solid case against him, though it looks like that will happen in the near future.

"For now, you should get some rest. You've been through a lot. You deserve a break. We'll reach out soon to ask more questions and update you on any progress being made on the case. We'll file a restraining order against Brian for you tonight, to protect you until he's arrested. He'll be allowed to collect his things, but another officer will be there with him when he does.

"I'll provide you with my number along with other resources to help you out during this tough time. You can look into getting a lawyer for your husband if you'd like. He'll certainly need one. But I'd suggest getting a lawyer for yourself and filing for divorce as soon as possible to separate yourself from this mess as much as you can."

"Of course. I can't stay married to him now."

Can't. That sounded so final. It was always shouldn't before. *Now...?* Now it was finally over.

"That's a smart decision. In the meantime, surround yourself with family and friends. Recuperate. You have help now. You'll never have to see him again. Until the trial of course. Will you be willing to testify against him?"

"Definitely. Whatever you need."

"Good." She nodded. "We'll talk more about that later. Do you have any questions for me?"

"Um." It was kind of an awkward one. *But since I'm free to leave...* "Well, we came here in Brian's car. I don't have the keys..."

"Of course." She smiled. "I can bring you home if you'd like, or we can try to get those keys for you."

"If you can, I'd like to drive myself home." I needed time to myself. I didn't want to be at the police station any longer. I certainly didn't want to be driven home in a police car. *What would the neighbors think? What would everyone think once this was out there for the whole world to see?* There would be no hiding it.

My whole world was shifting. All I wanted was to get back home, to a familiar place. Except it wasn't familiar. Not anymore. My house had morphed by the time I returned. Eerie morning light twisted it into alternative dimensions. The kitchen was empty. Brian should've been in it getting ready for work. And I should've been helping him—or upstairs trying to get some rest. A blanket lay on the couch. I never left blankets lying on the couch like that, all sprawled out. A baby didn't cry from the nursery.

In the span of twenty-four hours, my whole family had been ripped away from me. And if I were being honest, I had dreamed of that day—over and over again as I'd flinched at Brian's screams, when Abigail wouldn't stop crying. I knew life would be so much better if I just had a moment alone, time to breathe.

Now I had all the time in the world. Those moments waited, strung out in front of me, daunting, empty, waiting for me to fill them. I didn't have the energy, didn't know what to do. I wished

Abigail were alive. *I wish Brian were still here?* I was so tired, but I couldn't sleep in the bed we shared, so I sank down on the couch. I hoped that when I woke, things would be a little easier, a little more familiar.

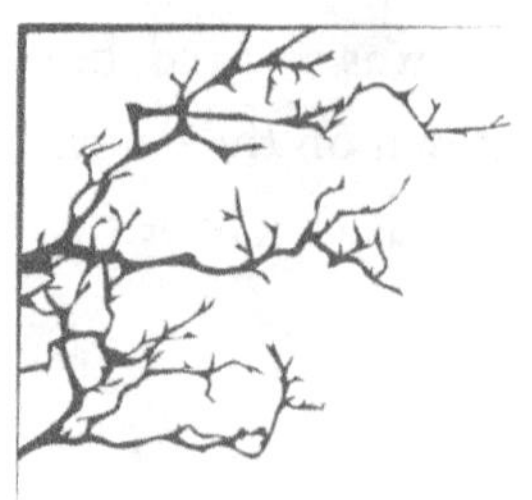

Chapter 5

I was certain that time. I tossed the pamphlets on the counter so I wouldn't have to look at them anymore—that vile information about the funeral I had spent my afternoon planning. For Abigail. For my own daughter. A child. A baby. I clung to a dangerous distraction as I went to the window and pulled back the curtains just a little.

There was that same black car, windows tinted just enough so I couldn't quite make out who was inside. I'd seen him outside the police station when I'd helped build a case against Brian. He'd been there when Brian had come to get his stuff, when I'd gone to the grocery store, when I'd picked out a dress for Abigail to wear—the last dress she would ever wear.

Someone was following me. It couldn't be Brian. He had been arrested earlier that day. *But who then? Someone connected to him? Has Brian, my original stalker, been replaced by another enemy for the time being? Will he kill me if Brian gets convicted? Will Brian kill me if he's let out on bail?*

A half-hearted wave distracted me. Allison walked up the driveway. She had stopped by five times in the last five days. That time, she was carrying an envelope and flowers in one hand, a mysterious bag in the other. *Does she know her brother was arrested for the murder of Abigail? For abusing me? Does she know that my words put him in jail?*

I'd avoided her because I didn't have the energy to face her, didn't ever want to. Brian was cruel, but Allison was always kind to me. She and Cassandra had become sisters to me even before Brian and I got married. They'd thrown my baby shower, and we often spent time together without Brian. Her anger would hurt more than his bruises. I didn't have a choice. I would be forced to face her rejection. I couldn't put it off forever.

The curtain fell, followed by a knock on the door. I took a deep breath and closed my eyes for a second. I could get through it. I'd lived through much worse. Once I dealt with it, I wouldn't have to talk to her ever again.

Still, I perspired as I walked to the door. I had put on makeup for the first time since before Abigail died, and it was about to be ruined. I braced myself for her awful words as I twisted the doorknob.

"Madeline." My name brought tears to her eyes. "I... I'm so sorry." Allison somehow balanced everything as she wrapped me in a hug, a touch of warmth I hadn't been granted since that interrogation.

I didn't realize how much I needed it until I was able to sink my body against someone else and feel how much she cared. It was nice to have someone there—different than last time. I let her go. I couldn't get all soft. That would only make it harder when she found out about Brian. Clearly, she didn't know yet.

"Can I come in?"

I shouldn't let her in. Then I would have to tell her inside, and that could get dangerous. She would be hysterical. I didn't want that in my house. *How would I deal with it?* I was already so fragile.

"Sure," I said. *What else am I supposed to say?*

She took off her shoes, well accustomed to our house rules, my rules.

"These are for you." She offered me those gifts she would soon regret giving me.

White roses, white lilies, and pink carnations, my favorite color, tied together with a gold ribbon. They reminded me of Abigail's nursery, not in a bad way though.

"And I brought food. We thought you might not feel like cooking, so Cassandra made lasagna, garlic bread, and your favorite, strawberry cheesecake, to go with it. She's working today, but she sends her love."

"Thank you."

I accepted the flowers, accepted the bitter knowledge that I would never spend time with Allison or Cassandra again, which was fine. I didn't care about them anyway. They were just my in-laws. I led her into the kitchen and looked around for a crystal vase as she put away the food. *When is a good time to tell her?*

"I just..." She turned to me. There it was. Maybe she did know. Maybe she was waiting to trap me like he always did. "I wanted you to know that I didn't know what was going on. I thought you and Brian were doing great. I never suspected..." She paused.

I hoped she wouldn't continue.

"That he was... that my brother was hurting you in any way. I would've gone to the police with you. I would've done anything to help. I'm so sorry you suffered through this for so long. After Cory, I hoped people would see that I'm not like my parents. I won't defend my family when they've done something indefensible. And I'm sorry you didn't see that. I'm sorry you felt like you couldn't come to me about this."

For a moment, I just looked at her. *She's sorry?* Brian was her brother. I helped put him behind bars. She wasn't angry. She was sorry, so sorry that tears rose in her eyes.

"It's okay." I took her hands, unsure after the unexpected response. I was prepared to defend myself, not to accept her level of understanding and empathy. "It's just, Brian turned on Cory, too, and you can see how that worked out. I guess I worried you would be like him. But I should've known better. I should've told someone before... before all of this could happen. I'm sorry for not doing something sooner."

We hugged, a real hug that time, without unspoken knowledge to separate us. We cried, mourned Abigail, mourned the Brian we thought we knew, and for the first time, I wasn't alone. Allison understood, at least as much as anyone else possibly could. Brian was her brother. She loved Abigail almost as much as we did. She probably felt trapped in a nightmare too.

"I'm sorry." She wiped away her tears. "I probably shouldn't even be here. I'm sure I'm the last person you want to see. I just wanted to—"

"I'm glad you're here." And to my surprise, I truly was. I was desperate to keep her there, for a little longer at least. I didn't want to go to that dark, lonely place with nothing but my thoughts to torture me. "Stay for a while? If you have time. I have wine."

"I never say no to wine." She laughed.

I had yet to turn to alcohol to get through my grief. I was afraid that if I started, I wouldn't stop. My guard might slip just a bit too far, bringing down my defenses. I needed them more than ever.

It felt safe with Allison there, though of course it was far more dangerous. So, we indulged in glass after glass paired with cheesecake and lasagna. We watched movies to forget about our troubles for a while and talked when we felt strong enough to face the things we could never truly accept.

I'd already told the police everything. I had nothing new to say about what exactly had happened that night. I didn't want to talk about it again, and Allison didn't ask for details. Instead, for the very first time, I expressed how I felt about it all. The confusion, sadness, and regret came pouring out with each glass. We laughed over memories, cried over things that were never to come. And late into the night, I shared my darkest secrets.

"I just feel so guilty," I confessed. "Abigail would be here if it weren't for me."

"Don't say that." Allison leaned against the back of the couch, blanket wrapped haphazardly around us. "It's not like you could watch her twenty-four seven. And you couldn't have known this would happen. No one could've. Despite his flaws, Brian always seemed like a great dad. He was until that moment—until he wasn't."

"I could've prevented it though. Things were so awful, and I thought I could make it through. I thought he would change. I thought we could have the perfect family I'd always dreamed of. But clearly that was the worst mistake. I could've left—should've left."

"You don't know if that would've helped. If Brian was already violent toward you... you just..." I could see on her face she didn't want to go there, and I wouldn't push her to. I heard the words she wouldn't say. *You don't know what would've happened. You did the best with the knowledge available to you. The only person responsible for Abigail's death is the person who killed her.*

She was right. Even if I left, horror was bound to follow. Brian and I would always hurt each other. It was an inevitable path set into motion the day we met. But I could've prevented Abigail's death.

"If I were a better mother," I whispered. I needed to stop. I was sharing too much, letting my guard down too far. I shouldn't be saying that. "She wouldn't be dead."

"You were a great mother, Madeline. Truly, the best. You did your best, and that's all a mother can ever do. You loved your daughter, and I saw just how much she loved you."

I nodded. She was right. I did what I had to do, as much as I could do. I was a good mother, far better than my own mother. I loved Abigail with all my heart. It was time to let go of the guilt. Another glass of wine eased the burden, and thankfully, I shut up about the feelings I shouldn't have shared. I fell asleep while I was lost in the world of a romantic comedy. Their issues were so silly, so much simpler than mine. Still, my problems only grew.

I WOKE THE NEXT MORNING with a headache, an angry stomach, and eyes that couldn't stand even a touch of light. But I wasn't alone. That was nice. Allison was already in the kitchen cooking breakfast. Despite all I'd eaten last night, I was starving.

"How'd you sleep?" she asked as I got off the couch.

I glanced at the window. It had become part of my morning routine. *Should I look with her here though? Would she notice?* She didn't look up from the stove, but it was easy to see from the kitchen into the living room. If she did look up, she would see. *Would that be so bad?* If I had a stalker, then it would be good if someone else knew—in case something happened to me. It might even be good to go to the police for protection. *Unless he's stalking me because...*

I tiptoed across the carpet and pushed back the curtains just a little. Relief. His car wasn't there. Maybe I didn't have a stalker at all. All the drama put me on edge, making me suspect things when everything was fine. Maybe my anxiety was creating false monsters. I needed to find a way to relax.

Except black caught my eye as I was about to look away. He wasn't in the spot he'd been in before. He was closer to the neighbors, hiding in the parking lot to the little park close enough for a child to walk to. That park had been one of our deciding factors when we'd chosen our home. We'd hoped our future children would love it. Ironic that it haunted me now. It didn't seem so safe anymore.

"Nice outside?" Allison's words shone on me like a bright light. Unbearable.

"Yeah." I turned around, put on a smile, and tucked away my concern. Maybe I should get a guard dog, protection that could never expose my secrets. "I thought it might be nice to get some fresh air," I lied. That was the last thing I wanted, but it sounded like a good excuse. "After being shut up since... you know. I don't think I'm quite ready for it yet though."

Guard dog. It would keep me company, but maintaining a clean house would be too difficult with a dog, and I didn't know how to take care of one.

"You'll never be ready," she said. "But it might be easier with the help of a friend. How about we go together?"

I didn't want to leave my house. Families would be walking about, children. Too many reminders. Too many strangers. Too many people I knew who would know what had happened. The world would move on, and I wasn't ready. People would stop and stare with sympathy, and that would be worst of all.

"I don't know. It's a bit too daunting right now. I have gone out a bit every now and then anyway—to the police station, to make arrangements for Abigail." When I said it like that, it could mean anything, arranging a playdate, a doctor's appointment, a babysitter.

"That makes you feel worse. You need to do something that convinces you this world is still good, that there are things worth living for, so you can get through this. Why don't we go out for coffee? That's a small start."

"But you're cooking breakfast right now."

"And it's just about ready." She flopped some waffles onto a plate. "We'll eat. You can get ready. I'll run home and get cleaned up myself, then we'll go out for coffee. Maybe we can grab lunch if we're hungry by then. Baby steps."

Baby. I tried not to cringe at the word. I did. Thankfully, Allison was too focused on breakfast to notice.

"I guess we can do that."

The sooner I got on with my new life, escaped my ghosts, the better off everything would be. *This is my chance, isn't it? To get away from Brian. Away from the abuse.* It was the escape I'd always wanted. Except even though Brian was the one in prison, Abigail had paid the true price. My innocent baby.

"Do you want some juice to go with breakfast?" Allison asked as a plate clinked onto the kitchen table.

"Yeah," I croaked. "That would be great, thank you."

In the shower that followed breakfast, I tried to wash away that night. The guilt. But a hint of blood lingered on my hands, thick, with an iron smell. *Is that what he's looking for? Can he see it from here?*

I tried not to look as I waited for Allison to return because I knew it would be bad for my mental health. I busied myself by cleaning the kitchen. And I tried not to look when we left the house. I didn't want to make Allison suspicious, didn't want her to see what I'd seen. Yet, I desperately wanted her to see what I was seeing so I would know I wasn't crazy.

I wasn't crazy. That car was still there. His eyes burned me from behind the safety of those windows, accusing me. He would expose all my secrets if I wasn't careful. *Is this being careful? Is going out for coffee so soon after Abigail's death appropriate? Will it look suspicious? What if he's a cop? Cops follow suspects in unmarked cars, don't they?* I was questioned for Abigail's murder. *What if they still suspect me? What if they already know everything?* They didn't. They couldn't. And all my anxiety would look suspicious. I needed to relax, find an outlet.

I'd always wanted a pet. Brian wouldn't let us have one. And once I had that sense of safety, perhaps I could return to the person I was before I had a child, before I met Brian. *What was I like before? What do I want now? What are my dreams? Do I actually want a pet?* I had money to last me until I figured it out. Or I could use it to get a head start on life, to make my own way, carve happiness out of the sadness.

My smile felt awful, a crack being forced upon my face, as I stepped into the passenger side of Allison's car. I shouldn't smile. My daughter was dead. My husband was in prison. I had so much to be unhappy about. But there was also a glimmer of hope, something I hadn't had in so long. It was a shard that dug into my skin and threatened to kill me. But if I was careful, I just might manage to craft something with it, something truly beautiful.

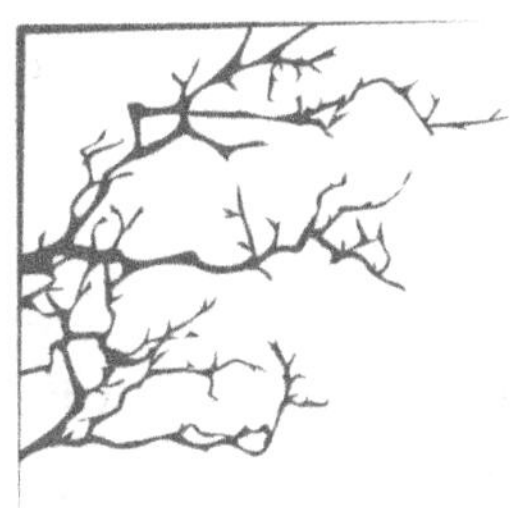

Chapter 6

"I want you to know I'm here to support you," Allison said. "No matter what."

Soft indie music paired with the clatter of people living turned out to be exactly what I needed to start feeling alive again. The warmth of the tea and the smell of honey reminded me I wasn't alone. Paintings moving with brilliant colors awoke my aspirations. Rich purples and blues soothed my nerves. And I tried not to think about bruises.

"I appreciate it." I meant it, even though I had been reluctant to leave my house. "I really do."

"Where do we go from here?" Allison asked. "What comes next?"

"Abigail's..." I couldn't say the words. They were wrong, cold, harsh. "The funeral is in two days. Brian will be allowed to go, with a police escort, of course, as he hasn't been found guilty of anything yet."

"Our parents plan on bailing him out as soon as they can."

"He was denied bail, though, wasn't he?"

I didn't go to the hearing. I couldn't face something like that, but Felicia kept me updated. I was rather surprised he wasn't allowed out. It still hadn't sunk in that he was trapped. I was waiting for him to come out of the shadows and punish me for all I'd done.

"He was, but my father hired the same lawyer that got Cory off." She shook her head. We all knew Cory was guilty. Brian detested him. "And they've been trying to find something, anything, to get bail granted to him. I'm not sure it'll work, but you know the ties my father has to the legal system. I'm disappointed but not surprised. They're convinced of his innocence."

Of course they were. Brian's mother was always kind to me, but his father didn't trust me. The only women he ever treated with kindness were his daughters, granddaughters, and occasionally, his wife. Either way, they would never believe Brian could do something like that. Their precious children could never do wrong.

"He's going to plead not guilty to the charges, of course," she continued. "But you probably already knew that. He's getting tons of people together to testify that Brian was a good dad. I just thought you should be aware—so you can prepare."

"Thank you. I want to do everything I can to get justice for Abigail." I paused. *Should I say this out loud? If I don't, how will I know if this is an okay thing to do?* It was better for Allison to think I was cruel than for anyone else to. "Though I also want to try to move on. Do you think that's okay?"

"It's essential," she assured me.

"I..." She would judge me for sure. "I have a life insurance policy on Abigail. I don't want to profit from her death..."

"But you need to do what's necessary. Brian was the sole breadwinner. I'm sure losing his financial support will be difficult. If you ever need help—"

"I won't." I wouldn't share the exact amount of the policy or all we had in savings. In the name of politeness, she wouldn't ask. "I plan to start working eventually, as soon as I can."

"That'll be good for you. Don't rush it though. Take some time to heal. Figure yourself out. You've changed so much since you met my brother. I should've seen it as a sign."

"You couldn't have known."

We kept it well hidden. Our secrets drew us together in a way. The darkness between us was something we protected, nurtured in the same way one would a child.

"But I do now, and I want to help in any way I can. I saw a flyer for a pottery class on the way in today. You were rather artsy before. We should go together. It's always fun to learn something new."

I wanted to fill my life with new things, rebuild it. I thought about moving again, far away, like I did last time. But I liked Allison. For the first time in my life, I had someone who truly supported me no matter what. "I'd like that. As long as it's after..." Perhaps I would need a distraction after the funeral. But in the days leading up to it, I needed time alone to cry, to mourn, to try to stay alive.

"Of course. It starts next week. In the meantime, what are you going to do to take care of yourself?"

Her question caught me off guard. I didn't really know. When people told me to heal and all that jazz, they didn't usually ask for solid solutions. No one actually held me accountable for that kind of thing. I figured most people didn't know how to heal themselves, which was why so many people in the world are broken, carefully stitched up so no one would see but never really better.

But as I talked to Allison, a rough path mapped out before me, back to a place I loved, a person I was proud of. College me, studying philosophy because I was young and didn't realize how silly that was. Eating healthy, meditating every day, cultivating a tiny garden in my dorm room, and working as a yoga instructor.

I had dropped all that when Brian came into my life. He'd opened my eyes to how useless philosophy was, taught me how working out in the gym was far more effective than yoga. He gave me a place to grow a bigger garden when we saved up enough money to put a down payment on a house with a backyard. I traded in meditating for cleaning a house. We had a baby just like he wanted. *Had I wanted a child?* I couldn't remember.

WHEN I GOT HOME, I was determined to find out. I was going to discover myself no matter how long it—*wait. Was that?* I stopped right before the kitchen met the living room, before black tile turned to carpet. Despite my grief, after that first day, I kept everything clean, as immaculate as it'd been before. Old habits died hard, and I'd yet to convince myself Brian wouldn't come back and get furious if he saw the slightest flaw. Break me all over again.

So, what's this gray dust in the rough shape of a shoe print? It wasn't there before. I never wore shoes in the house. I never let guests wear shoes in the house. *Did Allison take off her shoes before she came inside?* She knew the rules. Everyone did by then. Even Brian listened to that one. I wasn't one for confrontation, but that was one thing I was stern about. It was one thing I was willing to step out of my comfort zone for, knowing I would experience more discomfort if I didn't.

Yet our reunion had been so emotional. *Maybe she forgot? What did her shoes look like? Could that print be hers?* It looked like a man's shoe print. It looked too big to be Allison's. No. That was the anxiety talking. The shoe print was a whisper, too faint to really make out what kind of shoe it was or even if it was a shoe print. It could've been something else. But there it was. Gray dust against black tile. *Was someone in my house? That stalker? A police officer? Are they allowed to do that?*

I went straight to the window. One of my neighbors jogged by with her dog. *Kelly? Katie? Katarina.* Her dark hair was pulled back. Brian had checked out her perfect body more than a few times when he'd thought I wasn't looking. *Was she sad he got arrested?*

Perfect flowers reached toward the sun. A blue car drove by. An elderly couple held hands as they walked. He was gone, but he had tricked me before. Never again. Farther out, a young guy played football with an even younger girl. A truck was parked on the street, an exterminator. I looked again. And again. Again.

Stop. I was being obsessive. My therapist had warned me about that before Brian told me I should stop going. I stayed on my meds. He couldn't handle me without them. *Did I take them today?* Of course I did. I always did. *So why am I so on edge?*

It was that gray dust. I forced myself away from the window to sweep it up. And finally, once everything was in its place, I could breathe again. No intruder was in my house. It was just Allison. No stalker was trying to expose me. And if they were, that was okay. They wouldn't find anything. My secrets were safe. I was safe.

Back to my mission. Find peace. I went over the checklist in my head again and again, repeating the steps I would take to get back to that place I'd given up so easily. It wasn't a great start, but it was something.

MY FIRST STEP TOWARD my new life waited in the closet. His pressed shirts, waiting for him to come back, grabbed at me, monsters lurking in our closet. Suit jackets complained. *Didn't I know Brian had a job to do?* I was keeping him from it. What a terrible wife. Cruel woman.

It was torture. Brian had picked up the things he needed, but he'd left so much behind. I would have to get rid of them as soon as possible, all traces of him, purge him from my life.

But first... I grasped the rubbery feel of my mat. Finally. It lay underneath all the things that had replaced it, tucked by the shoes he didn't wear anymore but was too lazy to get rid of. I pulled it out. *Am I ready to unroll it?* Not yet. I tossed it on my bed.

It will wrinkle the blankets! My hands hovered. It was fine for the moment. The surprise delighted me. I could leave it there. A slight pull of fear reminded me I shouldn't, but I ignored it. I was able to.

I dug through my dresser. Tucked underneath soft cardigans, light dresses, and fancy underwear I didn't wear anymore were my workout clothes.

"You might feel better if you get back into working out." His voice reached me even from a prison cell. "Less stressed."

Brian had hinted for weeks that I should go back to the gym until he'd finally said it out loud. It wasn't about stress. He didn't care how I felt or he wouldn't always make me feel worse. He just hated that I'd yet to lose the baby weight. His comments hurt. They always did but not enough to outweigh my exhaustion.

I'd slept better over the last couple of days than I had in forever, so pulling on those yoga pants seemed less like a punishment, less like something I had to do to make Brian happy. I was doing it for me.

I didn't mind that my clothes hugged my body a little tighter than they once had. I was free. I didn't have to answer to anyone. No one was left to make me feel bad about myself, so maybe I could find some space to feel good.

My gym clothes were wrinkled after all that time. The blankets were wrinkled as I picked up my yoga mat. I'd always hated them anyway—gray, like a storm cloud, like smoke, like depression, made worse by that awful, dreary blue. He had insisted. It was dreadful.

I would change them soon enough. *Lilac maybe? Pink?* The possibilities were endless. So many choices. So much freedom.

I leaned into that as I rolled out my yoga mat, cool grass under my feet. Our backyard was shielded by a tall white fence, so even my stalker couldn't find me—or the police. Colorful flowers guarded it like knights.

So much wildlife grew in my yard I'd once loved, so much to care for, that we'd hired a gardener to keep up with it—well, really an aspiring gardener, a high school kid who did great work but was cheaper than a professional. I would feel guilty for letting him go, but it was necessary to bring my roots back to life, to remember why I'd wanted that backyard in the first place.

My muscles protested as I stretched in ways I hadn't in a long time. My arms had grown stronger from carrying Abigail. My legs were used to walking, pacing all night, a surefire way to calm her, a surefire way to drain my already exhausted body.

I wasn't used to stretching though. I used to be stronger, flexible. I could easily touch my toes and lower myself completely when I moved into a seated forward fold. And I'd advanced over time. I'd mastered bakasana, kapotasana, halasana. Well, not really mastered. With yoga, people were always growing.

But I was a seedling once more, returned to the ground but not buried. My knees stopped me about halfway through my forward fold. Yet the sun loosened my muscles, warmed them, awoke them, reminded them.

I didn't scold myself when my legs shook after a few minutes in warrior pose. I moved carefully. I treated my body with love. I was gentle, and exploring all it could do was wonderful. I tested my boundaries, reaching a little further than I thought I could go while being kind to myself. I kept at it perhaps a little longer than I should've. I would feel it tomorrow, but it would be a good kind of pain, the kind that helped me grow instead of doing its best to break me.

Cheesecake was my reward, followed by a long shower.

Thin black plastic felt like freedom, strength. I trusted it to contain the memories. All of Brian's clothes went into that trash bag. Three of them to be exact. His parents would come by and get the rest of his things soon, and I didn't want them to stay long, tainting my house. So much needed to be packed, but just that had drained me, so I allowed myself to take a break. I allowed the bags to stay in the bedroom, a stain on perfection. I warmed up some lasagna, pulled a blanket over me, and settled in for a movie. I started to acclimate to my new life.

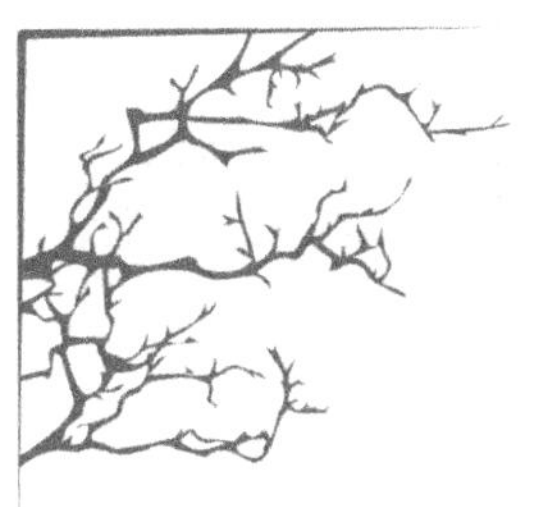

Chapter 7

Three a.m. I threw his games into another bulging trash bag. Plastic cracked. He always played them while I took care of Abigail, relaxing in a way I never could. He had never been a good father. Never. And I needed his stuff out of my house. I needed him out of my life.

I would be justified in getting rid of everything. He had already come by with the police to get the stuff he wanted. He'd had his chance. I couldn't get in trouble for throwing it away. I didn't want to see him ever again. *But today... don't think about that. Can't think about that.*

Another trash bag. His stupid books on programming. He always cared more about that tech company than he did about me. He always thought his ambitions trumped mine.

"I wish I could be there for you more," he'd claimed, an attempt to comfort me after I'd spent the whole day crying, after he'd stolen everything from me. "But now that we have a baby, it's more important than ever to support this family."

He never truly supported us though—never truly supported me, not in a way that mattered. Financial stability wasn't the only thing a wife needed from her husband. Abigail died because of it.

My life spun. I stopped—a mistake. Stopping only allowed the pain to catch up to me. Abigail was dead. My baby. Her crib would remain empty, her nursery locked, shut away. She would be trapped forever in that coffin.

His stupid books, he had so many of them. Sci-fi and fantasy, and he didn't look like a nerd, but he was one. He lived in his own fantasy world instead of being the hero I needed in real life. He was a villain in real life. I hated him more than anything. Spines broke as they tried to make room for each other in a bag that didn't have enough space. Just like Brian never made enough space for us in his life.

I grabbed another trash bag. If I stuffed it too much, it would break. His family would be stuck there for longer when they came to pick up his things. They would trap me with their awkwardness.

Abigail would never be there again. *All his fault. All my fault.*

The book in my hand was so heavy, weighed down by the worlds that would always be one step ahead of us, a perfection we could never attain. It dropped, thudding against the others.

The room was too small, too familiar. There was only one place I wanted to be. The door handle was a cold warning. I would only find death in there. I would only find coldness beyond that door. I unlocked it and peered inside.

I didn't know what I expected, because I wasn't really thinking until I opened that door. It was so much the same, so unchanged, and that was right. That was the life I knew. A chance to take back things I regretted.

Touches of pink invited me. I followed the fairies dancing on the walls and shut the door behind me. White teddy bears, tiny rattles, ruffles on the crib, the rocking chair, even the changing table whispered of innocence. Finally, I was back where I should be—a portal to return me to when life was better.

I ran my fingers over books with colorful characters and their wacky adventures. A hope for the future. One day I would read those to Abigail. One day she would learn to read them herself. Toys lay tucked away in her pink toy box for when she was ready for them. We wouldn't rush her. That time would be different. The little girl would celebrate all her birthdays.

I sank into the white wooden rocking chair. I focused on the soft pink curtains shielding our secrets from the outside world. I couldn't quite look at the crib tainted with the touch of the grim reaper. Its darkness didn't fit in that room of hope and light. I'd tried so hard. I'd given raising Abigail everything I had. She had been difficult sometimes, but I'd tried. And I'd kept trying, but I had never been enough for her, for Brian, for anyone.

All I'd ever wanted was to be enough. Falling short all the time broke my heart for good. But I couldn't cry. I would cry enough later because today was the day when we would return Abigail to the earth and hope her soul made it somewhere better.

I sobbed. I shouldn't have thought that thought. I had tried to avoid it. But once it came, there was no stopping the tears. The pain was worse than anything I'd ever felt. Childbirth in reverse. Stunningly sharp. *Why isn't blood pouring out of my heart?*

My baby didn't belong in a coffin, buried deep within the ground, away from me. Less than a year ago, she had been protected, safe within me. I wished she'd spent more time there—less time out here. I wished she could have grown in that bubble until she was at least a year old, maybe two. Maybe then she could've survived in our world.

Black-and-purple bruises blurred my vision as I cried for the pain she'd suffered, the desperate feeling of trying to breathe but being unable to. Brian had gotten me to that point once before, but there had been hope even then. I hadn't thought he would actually kill me. *How would it feel, in those seconds, if he did? Was she old enough to recognize her own parent was killing her? Did she know those hands wrapped around her throat had comforted her, taken care of her, eased her tears? Did she realize, when she cried, that no one was coming because one of the people she'd always cried out to was the person doing it?* I hoped she hadn't known, that she wasn't quite old enough yet, that somehow, she hadn't felt any pain, that somewhere she was safe, taken care of.

"I love you," I whispered in case her ghost still lingered. "Mommy loves you, Abigail, so much."

And I was finally able to catch a breath among the tears. As I looked at the crib, I could feel her presence—a mother's intuition. She wasn't dead, just sleeping. *Rockaby, baby.* I hummed the tune then sang it quietly so I wouldn't wake her.

A touch of warmth as I wrapped my arms around myself. Brian was gone. Allison was a great friend, but I would have to comfort myself many nights. I felt painfully lonely, but that would subside. Things would get better. They had to. Nothing could be worse than that.

The movement of the chair. Back and forth. Back. And forth. I closed my eyes. The motion soothed me. I hugged Abigail's favorite teddy bear and nuzzled its soft fur. I kissed its forehead as I had Abigail's each night.

They were trying times, but things would get better. That day was the worst of it. Then, the pottery class. I had also signed up for a yoga class to help me get my body back into shape. *And a pet maybe? A guard dog?*

Eventually, I would move out of the house, away from the cobwebs of dark memories. I couldn't right then, though. I couldn't buy a new house and not look suspicious, so for the time, I would sweep the memories away with paint. I would create a new life, a better life, if I could just get through the day.

Hours after I stepped into Abigail's room, I was strong enough to leave it. I shut the door behind me. Let the baby sleep.

The chill dew cuddling my toes brought back my focus. I stood for a moment and breathed in the fresh air before it was stained by the day's activity. I laid out my yoga mat on the grass.

Dashes of baby blue, lilac, and it's-a-girl pink colored my background. As a swan, I moved in the gold light, elegant, flawless. Even when I shook, stumbled, it had a purpose. I was undefeatable, strong, and I would prove it. Birds called out to me. The sun rose to meet me. I rose to the challenges of the day, daring them to take me down.

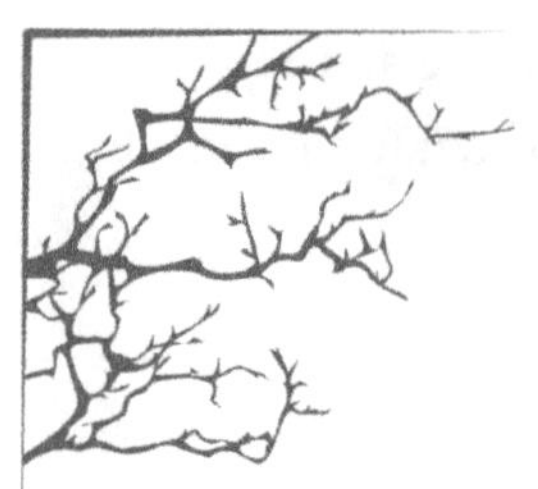

Chapter 8

Black dress, black tights, black ballet flats, black necklace, black flower in my hair. Black heart. Wearing my pain like that gave me a strange relief, a physical manifestation of the darkest feelings locked in my heart. Grief weighed less once I let it out into the world, once I fully indulged in it. Black purse draped over my shoulder. *Keys? Check.*

A bouquet wrapped in pink sat on the counter like Abigail wrapped in her pink blanket when I first brought her home—a bundle of joy. There would be no joy today. Still, I picked it up just as carefully as I had held Abigail for the first time, gently. White lilies, white roses, white orchids. Purity. Innocence. Peace. My daughter had been so young that she would leave the world as she'd entered it. *Unblemished except...*

Dark blue settled over the sidewalk. Purple clung to my car. Gray. The brilliant day I'd indulged in while doing yoga just that morning turned on me. Bruises gathered across my windshield, making it hard to see as I drove to the funeral home.

Her skin had been perfect when I'd found her. She'd looked untouched, like she had died in her sleep, carried off by dreams. *Was color already beginning to reveal those secrets when we held her at the hospital? How long does it take for bruises to show? Were we too wrapped up in grief to notice?* Maybe we just didn't want to know.

Why didn't the moon protect her? Why didn't the stars step in? They knew she was in danger. They had to. They always watched. Each night. They woke her, played with her.

Why didn't I protect her? The thought was an arrow that ripped through my heart and pinned me to the seat. It wouldn't let me go even once the car stopped at the funeral home. For my daughter.

I closed my eyes. Abigail was behind them, waiting. I opened them.

The arrow dislodged just enough to allow my body to shake, hunch forward as I sobbed. We weren't supposed to bury our daughter. Burying us was her pain to bear. I curled into myself as if I could somehow protect myself from it all. But it was within me, a thorn that became more deeply entrenched with each movement.

If any of the many people who had come to send her off noticed, they didn't disturb me, help me. I was on my own—safe—for the time being. I had to find a way to control my tears. Alone. I needed to gather myself so I could go into the funeral home.

I didn't want to go in there. *Is that strange? To not want to go to my own daughter's funeral?* I would've skipped it if I could. Abigail wasn't there. Seeing her like that wouldn't bring her back. It only made everything worse.

I saw a second possibility though. Everyone would expect me to go, and maybe I had to be there for Abigail through that. It was my punishment for failing her. My responsibility. Maybe I had to say goodbye. There would be plenty of time to cry later.

No one looked at me as I left my car and walked across the parking lot. I barely held myself together. *They don't expect me to, right? How could I?* My daughter was dead. That truth ricocheted around my brain and into my bloodstream, creating gaping holes in the various parts of me it slammed into. Tears returned as I stepped into the funeral home. Safe because no one looked at me.

Except once I walked through the door, everyone looked at me. My shadowed presence was their cue. I became approachable, so everyone saw the tears water the flowers. So many flowers led up to a tiny white casket—roses and lilies, lilacs, carnations—cards and a white casket ringed with gold, lined with pink satin.

Brian leaned over it. Despite the restraining order, I had requested he be allowed to stand near me, with me. I was willing to endure his presence for that. He was still her father—a great father, until he wasn't.

Now I regret it? No. I still didn't. Abigail needed both parents at her funeral. He hadn't been found guilty yet. It was the right thing to do, but it was difficult to see him there, to be there. Everything hit me, and I didn't know how I stayed standing. I couldn't even try not to cry.

Allison broke the invisible barrier around me. We cried together as she gathered my pieces in a hug, tight, warm. A human. I was alive, not alone. I buried my face against her and cried even more.

"I'm so sorry," she whispered. "I'm here for you through this. You're going to get through this."

Cassandra joined us. She put her hand on my shoulder, and the touch was so gentle, so caring.

My resolve from earlier wavered. *Can anyone get through this?* I hugged her for as long as I could. Then, I hugged Cassandra. I avoided everyone else around me, everything else going on. It would be okay if I could just be with the two friends I had left in the world. Avoid that one thing.

But no hug could last forever. No life lasted forever. And after Allison broke that barrier, others slowly approached me, a blur of faces, many I didn't know or, at the very least, didn't recognize.

"I'm sorry for your loss."

"I lost so-and-so not long ago, so I understand what you're going through."

"She was such a sweet child."

"You're so strong. I couldn't do it. I wouldn't be able to make it through if that happened to me."

That was a hard one to deal with. I wanted to scream in protest. *Strong? How am I being strong? Just by existing? What else am I supposed to do?* My heart didn't stop beating just because it was broken, though I wished it would. That wasn't anything special on my part. I couldn't do this either. *Can't they see that?*

Worst of all, yet most common, nearly everyone asked, "How are you doing?"

"Are you holding up okay?"

"How are you feeling?"

How do they expect me to answer that? How do you think I'm feeling? My child is dead. My husband has been charged with her murder. I'm miserable, and I don't want to be here. Don't want to live. Or I do want to live, but I want to live the life I used to have but better. Premarriage to Brian with our precious daughter. I hate everyone, hate this world, hate myself. I'm not okay—of course I'm not. I've never been less okay, and the questions don't make it better.

But that was far from the polite answer. It was the kind of answer that would get me glares and stares and maybe even a stint at the psych ward. No one expected the truth. Most people didn't even want it. They probably knew how ridiculous their words were. They just didn't know what else to say. Life never truly prepared us for the worst situations. *How could it?*

So, I forgave them. I didn't even know what I wanted them to say or do. I didn't know what would be helpful to me in that moment, and I wouldn't have known if I were in their position. I would probably do the same if I were in their position. I probably had said the same stupid things to grieving people in the past.

I ignored the flowers weighing down my arms. I ignored Brian. I was hyperaware of him. He was hyperaware of me. Every time I looked over, he looked back at me. We would both look away, then back. Uncontrollable. We always had been drawn to each other, like riptides we couldn't quite escape, even though we knew we would drown.

Still, for the most part, we managed to stay as far away from each other as possible. It wasn't too difficult. Most everyone had separated. Those who believed him were on one side of the room. On the other side were those who believed me.

It was some comfort that those who believed me expanded farther than those who believed him. Even that woman Brian sometimes went jogging with, Katarina, was on my side. It seemed he didn't have a whole lot of friends left. It was somewhat of an annoyance, as that meant I had more people to talk to, more people to comfort as I dealt with my own grief, more people to watch as finally the flowers became too heavy.

That white coffin, cursed with gold, beckoned me. Unavoidable, it dragged me down a path bordered by flowers, so pretty, so innocent. Dread. I couldn't take another step. Dead. But I kept walking. *Until...* I wouldn't look down, couldn't.

She lay among the pink, peaceful, eyes closed, snuggled by a white teddy bear. Wrapped in a pink blanket, just like the one we brought her home in, she looked like she was sleeping in the late afternoon, as she always loved to do. The sun was her comfort, when she felt safe enough to close her eyes. Safe. If cold colors had ever stained her skin, they were gone. Nothing was left but a flawless little angel, my angel.

I laid the flowers on the casket, my final gift to her. *Stupid. What baby wants flowers?* It wasn't nearly enough. I could never give her enough. I couldn't cry. I didn't want my baby to see me like that as I reached down and touched her cheeks. I ignored that they were a bit too cold.

She was sleeping, finally. She'd grown so big that she could sleep through the night. Oh, how the moon would miss her. How I would miss her. I teetered against the coffin as grief shot through the delusion I had worked so hard to build. It shattered everything. She was dead. Abigail was dead. I almost lost it then and there. Tears threatened to destroy me, but I needed to do one more thing. I wouldn't allow her to see my pain, not then, not ever.

Deep breath to get through this. I turned back to my daughter, so perfect, an angel. And I hoped somehow, somewhere, she could feel how much I loved her. My lips on her forehead. One more whiff of that baby skin that smelled different, tampered with.

"I love you," I whispered. "Mommy loves you so much."

A tear dripped onto her cheek. A sob shook my body. I turned before she could see me dissolve into a mess. And I dissolved into a mess, doubled over as the pain took me to the core of the earth.

Abigail was dead. My family was broken. *My baby. My baby.*

"My baby." I sobbed as arms wrapped around me. "My poor baby."

If I said it over and over, maybe the world would see how unfair it was. It would stop like my world had. Or fate would change its mind, return her. She was too young, too innocent. My love could make up for my past failings. My love would bring her back.

But my pain was just as strong as my love. Maybe stronger. My love and my pain must've negated the effects of each other because the day went on. Allison and Cassandra led me to a chair near the coffin and sat next to me. Cassandra held my hand. Allison rubbed my back.

The second the tears let up just a little, more people approached me. Even as pain leaked out over cheeks eroded by a river, people approached me. Any spare moment when I wasn't breaking down completely, they rushed in, eager to be part of it.

Except one person. Two really, if I counted Brian. She stood in front of the coffin in an elegant black dress. Her blond hair leaned toward gray, sharp features adorned with black diamonds. Her wealth was apparent to anyone who glanced at her.

I hoped she wouldn't look at me. *What is she doing here? How did she know? Why did she wear so much grief for a child she only met once? A baby I kept her well away from.*

She lived in the South, on the East Coast, the other side of the country—where the warm weather and fake smiles hid the darkest secrets. It was a world so different from our own, so different from the life I had created. They wouldn't have heard about a baby murdered there.

Her ice eyes froze me as she looked over. *What is she going to do? Approach me? Here, in front of everyone? Reproach me? Does she know? Does she suspect?* She looked away from me. And though my pain dug its claws into the earth, begging for more time to give my love a chance to right the wrong, the day wore on.

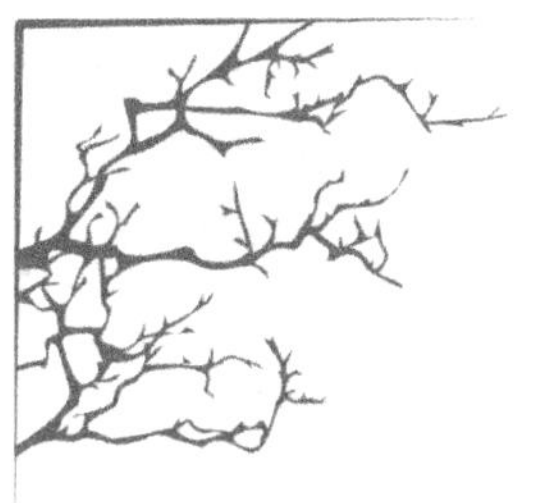

Chapter 9

The street wore on. I'd given my keys to Cassandra, too ruined by grief to drive. They herded me into Allison's passenger seat. The hearse drove in front of us. Unknown houses, shops, trees blurred together as time slowed enough for me to focus on the hearse and change the corpse it carried. To Brian. Losing a husband would be easier, especially one who was so often awful to me. It would be difficult for Abigail as she grew up, but maybe not too difficult, maybe not as difficult and complicated as actually having Brian around.

Maybe I would marry again while she was still young so she would have a strong, admirable male figure in her life. She would hear stories about her father and how much he loved her, but she wouldn't remember him enough to miss him. We would say all the right things. I would never talk bad about him to her, and our life would go on.

Allison drove through the graveyard. Stones were all that remained of so many souls, carved with beautiful designs, thoughtful words. Humans would do anything to make it better, easier. It was just a cover, a distraction from the corpses locked in the earth. Death was unfathomable.

Brian would join them soon. I would mourn him like I cared, like the dutiful wife I had failed to be. Then I would go back home to my daughter, and we would celebrate with a new toy and a glass of wine. Once no one was there to watch, of course. Maybe then, without him in my life, I could finally be enough.

The car stopped. Allison gave me a hug, armor against the monsters we would face out there. *The prying eyes of fellow mourners who don't actually care about me or...* My delusion teetered dangerously. More tears waited. It couldn't be. Couldn't be.

We walked out together, toward the hearse in front of us. Most everyone waited for us to pass. They fell in line behind us, respectfully, to give me full view of the coffin that held a person I loved dearly. As if that was something I wanted to see.

Most everyone waited except for those who would carry it—Brian's father, Brian's brother, Brian. He looked at me. His pupils were black question marks, irises angry. It wasn't him in that coffin. *It wasn't him so...*

They pulled a white coffin decorated with gold out of the hearse. I covered my mouth to stop the screams because, once I started, I would never stop. Still, a tiny protest rang out. It was so small, too small. No coffin should ever be that small. No one so little should ever see a graveyard.

Tears were determined to soak every moment of the day. Just like the sun was determined to stay hidden behind the clouds to show everyone it wasn't guilty. The moon was the one who had let the travesty happen. I was so guilty—of being a bad mother, not leaving sooner. I could've prevented it.

Those men carried the coffin so easily. It was too light, too tiny. We followed them like cult members, worshiping their path. We followed the earth's screams to a gaping hole in the ground. They laid the coffin over it, a Band-Aid for the wound. Once she was placed safely inside the embrace of the earth, it would begin to heal. My heart never would.

When I had made arrangements, I'd decided Brian could stand next to me in front of the grave, just like parents should. I regretted it. Didn't regret it. As we stood like we were still a happily married couple, people whispered about him, about me, even there. We didn't whisper, didn't speak.

We looked at each other. For a moment, the anger was gone. All the various ways we had hurt each other were cast aside. We were together, or else we would be completely alone. And I didn't want to be alone in this. It didn't matter who had done what. She was our child, the daughter we created together. We were chained in pain. Perhaps we always would be. A link ever enduring, together, for her.

The priest stood at the head of the coffin. We looked away from each other to gaze at him, hoping for answers, needing direction. Maybe he would show us the path to lead us from this, grant us hope. Anything. We were desperate for anything.

"Nothing is quite as difficult as losing a child," he started. "A young soul, so innocent, so pure." He was just as bad as most of the people who joined us there. Useless. He didn't know what to say. He didn't know what it was like to lose a child. Didn't know what it was like to lose our child. He couldn't feel our pain, so he couldn't offer us any true answers.

I looked back at Brian and stopped really listening. It was just a show, an awful one, a stupid ritual we had to do so we could do something, pretend like we had grasped what had happened when we couldn't. It was impossible to make sense of it, to ever move on.

I couldn't look away from that tiny coffin. I tried not to imagine Abigail in it. I saw her in it, alone, trapped in pink satin, suffocating—never to sleep under the afternoon sun again, locked away from the moon who had failed her.

No. She was sleeping peacefully in a crib that fit her better than the one we had bought ever would. She had escaped to a better place, free of pain. She would be happy all the time, in a way we could never provide. Mother Nature's care was superior to what I could offer. She would be fed, loved, warm.

Stares warmed my skin. I looked up. The priest offered his hand to me. My turn to speak. *What is there to say?* Abigail was dead, too young to be dead. Even I didn't know the words to make it better. *Who ever could?*

"I want to thank you all for your support," I said because that sounded right, appropriate, though only a couple of people's support had helped me. I looked at Allison and Cassandra. "It truly has meant the world to me. As cliche as it sounds, I couldn't make it through this without you." I still might not make it through the pain. Not again. But Allison and Cassandra had made it a maybe. *Without them...*

"Since I lost Abigail, my life has been agony. The pain of losing a child is more than I could ever describe, and..." I grasped for words and found the truth. "I don't even want to try. It's useless. No one could understand the depth of the pain I'm drowning in. We all know it hurts, but we don't know how much until us unfortunate parents are forced through it.

"So, instead of trying to explain the unexplainable, I'd like to focus on Abigail. As she was. My daughter... she was perfect. A little angel who screamed her way into the world. She was gorgeous in her pink dresses, wonderful to snuggle. A fire grew within her, curious already, stubborn. She was a unique gift, our little night owl. A gem blessed by the stars and the moon. And I hope they'll watch over her now, as I'm unable to." I lowered my voice because the tears were already coming, and my words would unleash them. "I love you, Abigail."

Tears cut me off as I stumbled into Allison's and Cassandra's waiting arms. I wished it could be Brian. For that one moment, I wished I could find comfort in him, in the only person who actually understood. But he had hurt me so many times. He was suspected of murdering our daughter.

Even before that, we had both known we'd crossed a line in our marriage. We had reached a place we could never come back from. We could only ever go farther into the darkness where we transformed into monsters we couldn't recognize. The physical distance was the thunder. The broken connection was the lightning that had struck years ago and zapped the love from our life. Allison was safer. Cassandra was kinder.

Yet I had to admire Brian as he stepped forward to speak. Whispers started again. *He killed his daughter. How dare he come to the funeral? How dare he speak on her behalf?* He was innocent. It was plain to see by how hurt he looked, how distraught he was. Folks on both sides kept him under scrutiny. I didn't know what to think, about him, about anything. But I listened.

"I have never felt such immense joy, such pride, as I did the day I held my daughter for the very first time," Brian started. "Never before, and yet those feelings returned day after day as I watched her grow, cared for her, loved her like I've never loved anyone else. That little girl was my entire world, and though she was only with us for a short time, she became everything. It was a privilege to be a part of something so precious. Nurturing her was its own reward. I loved every part of fatherhood. From feeding her to the endless snuggles and even staying up with her while she fussed, easing her distress. It was everything I could've dreamed and more.

"And even though it's ended as a nightmare, though the future is uncertain, it was worth every bit of devastation that her death has brought me. No matter what happens, I love my daughter. I always have and always will. She is the highlight of my life. And I know our little owl will fly among the stars, play on the moon, and become even more brilliant until we can all be reunited as a family once again."

Would we ever reunite as a family? Would, somewhere, someday, Brian return to the husband I loved? The man I needed? Would we watch Abigail grow together? Would we find happiness together again? It was such a lovely dream, but the thorn of the white rose pricked my skin as my fingers closed around it. I felt thankful for a brief second of manageable pain.

Then, it was gone. Roses lay on the coffin. A last gift. Remembrance.

I couldn't leave her there. I couldn't leave my daughter alone in the cold, dreary day, abandoned. She would think we'd forsaken her. I couldn't leave her alone. Cold grass felt hard beneath my knees as I fell to the ground. Just like that night, I would never be able to stand again.

"My baby," I cried. "I need to be with her! I need to take care of her!" I reached for the coffin.

It was so small, but there had to be room for me inside. Allison knelt beside me.

"Please." I turned to her. My voice lowered. "I need to be with her. That should be me, not her. This isn't fair. It isn't right."

Brian looked over like he wanted to do something, say something. And I wanted him to. I wanted to curl up together in our familiar bed and forget everything bad that had happened. I wanted to start over. *Why can't we just start over?* We would do so much better if given a second chance, I knew we would. We had learned our lesson, and we were so sorry.

"Losing you won't bring her back," Allison reminded me. "We need you here. We can't handle all that grief at once. You'll be together again when it's time."

When will it be time? How will we be together again? How will we know?

"She's safe in the stars," Brian whispered, quiet enough for only me to hear.

As my tears subsided, Allison gave me space. Mourners trickled away, thinking it was safe to leave. A get-together would be held at Allison and Cassandra's house, to eat, share memories, prove we could still live.

I couldn't, so I sat there on the grass. Allison waited off to the side. Cassandra left to deal with the guests. Brian knelt on the grass next to me, not too close, quiet until the shuffling footsteps made enough noise to hide his words. Then he turned to me.

"Do you really think I could do this?" he asked. "You know I love Abigail. You know it. Someone must've come in while we were sleeping. It's the only explanation. The true killer will go free if they arrest me, and I can't believe you'd think... do you really think I murdered our daughter?"

I couldn't get up, couldn't answer, but I could move easier than I could tell him the truth. So I started to stand.

"No." He touched my hand gently. "Stay. I'm sorry. I won't bother you anymore."

So, I stayed until most everyone was gone. I sat in silence with Brian, Allison, and a couple of police officers until it was so cold I couldn't feel anything anymore. Except for that ever-present, excruciating pain, the heartbreak that was as steady and constant as my heartbeat had once been.

"I can't leave her," I whispered.

"She's part of us," Brian whispered. "She'll always be with us. As close as she can be to anybody. We won't leave her, not ever. We can't, and it's impossible for her to be away from us."

That was the first thing anyone had said that made sense to me. That sounded true. So, I stood. I almost hugged him, but the police were still there. *What would they think of that?*

I turned to Allison instead. We walked to the car.

How dare he come to her funeral? Stalking me was bad enough, but this? That same black car waited for me to slip up, the one who had been parked outside my house. One of the few cars remaining, it stained the already-awful day. It was my daughter's funeral. I had already shed enough tears, had enough emotions crashing over the graveyard. And Allison was there with me. I couldn't confront him, so the anger simmered.

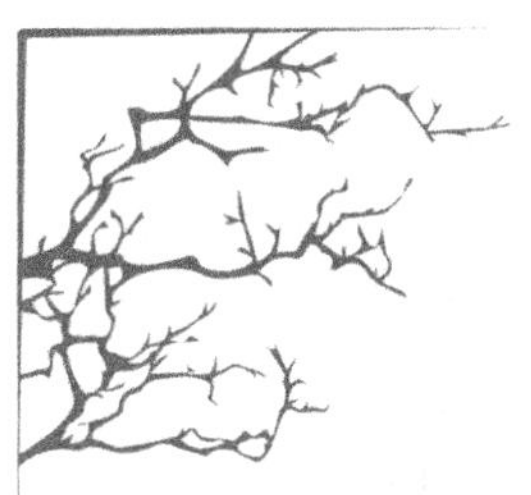

Chapter 10

Anger fueled me through that evening at Allison and Cassandra's house as I sat through something that felt too much like a party, like we were celebrating Abigail's death.

People gave me gifts, food, flowers, cards. Someone even started up a donation drive to pay for her funeral and court costs. So nice. So unnecessary. We should be crying, locked away in darkness, allowing ourselves to feel all the awful emotions that accompanied something like that. We shouldn't be there, doing all that—whatever that was. I had never realized how appalling it all was until I was right in the middle of it.

My anger fueled me, so I only cried three times while I was there. I tried to keep myself together near the end so no one would try to comfort me. It was far too obnoxious and hollow when they did. I tried to hide my hurt so no one would stop me from leaving. About half the other mourners had already left.

"You look so..." Cassandra looked at me. Dark hair only partially hid green eyes that were too perceptive. She was a therapist, though, the most difficult person to lie to and get away with it. "So worn down. Why don't you stay here tonight? We could use the company. I'm sure you could too."

I could, definitely, and I wanted to stay. But the anger remained, simmering. If I stayed, it might boil onto Cassandra and Allison. Scorching them was the last thing I wanted to do. I had someone else in mind to spill onto, and that anger just might grant me the nerve to do it.

"I appreciate the offer, but I kind of want to be home right now. Spend some time by myself, maybe in the company of something sweet and a bottle of wine. But I promise I'll reach out tomorrow, after I've had time to process a bit on my own and can move forward in my new life."

"That would be wonderful," she said. "And taking time to heal on your own is so important too. At least let me provide you with fuel for the night though. We have so much stuff here."

Others had already gifted me with food, but I suspected I wouldn't feel like cooking for a really long time, so I didn't protest. Cassandra found me bottles of Merlot and Moscato, a platter of dinner foods, and some dessert. She and Allison helped me load everything. I hugged them extra tight because it hurt to leave by myself—without a husband, without a daughter.

I was thankful I did, though. I slowly drove up my street. I found him parked near the neighbor's house, that same car again. I wanted to hit him with my car. *What if it's a police officer though?* I resisted the urge and pulled into my driveway, my confrontation already rehearsed, ready to go. That was the night.

Except another car already sat in my driveway, a white Jaguar, her favorite. My anger spiked as it mixed with fear and ancient hatred, a dangerous cocktail. I should leave, go back to Allison and Cassandra's house. Surely, they would understand if I told them I'd changed my mind. But I knew her too well. She would wait and keep on waiting until I returned. She was so stubborn, one of the many things I hated about her.

Deep breath. I couldn't shoot off in anger right away. Otherwise, no matter how much I thought she wouldn't be able to, she would find a way to make me feel bad, to make me feel like I was in the wrong. She specialized in becoming the victim.

No. I had to wait. I had to listen to her long enough to fully assure myself that my anger was justified, that any response I had was justified. Then I could avoid the guilt. I wouldn't end up regretting it, apologizing to her when she was the bad one.

Her anger radiated from her car as I got out. I ignored her and went to my trunk to load my arms with as much stuff as I could. I would have to make another trip anyway. I could feel her prying eyes through the car window as I walked by it. I refused to look, refused to act as if anything else was different.

I reached for my front door, and it opened. She stood in the doorway.

"Mom?" I hadn't used the word in so long. It sounded dirty coming out of my mouth—a word that shouldn't be used for her—but I was so shocked. I looked toward her car. No one was in it.

"Hi, sweetie." She reached for the things in my hands. "Let me help you with that."

"I've got it." I twisted away from her. My carefully stacked treasures teetered dangerously, just like my life whenever she was around. "How did you get in here?"

"The back door was unlocked. You were gone so long. You couldn't expect me to wait in my car all this time."

"It wasn't." I never left the back door unlocked—or any doors, any windows. "And I never gave you a key. So how did you get in?"

"I assure you it was. You really should be more careful. I thought I taught you better."

Before I could fight her on it, she slipped past me and walked away. *Leaving? It couldn't really be that easy, could it?*

"You start taking care of that stuff," she said. "I'll get the rest."

And she walked right up to my car like it was hers. She reached for stuff in the trunk. So surreal. So her. I walked into my house.

If I shut the door, I could lock her out. I wouldn't have to deal with her. I couldn't deal with her that night—or ever. But I would have to deal with her eventually. She would knock and knock until I let her in. Or she would leave and come back. Always until I faced her. It was better to deal with her, get it over with, or it would only get worse, like a splinter. I just had to suck up the pain and pluck it out.

I went to the kitchen and tried to rewrite the script. Forget about the words I planned to say to my stalker. Think about what I would say to my mother. They were quite similar anyway. Both were intrusive, dangerous.

I put the casserole in the fridge, made up an excuse as to why I'd left without telling her, set the cookies on the counter, thought of an excuse as to why I'd stayed gone, gathered the cards into a pile. *What does she want anyway?*

A thud. I jumped and looked up. She opened the bags and put stuff away like any of it was normal.

"What are you doing here?" I asked.

"Well, right now, I'm helping you put your things away, though all you want to do is shut me out. I'm trying to keep in mind that you're grieving, so I'm not too harsh on you."

"Like that's ever stopped you."

The fridge door slammed shut. Frozen eyes turned on me. Her hair fell in soft waves, but they didn't make her look any softer—or any kinder. "I've done my best," she snapped. "I was the best mother to you that I could be. I bought you everything you needed, took care of you when I could, and hired the best nanny to be there when I wasn't. I encouraged you, scolded you when necessary, but I also loved you. I loved you, Madeline. I still do.

"But you hurt me, truly. You ripped out my heart when you left. I cried for days. I worried, hurt that you didn't tell me you were going. You didn't tell me where you were going. Yet, I forgave you. I tried to understand. You were grieving, and grief does strange things to people. Sometimes it makes them act in unreasonable ways.

"I was delighted that you reached out to me when Abigail was born. Bitter at first, infuriated that I didn't even know you were pregnant, but I tried to put that aside because meeting her was so wonderful. She was a beautiful baby, and I thought things could be better. We could reconcile.

"And yet, the second I flew home, things returned to the way they had been. I called and called. You didn't answer. You made it clear you didn't want me to come back. You never showed me pictures of Abigail, never updated me on her well-being. And when I finally flew down to see you, you just happened to be on vacation for the week. With a four-month-old? No."

She shook her head. She looked like she was about to cry, but that was the one thing I admired about my mother—she rarely cried, even if it would be to her advantage. She refused to stoop that low, though of course she would find every other way to make me feel bad. "You left to avoid me. You were still in town, hiding out. But I was determined to be part of your life. So I tried to give you space, tried to do whatever I could. I vowed to see Abigail before her first birthday, then..."

She was going to cry. Tears gathered in her eyes. Not for me, never for me. *For Abigail? For the baby she saw once?* The ice was cracking. *After all the things she's gone through, this is what's going to break her? I'm going to break her?* She blinked. Eyes closed for a moment longer than they needed to be. When she reopened them, those tears were back in their place. The only tears she'd allowed were the ones at the funeral.

"She died," Odette whispered, the words too awful to be said at full volume, I guessed. "Murdered. My granddaughter was murdered. And you didn't even tell me."

"How did you find out?" The second the words were out, I realized they were the wrong ones.

Fury colored her normally pale cheeks. She leaned over the table. She was finally finished with hateful looks. That time, she would actually kill me, which would be mercy.

"Brian told me," she hissed. "He called me, explained everything. The person suspected of murdering my granddaughter had more respect for me than my own daughter does. If it weren't for him, I would have missed my granddaughter's funeral!"

Of course he'd told her. He always tried to get me to rebuild my relationship with my mother. She adored him. They didn't know each other's dirty secrets. If they got together, everyone would know mine.

"I thought it might be difficult for you," I said.

Her eyebrows rose through my cloud of excuses. She had made it so hard for me last time. She always cut me down with her words, twisted my emotions. I couldn't handle it right then.

"It was so hard for you last time, and—"

"And you thought you'd just not tell me? That when I came for her first birthday, you might mention it then? Maybe you'd just pick up the phone one of these days, and when I asked how Abigail was, you'd tell me she was dead!"

"Of course not." I had planned to never see her again, never talk to her. I had planned to change my number and move somewhere she wouldn't find me—where no one would. I would start over.

I had never meant for her to meet Abigail in the first place. Brian had insisted, and I got so tired of fighting with him, with them. They were the same, really.

"It's just... so difficult." I grasped for words that would make it better, would make her go away. "It's all so much, and you know I like to be alone during the worst times. Besides, everyone from back home is a reminder of dark memories I'd rather forget. I couldn't deal with it all at once, so I was selfish. But I never meant to be cruel."

"Oh, sweetie." She softened—for the first time ever, toward me at least. "You never mean to be cruel. Yet you are so often. You're the worst type of person really."

Guess not.

"So wretched. Maybe you need to be reminded of those dark memories because something isn't right here. This shouldn't keep happening. Have you spoken to a doctor?"

"Odette, I am not doing this right now."

"You know I don't like it when you call me that. I'm your mother!"

"You have never been a mother to me! You took away the one true parent I had. I know what you did to Daddy!"

"And I know what you did to your daughter." She wasn't as blunt about it as the police officers had been. She didn't need to be. She could always say so much while speaking so little.

It hurt so much. That way, if I called her out on it, she could deny she ever meant it like that. If I was cruel, it was because I was raised in cruelty.

"I want you out of my house," I said in an even, controlled tone. "This is why I didn't tell you, why I ran. Though I may be cruel, you're absolutely vicious, downright horrid to even suggest I might have caused this."

"Not you." She stepped back as I approached her, raised her hands. "I don't think it's completely your fault anyway, even though you physically did it. But maybe there's something biologically—"

"Yeah, there is." Finally, it was an appropriate time to let out all my anger. She deserved it. "I'm biologically fucked up because of your genetics, because of the rotten pieces of you that make up who I am. You've tainted me, infected my life. And I want you gone before you can cause any more damage."

"Madeline!"

"Now!"

Our screams matched each other's, building a tower that one of us would knock down someday. One of us would go just a bit too far because, somehow, we hadn't quite reached that boundary yet. We hadn't pushed past the other's limits.

"Where am I supposed to stay?" She lowered her voice, fishing for pity.

"You have a hotel lined up."

She looked away. I knew it.

"You ungrateful, wretched, spoiled, awful..." She almost got to the door and turned back. "Child."

"Your own creation." I smiled through the pain, just like with Brian.

Whoever hurt the other most won. Always trying to break me down, just like Abigail broke me down with her ceaseless crying no matter what I did. I was never good enough for either of them. She spun in a huff and opened the door.

"Wait!"

"Yes?" She turned back, proud, like she expected an apology.

"How did you get in here? Really?"

"I already told you. I used the back door." She rolled her eyes. "I'll be back when you get your head straight." She finally left.

No relief. She would be back. She always came back. I always ignored her, avoided her until I had no other choice. Then we would tear each other down, run off to heal, and try again—until we found that ledge and someone got pushed off and didn't come back.

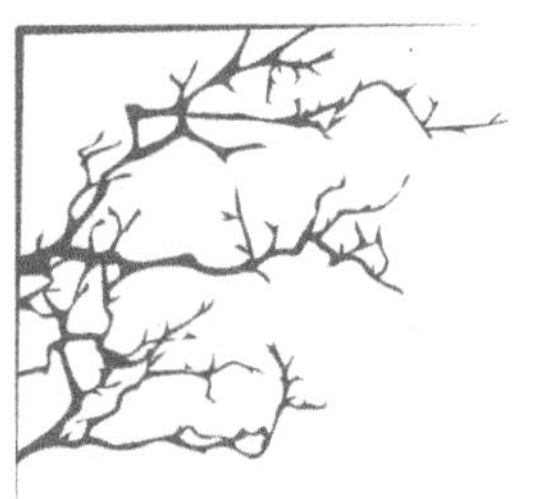

Chapter 11

I had my reservations, but it was time. I couldn't keep letting people break into my house, and locking it up didn't prove to be much of a deterrent. I considered getting a security system, but it might take more time than I had. Besides, security cameras made me uneasy. I didn't want to be watched in my own home.

How do I even take care of a dog though? That almost made me stop the car right then and there. I'd never had a dog. *What will I feed it? How do I train it? What do dogs do? That's why I'm getting a dog from the humane society though, right?* I could get an older one who was already trained. I could google how to take care of one. My father had gotten me a kitten when I was younger—a cat my mom hated, a cat I couldn't protect. Dogs and cats couldn't be that different.

I stopped the car in front of the humane society. The building was bigger than I'd thought it would be, though rather plain. I only knew I was at the right place because of the animals painted on the sign over the entrance. Then, once I stepped out, there was the noise. A chain-link fence reached around the back, and people with dogs of all kinds enjoyed the summer sun outside. I loved the sun—usually.

That day, it was too bright. It revealed just how crazy dogs could be. They jumped and barked, drooled and got dirty. Some were big, others small, but each looked like a handful. I should have turned around right then. I didn't even have anything for a dog.

That's the perfect excuse, isn't it? I didn't have anything for a dog, so if I didn't find one I liked, or if I was too overwhelmed, I could say I would come back, that I had to buy supplies first. *They won't judge me that way, right?* I could promise to pick one out another time and never return. *I don't have to leave with an animal, right?*

Before I could think about it longer, my hand was on the door handle. I stepped into a warm room with rust-red walls and wood floors. A young man looked up from the computer at the desk and smiled. He looked nice. *Aren't all people who work with kids and animals nice?* Also young. His hair was dark, his eyes brown. He didn't look like Brian, so maybe I could trust him.

"Hello." His voice was pleasant. "Welcome to the Seattle Humane Society. How can I help you today?"

"Well..." *How can he help me? What do I want?* "I'm interested in adopting a dog, a good guard dog. Maybe not anything too big though, just big enough to keep people away."

"Have you ever cared for a dog before, and do you have any pets now?"

"I don't have pets now, and I've never cared for a dog, but I did have a cat when I was younger."

"Dogs and cats can be a little different, but we can help you adjust. I'll tell you everything you need to know to take care of a dog. Do you have a specific breed in mind?"

Dog breed? I ran through a quick list in my head of the ones I knew. That wasn't too many. *What if I name a random one and adopt a dog I hate?* "Not really," I replied. "Could I just look at the ones you have for now? Get a good idea of my options?"

I sounded cold, even to myself, like I was looking at cars. They would never let me take a pet home.

But if he noticed, he didn't say anything. He just smiled and stepped out from behind the desk. "Of course! Some of our dogs are outside right now, but I can give you a tour of the kennel, and we can go from there."

I nodded, glad to have someone to follow. I'd felt a little lost since Brian was arrested, so it was a bit comforting—though, I already kind of regretted coming. I felt out of place. I didn't belong. We never had pets because of Brian, but maybe I wasn't a pet person either. *Who was the one who didn't want a pet after all?*

"I'm Calvin, by the way." He offered his hand.

"Madeline."

The door to the kennel opened, and I jumped back. Dogs went crazy, barking, jumping at their cages, wagging their tails. There were so many, so much to deal with all at once. *So loud. So dirty. So—*

"Are you sure a dog is the right choice for you?" he asked.

Did I catch a hint of arrogance in his voice? Is he looking out for my best interests? Or is he being condescending like everyone else? "I don't know." I walked inside and tried to act like I wasn't bothered by all the noise.

He reached into one of the cages and pet a dog with drool running from his mouth—big head, floppy ears, kind of cute. I would never touch him.

"Dogs are... nice," he said.

I walked farther down the row of cages and saw a light-brown pit bull. I'd heard pit bulls weren't the vicious monsters some people made them out to be, but they could be intimidating. And that one was far from the biggest dog there. I walked up to—*her?* The dog wore a pink collar. She begged to be petted.

"This little lovebug's name is Luna," Calvin said.

Luna jumped up and rubbed her head against him.

"She's a great choice. Not much of a guard dog, but she can be protective, especially under the right circumstances. Would you like to pet her?"

Luna's eyes were so big and lovable. The name was perfect of course. But I wasn't sure I was ready for a reminder of the night, of the shadows the moonlight had failed to illuminate. I wasn't sure if I was ready to have a dog. I couldn't seem to find a no though.

"These guys can be a lot all at once," Calvin admitted as he stepped away from Luna. "You said you had a cat before. Would you like to see our feline friends?"

I liked cats, sure. Still, I had no interest in seeing them. I didn't want a cat, didn't need a cat. A cat wouldn't keep people from breaking into my house. It would just be another thing to make my house messy without any value.

"Sure," I said because I did like cats, and maybe it would be easier to get used to the cats, then return to the dogs. Maybe it wouldn't be such a shock.

I braced myself to walk all the way to the end of the cage row, to the door at the other side of the room. To my relief, Calvin turned right back around, saving me. I took a deep breath once the door closed behind us. I could still hear the dogs barking, but it was quiet enough to not be overwhelming. I could own a dog if it was always like that. Maybe one dog would be manageable. I could get used to it.

"Our cat room is on the other side of the building," Calvin explained as we walked toward another door I didn't want to go through. I wasn't ready to face all that again. "They don't seem to appreciate all the noise that sometimes comes from the dog kennel."

"I can't blame them." The words were out before I could stop and think about how bad that would sound.

Calvin laughed though. "Me either."

He opened the door to the cat room, and it was nice. I walked inside and wasn't bombarded by noise. Some of the cats looked up, stood. A few even went to the doors of their cages, but they didn't go crazy. Many of them didn't even seem to notice we were there.

"Some of our kittens recently became ready to go to a new home." Calvin walked over to a fluffy, square bed in the corner of the room.

Tiny kittens meowed as they scrambled over each other, a quiet noise I could handle, adorable. I knelt in front of them. The tiny white one with blue eyes reminded me of the kitten I'd had when I was younger. I had picked her out because of my favorite Disney movie. I picked her up. She fit right in my hands, a ball of fluff, helpless.

"They're precious," I whispered. I brought her to my chest.

"You know, I kind of suspected you were more of a cat person." Calvin crossed his arms over his chest. "Working with animals and people gives me a good sense of these things."

"I still want a dog," I assured him as I set the kitten back down with her siblings. "I like cats, but I don't need a cat, nor do I want one. I want a guard dog. But I guess I'll look around here a little longer."

Being there was oddly like doing yoga. I found peace in the room of cats. I pet every single one and whispered sweet reassurances to them, the kinds of things I wished my mother would have said to me, the kinds of things I used to say to Abigail—when she was quiet enough to hear them, that was. They didn't cry like she did though. They purred. They listened. And I kind of didn't want to get a dog anymore. I wanted to take them all home.

I left the humane society empty-handed. I went straight to the closest pet store. It had so many aisles of colorful toys, different foods, collars, treats, etc. It was overwhelming. It had been too long since I'd last had a pet. I didn't know what to choose, what exactly I would need.

Yet I'd always been a perfectionist, patient with most things, except maybe Abigail. So, I walked down each aisle and enlisted the help of an employee. I analyzed the different products and decided on a purple-and-gold color scheme. I spent hundreds of dollars on supplies and still made it back before the shelter closed.

"She's all ready for you." Calvin looked fondly at the pink carrying crate on the counter. "We just need you to finish signing paperwork, and you're good to go."

Plus, I had to deal with the fees, of course. As I filled it all out, I was filled in about her background—where she came from, how she had behaved since they'd gotten her, how old they thought she was. Her name was Cleo, like the queen. I tried to be patient, but it took forever.

Will she howl in the car? I hadn't thought about that until I put her crate in the front seat. *What if something happens while I'm driving to my house? What if this isn't a good idea after all? What if I can't take care of a pet?*

She was quiet the whole ride home. I drove extra slowly, and not many people were on the road anyway. I didn't even think about checking for that black car until I was already in the house, Cleo still in her crate, a pile of cat supplies in the living room.

I sat down on the rug in front of the crate. Her eyes flickered open. She stood and stretched, ready to get out and explore her new home. *Am I ready for her?*

I intended to leave her in the crate for a little while, let her get used to being there while I set everything up, maybe ate something. I felt so nervous. *What if she dies like Abigail did? What if I can't take care of her?*

Green eyes dared me to leave her in there any longer. I'd spent some time with her at the humane society, but I was excited to get to know her, really know her. I was excited to not be alone anymore.

I slowly opened the crate door. She looked out, peered around for any enemies, and slowly stepped out. I guessed we were both a little reluctant, a little apprehensive. She'd had a home before but had been given up when she hadn't gotten along with the new kitten. *Does she remember that? Does she remember them?*

That black hair was going to make such a mess, but I already loved her. I pet her gently, barely touching her at first. I didn't want to scare her. She rubbed against me for a few minutes. Then she went off to do some exploring. I went and got some dinner.

That night, we curled up on the couch like we'd always lived together. And for the first time in a long time, I was truly comfortable with another living creature.

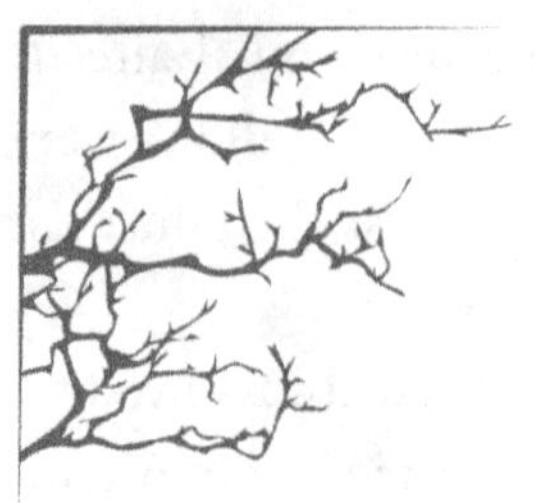

Chapter 12

The light-green abyss was perfect, so flawless I didn't want to disturb it. It was vines growing up a secret wall in the garden. It kept flowers safe before they blossomed. It was the color of my father's eyes before he died, the color of my mother's jealousy when she saw how close he was to his secretary. It was Cleo's eyes.

It rippled as I dipped the brush into it, slowly, so I could watch the transformation. Mesmerized, I took the brush out. Paint dripped from it.

I turned to the dark-blue walls that were almost black. I didn't bother to cover the gray carpet. It would be ripped out in a couple of days, anyway, giving me enough time to paint over his decisions.

Get rid of Brian. Exorcise the house. Evil spirits had dwelt in it for far too long, evil intentions. There would be only peace and harmony. I would fill the room with plants, a scratching post for Cleo. I would stuff it with life. It would be the perfect space to do yoga when it rained, the perfect place to hide when it was cold. That room would be our sanctuary.

Green splashed against blue empowered me. I was in control. I could take back my life. My house would be how I wanted it to be. My future would be what I chose. *What would I choose?* It didn't matter. I was in control.

Before, painting was a chore. One that we would usually pay someone to do. I savored the moment. I still had enough money to hire someone to do it. I didn't want to. That room would be how I designed it, and if the walls weren't perfect, that was okay. The flaws would be a reminder of all the things I could do, would do, all the things I'd done to reach the flawed but whole person I'd become.

I started painting before the sun came up and finished sometime late in the morning. It was a little splotchy. I could tell I was still trying to get the hang of it and find my footing. But I would cover it with another coat, and that time, the strokes would be more steady, sure.

For the time being, it had to dry. I had to get ready. I took a long shower, but paint still stained my hands as I dressed in jeans and an artsy purple shirt, the kind that I hadn't worn in forever. I threw my hair up, a vain attempt to hide the green bits that wouldn't quite come out. I wasn't too upset about that. It was proof, a trophy I was proud to wear.

Cleo sat on the couch, watching me. I had a little more time before I had to go. But I was already dressed, and her hair was black. I turned away then turned back. I gave in and spent a little time with her, even though that hair got all over my clothes, just like I thought it would. I wasn't perfect, not enough for anyone. *Except maybe her? Except maybe me?* The stress faded into something different, something like happiness.

As I reached my door, the happiness paused, reluctant to go outside with me. It feared it would be killed if I saw one thing, that one person who could ruin my day. I never got a guard dog. *Would my new cat keep me safe?*

Deep breath. In through the nose. Out through the mouth.

I opened the door and scanned the perimeter for the enemy. The black cloud that had followed me didn't dare dampen my skies that day. It hadn't since the funeral. Maybe he realized what a creep he was—how awful it was to do that to a woman who had just lost her child. Maybe he was a cop after all, and they'd realized I was innocent. Whatever the reason, I was thankful he was gone.

I felt almost whole again as I parked in front of Allison and Cassandra's house. It was a symbol of modernity with sleek, dark stone walls crafted by the wind, an artistic sculpture really. It was small, only one floor, but had lots of windows to create a sense of openness. Tinted black to hide the secrets. I didn't bother knocking. I just walked inside. Chatter mixed with hot sauce sparkled out of the kitchen. I followed it to a room blessed with an abundance of light, a gift from the skylights.

"Maddy!" Allison hopped off the kitchen counter to hug me.

Cassandra was busy at the stove, making magic with bright colors and mysterious potions.

"I'm glad you actually came. I'm so excited for this pottery class. I hope you don't mind, but since Cassandra has the day off, I invited her to come too."

"Of course, I don't mind." The more company, the easier it would be to hide the moments when grief grabbed me, tore me from the world, and threw me into the darkness.

"I'm making us lunch," Cassandra said. "An offering so I might be worthy to join in."

It was pleasant to be in a kitchen talking to other people. I hadn't cooked a meal since Abigail had died. It was almost like living again. Almost.

"How have you been?" Allison handed me a cup of green tea.

"It's been tough," I admitted. "But I'm doing my best. I painted Brian's game room. I'm turning it into a calming area for yoga."

"That's wonderful! I haven't done yoga in so long. I'll have to join you sometime. You can help whip me back into shape."

"Oh, and I got a cat." It felt strange to tell her that. It seemed Cleo had been in my life all along. My new world didn't exist without her. "Her name is Cleo."

"That's wonderful! I can't wait to meet her. What's she like?"

That was that, the most we talked about the horror that had destroyed our lives. They seemed as determined to move on as I was, so we moved on. I told them all about Cleo.

When I slipped into that darkness, they kept talking. As I stared down at my lunch, they went on about the new plants Allison was cultivating at her flower shop. They didn't call me out. I found my way back to the conversation eventually, regardless.

Back to life. Back to darkness. The car's steady movement delivered me peacefully.

Stopped. Sunlight shocked me back, burning away the darkness. I wasn't quite ready to leave the shadows yet. I was facing an unknown. Every day was frightening. Every day was something new, and the darkness was safe, judgment free. Cassandra smiled at me as Allison opened the studio door.

What if my stalker saw me? What if the police saw me? What would they think about me going to a pottery studio?

"I'm going to be so bad at this," Cassandra promised. "But it's going to be so much fun."

I tried to smile back. The warmth of the earth vibrated off clay walls, humble bearers of colorful paintings, and bright chips of pottery. Mobiles hung from the cloud-scattered ceiling. Sculptures and various clay works rested in unique stages of development around the room.

Anxiety connected people in the center of the room, where a circle of pottery wheels waited patiently. No one would sit at them, not yet. Bodies slanted toward the friends they arrived with, and they cautiously stole glances at others, looking away when eyes met. I was thankful to have two people to hang around, where most students only had one. Three people were a group. It didn't look antisocial if I only talked to two other people.

Allison plunged right into the rest of the group, though, fearless. "You must be Camilla." Allison approached a tall woman protecting her black dress with a paint-splattered smock.

Her eyes were blue, intimidating. But her smile seemed genuine, and the streaks of blue and purple in her hair reminded me a bit of a mermaid. I would give her a chance.

"I am." She shook Allison's hand. Clay dusted her fingers. "Welcome to the class. You must be..."

"Allison. This is my wife, Cassandra, and my sister-in-law..." She paused.

The divorce nullified our relationship as sisters-in-law. She looked at me. I didn't protest.

"Madeline."

"It's nice to meet you all."

Camilla's hands were warm, though I didn't appreciate the feel of clay against my skin, grating and dirty. I allowed it because soon it would be all over my hands. I would have to challenge my perfectionism eventually—especially since I got a cat. I was okay with her mess. Clay couldn't be so bad.

"Grab a smock, and find a seat. We'll begin creating soon."

The others looked at the coatrack covered with smocks stained with other people's paint, other people's clay.

Other people's sweat? That was nothing like having a cat. Cleo really wasn't so messy, not like that. And I loved her. I hated this. *Why did I agree to this? Could I really do this? Did I really want to? No.*

They hesitated. Allison walked right over, forcing Cassandra and me to as well. We exchanged a look while Allison grabbed a smock. She had always been artsier than us—creative, fun.

Was I ever fun? I think perhaps I was once upon a time. Could I be that way again? Probably too damaged. Everything in me screamed, recoiled as I picked up a blood-washed smock. No, red paint. It was only red paint. Only a smock that had been around other people's bodies. I closed my eyes. Suddenly, it was around my body.

It was every bit as horrifying as I thought it would be. Their sweat soaked into my skin. Tainted my veins. *And the stains...* Brian would be so angry.

When we first got together, we never fought. He never got angry at me, even when I kissed that other boy two weeks in, when I stained his favorite sweater, was late to a date. I was so stressed back then, but he never blamed me—even when my mother came that one day and I cried. I freaked out, and he was there.

He took me on trips to the city, bought me gorgeous jewelry, flowers, roses. I led him on hikes, walks through secret gardens. I made him dinner, surprised him with coffee and beach trips. And that was enough for him. I was enough for him. Back then.

We adored each other. Everyone said we were perfect. We were perfect. But then there was that one fight. Over what, I couldn't remember. I didn't think it would be a huge milestone, a red flag. *Everyone fights, right?* But as time went by, he got angry at me more easily. I got angry at him faster. It would end in a fight. We would scream—and cry. *And it became physical?* I could never know anymore.

Camilla's hand on my shoulder brought me back to the pottery class, to the colors, away from the black. It was a new start. It would be fine. We would have fun.

"Looks great," she smiled.

Maybe genuine?

I thanked her and took my place between Cassandra and Allison. I appreciated the fact that I was between them, even though they probably wanted to sit next to each other. They knew I needed the extra support, and I was more than willing to take it.

A chunk of brown clay already sat in front of each of us, wet, slimy. It looked like a lump of mud, which was really all it was. I was supposed to touch that, touch mud, and turn it into something nice. It was almost like taking a clump of cells and turning it into a human.

I picked up the clay like Camilla instructed and centered it on the wheel. That was nothing compared to crafting a human. There was less pain, less pressure, lower stakes if I messed up. It wasn't quite so messy.

"Now dip your hands in the water."

Almost as messy.

"And wrap them around the clay."

Imagine how muddy that would be. How messy. Even worse than painting. The clay would settle in the lines of my skin like it had hers. It was far scarier than painting my house. It was creating something new. I couldn't do it. I could not do it.

Wet clay coated my fingertips. Carefully, I tried to get used to the feeling before I wrapped my whole hand around it. Grime coated my fingertips. *Careful.* My new fingerprint.

"Don't be afraid." Camilla was so confident, so sure of herself. Like I could trust her. "Really get in there."

I plunged in. Full hands wrapped around swamp muck. Shock. It was a horrible shock. Repulsive. Uneven sides smoothed a little.

"Keep adding water to it, smoothing it out," Camilla instructed as she sat in the middle of the group, working her own fresh lump into something malleable.

I watched her, the clay still whirling under my hands. It was getting drier. It would soon turn to dust.

I dipped my hands in water again, used them to shape my lump into a piece of mud that looked like a good start. I leaned in closer, like Camilla did. I anchored my elbows into my body, cupped my clay as I would a child. By experimenting, I learned I could put a bit more pressure on it without breaking it.

I was slow, meticulous, and it started to be a bit thrilling—a lot thrilling really. Everything else was lost as my full focus gathered to create that nothing into something. All my own choosing, if I tried hard enough. How it turned out was completely up to me. I could do that.

Even when I couldn't, when the sides got a little too thin, the bottom a bit uneven, Camilla leaned over me. She guided me, showed me how to fix it. She helped me improve without making me feel inferior in the process.

Cassandra was the first to finish her pot, and it took her hours to do so. She stood and stretched. I looked over for a moment. Glorious. My muscles ached to move like hers did, to feel the same relief.

My attention returned to the project at hand. It wasn't finished yet, and I didn't dare leave until it was. Standing, stretching, that would be far too tempting. I might never come back to hunch over mud. Cassandra left to get us coffee and snacks while Allison and I continued to form our art.

Some left. Others stayed just as long as we did. They were smudges of light on the day, flickers of movement. I barely noticed them through my own focus. Some talked, laughed. I didn't make a sound, and no one tried to talk to me. It was my escape, and I loved it. I never wanted to leave.

Eventually, my little pot was as lovely as I could make it. The sides were a little uneven. The top sloped a bit, and it was rather small. But it was mine, and it was pretty good for my first try.

That wouldn't be the only visit. I would have to come back anyway to complete the steps and turn it into a fully formed pot. Yet, even once it was finished, I wasn't. I would never be a master, never be perfect, never be good enough.

Except, I was there. I was good enough, even though I wasn't perfect. I was accepted, and I wanted to try doing better—not because I felt pressured to, but because I wanted to. I wanted to keep escaping, to see if I could find something beautiful among the dust and the mud. I wanted to create something different.

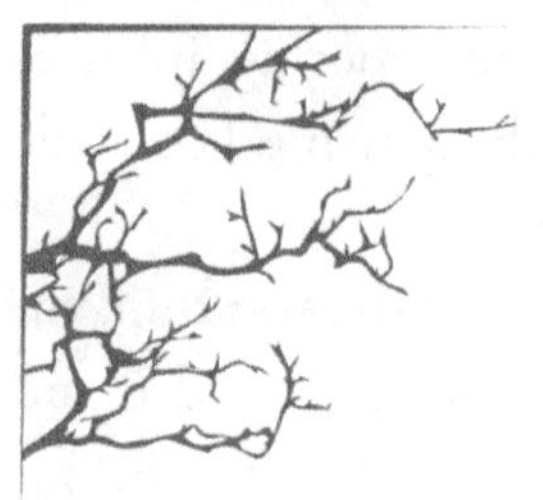

Chapter 13

The dust stuck to the lines of my skin just as I feared it would. Even though I wore a smock, some of it gathered on my jeans. I took a little bit of my creation with me. A little bit I wouldn't share with anyone else.

I didn't mind as much as I thought I would though. I didn't mind at all, really. And by the time I got home after a wonderful dinner with Cassandra and Allison, I was in a great mood. *The darkness banished for good?* For the time, at least. I couldn't wait to get home to Cleo, curl up with some tea, and watch a movie. I didn't even look for the car. Yet there it was.

I slowed down as I passed it, almost passed it without recognizing it. Amazing how many things we can see without really seeing them, how unaware we can be, how blissful those moments are. *Would I choose not to see if I could?* For that night at least, I think I would've. I did see it though. It was the same car, same tinted windows, but that close, I could see an outline of a figure, a man with blurred features.

Fury returned, having grown under all that happiness, tended by hope. *How dare he ruin my day like this? How dare he remind me when I was doing so well at forgetting?* As I parked my car, I had a few seconds to think about what to do, then reconsider. *What if it's Brian?* It couldn't be. He hadn't been released yet. If he had, they would've told me. *Right?* His parents were trying, but they hadn't succeeded. *Right?* I couldn't really think straight. Not with all the anger. I was barely thinking as I slammed the car door.

What if it's the police? What will they think of me confronting them like this? What if it only confirms their suspicions? What if I get arrested? I walked across the lawn. *Am I really doing this? Really? I should stop. Right here. Right now. Turn back around.* Cleo was waiting. The man could be dangerous. *What if I die? Who will take care of her?* She'd already been abandoned before. *If she ended up at the shelter again, would she think I abandoned her too?*

I could be crazy. That slowed my pace for a moment. *What if I'm making all this up? What if everything that has happened has finally taken its toll on me? Driven me over the edge.* Maybe I was losing it. Maybe I was about to confront an empty car, or an innocent person. Maybe I would be the one sent to prison, not Brian—or put in a psych ward, or a ditch.

I kept walking. I didn't think I was going crazy. And if I was, it was best to find out so I wasn't scared over nothing. If it was nothing, well I would figure that out. *If it wasn't?* I wasn't scared even as I marched across the street. The blackness drew me in. *Who's hiding behind those tinted windows? Brian? An officer? Someone else? Someone dangerous?* Certainly.

But I was taller than he was as I raised my fist to the glass window. I knocked as I would if I were knocking on a door, with confidence—nothing left to lose. *Kill me. Life already has.*

He looked up at me, his brown eyes bright with shock. At least they weren't blue. He was muscular. His dark hair was cut short, and in another situation, he might have been intimidating. Yet he looked scared of me, too scared to face me. *Too scared to open the window? Is he going to?* I would break it if he didn't. Slowly, the glass barrier between us receded.

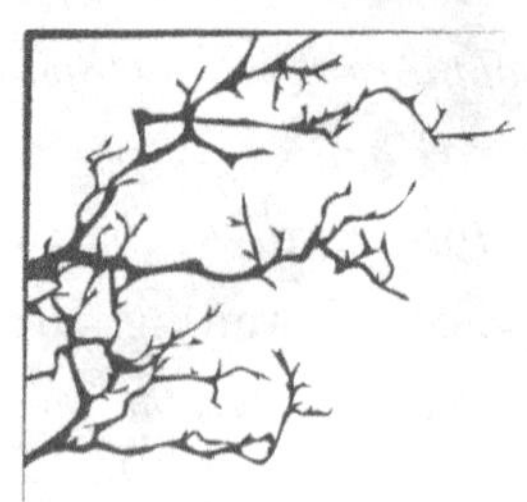

Part II
Declan

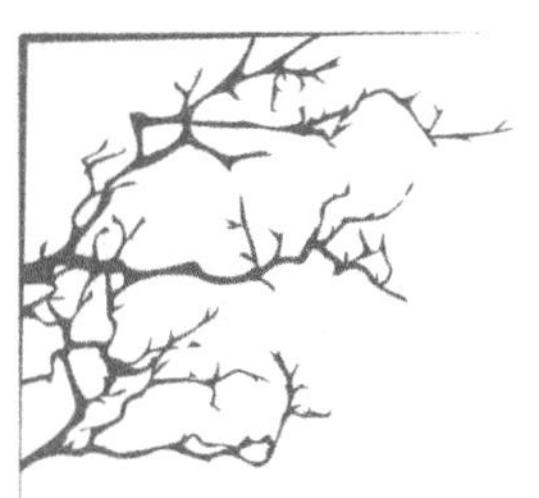

Chapter 14

F*uck! How did she know?* I knew she would notice. I wasn't cut out for that kind of work. I wasn't meant to be a criminal. That was why I owed Brian so much in the first place—because I wasn't good at sneaking around, though I tried so hard to be discreet.

Did I? Really? Perhaps not as much as I could've. The whole situation just felt grimy, and I was trying to be a better man. Digging up dirt on a woman who just lost her baby wasn't in line with that. But neither was watching Brian get punished for a crime he didn't commit. And he had helped me so much in the past. He gave me the second chance I didn't deserve but desperately needed.

No one was really focused on Madeline anymore. Everyone was focused on Brian and how guilty he looked. It seemed like no one believed him. I knew better though. He was a good person, and that was my chance to finally pay him back for all he'd done for me. Even if I hated stalking someone.

In trying to figure out what game Madeline was playing, I'd learned enough to know she wasn't as innocent as she looked. It wasn't enough to ease the guilt though. Not enough to justify my actions. *What would Leah think if she knew?*

As the window disappeared, the full weight of my repulsive behavior was forced on me. She was kind of hot, rather slender with blond hair and brown eyes. But she looked old in a way a woman in her late twenties shouldn't. Since I'd been watching her, she'd grown from completely hunched over to standing up straight. I wasn't sure what motivated her transformation, but it was apparent.

Yet the darkness hadn't quite left the bottom of her eyes. Her hair fell into her face, and her anger enhanced her exhaustion, her grief. My presence made it all come back. I was a monster, but I wouldn't be forever. Once I was done with all that, I would make up for it.

It felt like my life was a never-ending series of debts to pay off, favors people expected me to return, jumping ahead but only because I still owed someone else. Soon, that would all be over, and I couldn't fully fathom what a relief that would be. I just had to get through my task.

"Who are you?" Madeline's words were ice spears that worked their way under my skin.

What can I even say? How can I soothe the situation? I had talked my way out of worse before. But even I couldn't justify my actions. "My name's Declan." I offered my hand out the window. "It's nice to meet you."

She looked at my hand. Her wrist flickered. She was really going to shake it, introduce herself. It was going to work. She looked back up at me. "Why are you stalking me? I've seen you outside my house multiple times now. I've caught glimpses of your car at other places I've been. You were even at my daughter's funeral! How dare you go there?"

I wasn't going to go. That was one step too far. I had intended to leave her alone for that day at least, maybe even the day after, and let her grieve in peace. But Brian had needed a friend, and I'd needed him. It wasn't about stalking Madeline that day. It was only about trying to be a friend to Brian.

"It's Brian, isn't it?" she demanded.

I recognized that look paired with hands on hips. Leah used to give it to me all the time until she finally gave up on me, on us. I wished every day that she would give me that look again—that look that meant she at least cared.

"First, he murders my child. Now, he's having me stalked." Her frown twisted into a cruel smile. "But maybe this is good. Maybe this could work in my favor. I could call the police and—"

"No!" I sounded harsher than I'd meant to.

She stopped. Listened.

I didn't want to do it, but I couldn't risk that. Going to jail, even getting arrested, would screw me over in a way I might not be able to come back from. Even if I weren't charged with anything, it would ruin my chances of getting visitation with my daughter. I wasn't even going for custody. I knew I didn't deserve it. I just wanted to see her, and I was on my last chance—if I even had a chance left.

I opened the door slowly enough for her to back out of the way. She did. I was able to show her how much taller I was, how much stronger. She wilted as I looked down at her. It made me feel terrible. I'd never done something like that before, even during Leah's and my worst fights.

"You don't really want that, do you?" I asked.

She grabbed her wrist.

I didn't know everything, but I knew enough. "Brian may have secrets, but so do you. If I just happened to be at the police station anyway, those secrets might slip out. Those secrets might get me out."

"I won't let you keep stalking me," she snapped. "My secrets won't matter so much when the police find out my husband hired someone to stalk me, intimidate me. He'll be locked up for sure. And who will listen to someone hired by a murder suspect?"

Who would listen to someone who's had run-ins with the law? Someone with a past like mine? What would that look like to the judge? The hearing was only a couple of weeks away, so close. I couldn't screw it up. This had to work.

"Do you really want to risk it?" I asked. "Sure, they'll be interested in Brian's part, but you were a suspect too. They'll be interested in hearing about you. You and Brian will catch their attention more than I ever could."

She looked down at the street, uncertain. I could work with that. It was my only shot.

I opened my arms, more like a friend, to appear less threatening since she was listening. It was disgusting how manipulative I'd gotten. "Look, we both have our reasons for not wanting the police to get involved. So, why don't we try to work this out?"

"I won't let you keep stalking me," she repeated.

"The gig's up now," I said, though I wasn't sure it had to be. I could still find a way to continue the search. I just had to get creative. "You're right. Brian hired me. And he can't expect me to keep trailing you if you know about it. He won't."

"And if he does?" Madeline asked. "How do I know you won't just get sneakier? I know Brian. He won't give up that easily, especially when he's desperate. He can get a little... rash when he's cornered."

Maybe he would insist I stop. I would be a little relieved at that. *Or maybe...* "Then maybe we could work together," I suggested.

Her eyebrows rose toward the setting sun.

I couldn't blame her. *It's all crazy, but where else would I expect these last few years to lead?* Things could be worse. I knew that all too well. *So, why not make the most of this?*

"Just hear me out. Okay? Brian hired me, but I don't harbor any particular loyalty to him. He's just helping me out with something. So, if you don't go to the police, maybe I can lead him astray, be your inside man. I'll tell you what he's thinking, what he knows."

"What he knows because you told him."

"Not as much as your mother has told him."

I was expecting protests, outrage. I waited for Madeline to insist that her mother would never do such a thing. I didn't believe it myself until I saw her at the prison talking to him. I already had my comebacks rehearsed.

She didn't respond at first. Then she shook her head. "I can't believe her," she hissed. Her anger screamed her true feelings though. She believed me. She looked back up at me. "Tell him I found out, and if he doesn't call it off, then we'll talk. But if I see you or any of Brian's rats sneaking around here again, I will call the police. I refuse to stand for this." She turned, her anger a cloak that whipped around her.

"How will I contact you?" I asked.

"I'm sure Brian gave you my number."

I'd forgotten all about that. Of course he did. He gave me everything. Nothing was sacred between him and his wife anymore, nothing except his own secrets. But a good deal of those were expected to come out during the trial, and thanks to all the sins I'd gathered over the years, I couldn't blame anyone for theirs. Unless he or Madeline killed Abigail. Even Brian didn't think that though.

"Call me. If he doesn't call it off, then we'll set something up." She walked off in a huff, not waiting for my reply.

I didn't have one to give her anyway. I watched her for a moment, still shocked I'd just had my first conversation with the woman I'd been watching for a couple of weeks—someone I thought I was getting to know. I didn't know anything.

I retreated to my car and rolled the window up. My mind fired off in different directions, but all thoughts led to the same place. "Fuck!"

My fist thudded against my steering wheel. So much anger and tension remained, but it eased enough that I could start my car and drive away before I did something stupid.

It sucked being so helpless, to be the scum that stalked a grieving mother, blackmailed her. And honestly, I hated Brian just a little for everything he held over me. Knowing another man controlled my life infuriated me. But he wasn't the one in the wrong. I chose to do it for him. I needed to repay him, and he had only stepped in when

I'd needed help. It wasn't like he'd planned it. *Besides, what could I do about it now?*

Not think about it, that was what I could do. I blared the music. Someone screamed loud enough to drown out my thoughts. I would have to visit Brian, tell him everything. But it was impossible to do that right then anyway. It would have to wait until the next day.

Right then, I was parched. Only whiskey could satisfy my thirst. One of my favorite bars was right down the street. So far, I had refrained from taking a sip. I didn't want to say things I shouldn't, didn't want to get involved in yet another fight. But, God, my fists ached for relief. I deserved relief after my day. No. I couldn't. I had to stay out of trouble, or I would never see Grace again.

I took the long way round, resisting the urge to release my anger through speed. Even a simple ticket could screw me. I stopped at the gym, anxious to work my muscles so hard that the pain burned away everything else.

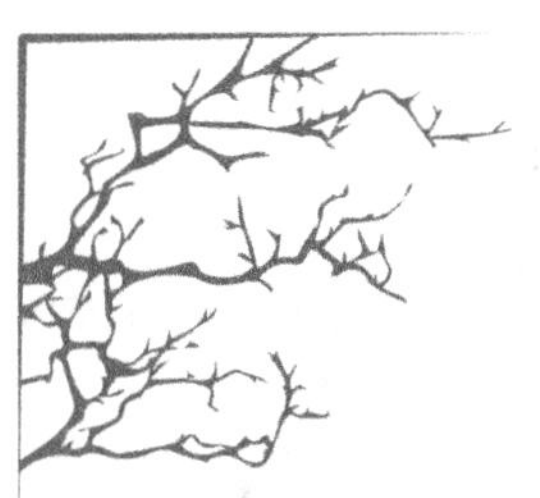

Chapter 15

I lowered my music as my car approached the prison. I didn't need to draw attention to myself. Not there. Not then. Still, the barbed wire fence saw me. It closed in on me. I still had time to drive away, cut my losses, and try to figure out my life without Brian's help.

But Brian was a huge reason why I lived outside prison walls in the first place, maybe the only reason. I couldn't abandon him. Especially because I owed him, and I was the type of man who always paid my debts. Or at least, I was becoming that kind of man.

Could I betray him? For real? Do I harbor any true loyalty to him? Even I didn't know, because I was still trying to know myself. *Is it true loyalty when you help someone because you owe them? Does my life have any real meaning when it's built off increasing transactions?* It was difficult to keep a friendship up with someone who could ruin my life.

I thought back to Leah. It was more difficult to pay someone back who had already written my bill up as a loss and decided to stop doing business with me.

I clenched my fists and forced myself out of my car. I focused on each footstep, each breath of fresh air, grasping for it as the prison doors shut. It wouldn't look good to come in already sweating, fists clenched, eyes wandering like a junkie looking for his next fix. They would think I was up to something. A couple of guards already watched me. Not me. They watched everyone who came in. I was getting paranoid, and that always ruined me.

I blinked, using the second of darkness to put on my facade. I never left home without it. My hands unclenched, making me look weaker, safer. I kept my stride in check—confident and not rushed.

I looked out the dirty window—gray sky, gray parking lot, dirty brown buildings, lonely cars. Mine was out there as an escape, not like last time.

Facing the metal detectors, I took off my watch, belt, and fear. I placed them all into a little plastic basket. I didn't care that the guards eyed me as I walked through. They were just doing their jobs, and I wasn't a criminal. I was visiting someone who'd been unjustly imprisoned.

As a reward for making it through the prison bs, the guards granted me entrance into a creepy gray room with black-and-white tile arranged to hypnotize me, convince me to never return. Cheap tables worse than the ones back in school were the only comforts. I bought a couple of sodas, some chips, cookies, and candy bars from the vending machines. Brian was always starving when he came out. Maybe that would put me on his good side, if he even had one of those anymore. I couldn't blame him with everything going on, but he hadn't been the easiest to get along with lately.

The stupidly small chair creaked as I sat. Older couples clung to each other as they waited. Young women sat, many with kids tied to their laps. Only one other guy my age was present. The rest were smart enough to give up.

God, it was so hot. I clenched my fists, unclenched them, opened a bag of chips so I would have something to do. I barely tasted them. By the time the second chip touched my tongue, the prisoners were led out.

Orange was a shock of color too bright for the room, drawing everyone's attention to the mess the people they cared about had found themselves in. The uniforms burned, but I couldn't look away. It was fascinating and horrifying to see the various types of people locked up, the transformation Brian underwent.

Unlike his ex, he was getting tougher by the day. His hair was growing out. His uniform looked a bit tattered. The blue in his eyes had faded to match all that gray. He had always been strong, but I was impressed by how muscular he was getting. Not that I envied him.

"Those are mine." He took the bag of chips right out of my hand and started eating.

I pushed the pile of snacks toward him.

"You can eat on the outside if you're hungry. The food here is complete trash, toxic at best. Please tell me you found something to get me the fuck out of here."

"Actually, that's what I came to talk to you about."

"Well, I assumed it wasn't a social call." He leaned closer. "What'd you find?"

I was tempted to make something up, neglect to share that Madeline had found out. But I wanted out of my mess, and if Brain found out I was lying, I would be worse off than I'd ever been. Besides, her catching me hadn't ruined everything. At least, I hoped it hadn't.

"You see, she found me."

Crunch. The chips turned to crumbs in his hands.

"How could you let that happen?" Brian punched the table.

The guards looked over—a warning. He sat back just a bit. His tense stance demanded answers.

I put my hands up. "I don't know," I admitted. "She's observant, I guess. You know I did my best. She was probably on high alert, considering everything. She confronted me last night. Threatened to call the cops."

He looked down then tipped the bag up, pouring its contents into his mouth. He tossed it aside, opened the closest package, and shook his head.

"It's time to call it off," Brian said. "This could get me into so much more trouble. If the investigators find out that someone connected to me is stalking her… I don't know, man. I have a good lawyer, but I don't think he could explain that one."

"I want to continue," I assured him. "After all you've done for me, I want to do whatever I can to help you out of this mess. You deserve a second chance. I am a little worried, though, that she threatened to call the cops."

"She wouldn't."

"Wouldn't what?"

"She wouldn't call the cops," he replied. "If you got caught, it'd be the cops spotting you. She wouldn't call the cops on you."

"You don't know that."

"I know Madeline. She doesn't do confrontations, and she wouldn't want the police to intrude any more than they already have. She's built a nest of secrets, and I want to untangle each branch. Build my escape. I don't think she killed Abigail. I know she wouldn't do that. But I do think she's the key to set me free, and I think she's well aware of that."

I agreed. She was too aware of it. Even though she seemed innocent from the outside, I suspected he'd underestimated who he'd been dealing with for all those years. I knew the kind of person she was because, in my own way, I was that kind of person—or I used to be anyway. I used to manipulate people, do whatever it took to get ahead. I had built a whole life off lies that had crumbled around me, revealing the harsh truth of who I really was.

Brian had helped me out of that awful cycle. He'd found me when I was broken, when everyone else had given up on me. He'd given me one of those talks that had stripped me bare to my soul. Then he'd helped me do the work to rebuild that outer layer. He'd helped me get a job, get out of debt, and get an apartment. He had even hired an attorney for me, one of the best, because he'd known I couldn't afford a decent one on my own. And when people did the types of things I'd done, a regular attorney would only ensure they never saw their kids again.

I had to help Brian, but it was risky. I could barely afford my apartment without Brian's help, even then. I was doing it, surely. I refused to take more money from him. But it was still a struggle. I was getting back on my feet, but one misstep would send me tumbling down the mountain. The path back up had already been destroyed. If I got caught, I would lose everything. If I couldn't help Brian, he could lose everything.

"Why don't you try again?" He started on his second can of soda.

Though he tried to remain cool and confident, prison had worn down the once successful man who had always been one of manners, of class. I'd looked up to him. Now, he scarfed down cookies while he spoke. *He's been in here what? A week? Two?* He would dissolve if he didn't get out soon.

"I thought you wanted me to give up the search," I reminded him. I saw in his eyes, though, that as scared as he was of what would happen if I didn't give up, he was more terrified of what would happen if I did.

"Can't you try to be more careful?" he pressed. "Hide yourself well enough so she won't see you. Or just quit stalking her and find information other ways. I have her mother'

"I'll take a trip there, okay?" It was the least I could do, a start maybe, a testament to a long-standing friendship that had always been crazy.

I had met Brian in college when we were both studying computer science. Unlike most of my peers, I didn't grow up with wealthy parents. I worked my way there, worked my whole life to avoid their fate, to do better. And it looked like I was heading in the right direction.

Great grades and an even better internship landed me a decent job as a computer systems analyst. When I was twenty-seven, I married Leah, a brilliant woman who worked alongside me. Her parents hated me at first. They were wealthy, and they didn't trust a nobody courting their daughter.

We proved them wrong, for a while at least. We were both successful in our careers. We carved out an impressive life without their help and had a daughter two years later. Their hate turned into fondness. Her father invited me to go on golf trips with him. Her mother doted on me.

Brian and I talked occasionally throughout the years. We were best friends upon leaving school, and though we didn't maintain our closeness, we caught up for drinks, watched the Super Bowl together, that kind of thing.

By the time I turned thirty-two, though, Leah's parents were back to hating me. Life had fallen apart. I was jobless, homeless, going through a divorce, though I couldn't afford a lawyer. I gave everything up to Leah in the end. She deserved it after everything I had put her through. When Brian called me up to hang out, I almost didn't go. But it was nice to cling to an old friendship. I had tried to be presentable, but it had all come out.

"And you'll continue watching Maddy in the meantime?" Brian pressed. "If you're going to do this, I need you to put your all into it. My freedom is on the line, my whole life. You know what it's like to lose everything."

The thing was, since Brian had gotten me a job at his company, I had finally started paying off my debts. He'd loaned me money for a crappy apartment until I could afford it myself. I had gone to therapy, learned how to move on.

Once I offered to help him, Brian bought me my car just so I could stalk Madeline, and I appreciated that. I appreciated everything he'd done. But taking so much time to help him was hard when I had a life to live. I knew I wouldn't have my life to live if it weren't for him though.

"I think I may have a solution," I said. "To get some answers but avoid getting the police involved. None of us want that. It'll be risky, but it just might work."

"I'm listening."

"I could try to befriend her."

I didn't think it would work. Brian's widened eyes showed he agreed with me. But it was my only shot. I'd stopped gambling at casinos. Now I was playing with higher stakes.

"Just listen before you argue. I already admitted to stalking her for you. To ease her mind, I told her I would team up with her, tell her all I know about you."

"You'd betray me? After all I've done for you."

"It was a ruse." Obviously, or I wouldn't have told him. He may have been gaining muscle in there, but he was also losing brain cells. "I can share inconsequential things with her, tidbits that won't matter. I'll make her think she can trust me, all while gathering information for you. It'll allow me to get close to her, dig up her secrets, while avoiding the police."

Brian leaned back and started in on a candy bar. His eyes narrowed. Then he laughed, a broken sound in there. "It's a crazy idea, absolutely nuts. Even taking a chance that Maddy would trust the person who stalked her, well, there's no chance at all. I'm surprised she even talked to you in the first place. But it's the last option we have, isn't it? And if anyone can pull this off, it's you. You're brilliant in a lot of ways, but lying is your best talent. You better not be lying to me though."

"I wouldn't dare," I swore.

"I still don't trust you." He shook his head. "I guess I don't have much of a choice. Try it. See where it gets you. Go to her hometown too. That might get you further. Just get me out of here."

"I'll do my best."

"Not good enough."

"I will find something that sets you free," I vowed.

And though I wasn't particularly known for keeping my promises, that was enough for him.

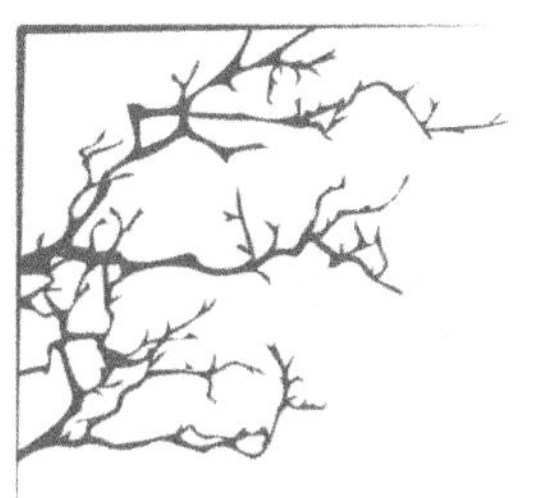

Chapter 16

Being a spy was thrilling. Digging up information on someone else excited me, but it also felt grimy. At first. I got fed up with it a few days in, when I understood what I had to lose if I got caught. Though I had always sought adventure, no rush had been as sweet as returning to work.

Computers didn't have feelings, and they always provided the answers I needed if I was smart enough to find them. I could do anything with a computer, learn anything. And though plenty was at stake at any job, especially a well-paying one, the risks were nothing compared to being locked up, nothing compared to losing my wife, my daughter—my mind.

In my old life, I had always looked forward to the weekends. I'd longed for those evenings spent with my buddies, my family, just hanging out and relaxing. In my new life, separate from my old life and my rock bottom, the end of the workday came far too quickly. Work was my risk-free time to take a break from fixing Brian's mess, time I did something good.

Once I was in my car, my time was Brian's, all because he'd cleaned up my mess, all because I couldn't clean up my own disasters. *That's what friends do, though, right? They learn all the horrible secrets about each other, then they help bury those secrets.*

Madeline: *Meet me at Mocha Mondays, a coffee shop right by the pottery studio. 2?*

I had no idea where the pottery studio was or even that we had one in town. The coffee shop's name sounded familiar though. The text had come at 1:24, a few minutes after my lunch break had ended. I never checked my phone at work—I didn't want to do anything to risk the job I desperately needed—so it was a quarter past six. A little late for caffeine when I had to get up the next morning. God, I was getting old, responsible. Finally.

Declan: *Sorry, just got this. How about dinner? My treat. It's the least I can do after everything.*

I sent the text and headed back to my apartment.

What if she takes me up on the offer? I hadn't showered lately, and office attire wasn't exactly what I wanted to wear if I could take her out. *Do I even have the money to take her out?* I did, but I was using it to save up for a better place. I was focused on building the kind of life that looked good to judges and paying Brian back. I wouldn't have to worry about that for a while though. He was in prison. *What would he need money for?* Certainly not to support his wife. I would take her somewhere nice but not too pricey.

Madeline: *I'll allow you to take me to Zola's.*

I paused, halfway to my door. She'd texted me back almost immediately, though I had missed it because I was driving. My phone stayed on silent while I was in the car. I didn't need that risk either.

I didn't expect such an immediate response, nor did I expect a demand for the priciest seafood place around. Some of the guys at work talked about bringing their wives there when they had done something particularly stupid. But I guessed I had done something particularly stupid.

The key jingled as I fiddled with it to unlock my door. The lights took a second before flickering on. Cheap tile, off-white walls stained with smoke, and a dingy kitchen stocked with the bare minimum welcomed me home. It was hardly a home. I tossed my bag on my ugly brown sofa and sat back for a moment.

Clearly, I couldn't afford to take her out. Not there. That was why she mentioned that specific restaurant. It was a test to see how far I was willing to go. As I picked up my phone, I ran through all the options. Like there was more than one.

Declan: *Sounds good. I'll meet you there at 7:30.*

I quickly pressed a pair of black pants and a blue button-up shirt, then threw on a black tie. I wanted to look like a man she could trust, the kind of person she was used to. I donned a mask no one could see behind. Only Brian could know how bad my life had gotten.

I didn't expect her to show up. Didn't think she would take me seriously. I drove to Zola's anyway. My wallet tried to divorce me as I parked on the street. Zola's stood out in our hipster town by having a touch more class than everything around it. The windows were tinted just enough to protect conversations yet allowed candlelight to dance along them. It had a classic white stone front, gold lettering, red drapes.

I walked toward it like maybe I was going inside but maybe I wasn't. I certainly wasn't going in without Madeline. I would never cough up that much money for a meal for myself. If she didn't show, it would be a ramen-and-veggie night, along with more digging, maybe a stupid movie as a reward. Even before, I didn't take much downtime. I had a life to build, and I had been lazy for far too long.

I walked slowly in case I was a bit early. I wouldn't go in without her, but I also didn't want to miss her. She wasn't there. She wouldn't come. *Would she still accept coffee tomorrow?*

"I didn't expect you to actually show." Her voice killed any hope of not having to pay for dinner.

A black dress hugged her curves, paired with red lipstick. I had stalked her, and suddenly I wanted her, the woman who had just lost her child. If it was possible to hate myself any more than I had a couple of weeks ago, I did.

"I'm a man of my word," I lied.

"Unfortunately." She turned.

I opened the door for her.

"I'm looking forward to dinner, though I do wish I had better company."

I laughed without knowing why. Maybe all the stress was getting to me. Maybe it was the serious distaste on her face when she said it, but I laughed as I followed her inside. She looked back at me and smiled, then turned straight ahead.

I couldn't afford that place with its crystal chandeliers, black-and-white decor, and red roses on the tables. I looked like everyone else dressed in evening wear. But as we walked past fancy drinks, extravagant dinners, and desserts straight out of one of those baking shows, it became clear that I could not afford it. I'd made a grave mistake, and my hope of having a reasonable place to live before the hearing melted in the candlelight.

But I was there. I couldn't take it back. So I did what I'd always done. I pretended I wasn't in over my head and acted like I could afford it. It was kind of nice—being there, dressed like I was someone important, like I had the lifestyle I could've had by then if I hadn't messed it all up.

A beautiful woman sat in front of me, in the type of restaurant I may have taken Leah to for a special occasion. I might have even surprised her with flowers beforehand. Not a bouquet though. She hated those. She thought they were useless. She loved potted plants growing all over the house instead. Maybe I would've brought her an orchid. They were her favorite after all.

God, I wished Leah were there. I wished she would forgive me so we could forget it all, raise our daughter together, rebuild. But she had given up on me. It was time to give up on her.

I smiled at Madeline and opened my menu. Drinks before the unpleasant stuff.

Illusion shattered. *Really? Thirty-five dollars for a glass of wine?* That wasn't even the most expensive one. *What if she has more than one glass? Would it be improper for me to order water?* If I had a glass and she had two, that would put me over one hundred dollars before the meal had even begun.

I had the money on my card. Brian would probably even cover dinner if I explained myself. He had a lot of money hidden away—money his wife never knew about. *But what if he doesn't? Is it too late to leave?*

Madeline peered over her menu as she watched me squirm. Her eyes dared me to call it off. She knew I couldn't afford it. I didn't know how she knew, but she knew I was sweating over it. She expected me to bail. She was far more perceptive than I'd given her credit for. I suspected she was far more perceptive than anyone had given her credit for.

"Good evening," the waitress said. "I'm Vivian, and I'll be your server tonight. Have you had a chance to look over the drink menu?"

"We have," Madeline said. "I'll go with the rose champagne."

Her eyes didn't leave mine. *Did they catch how I cringed at her drink choice?* It was one of the most expensive ones.

"And for you?"

"You know what?" *What am I doing?* I could not be that stupid. "I think I'll have the same."

Madeline tilted her head a little. I smiled back, though the smarter part of me was furious. I couldn't afford it. But it felt so much like a dare that I couldn't resist. The smarter side had been in control for so long, and I'd never gotten anywhere anyway. I was always one step away from losing. I'd already lost Leah, and I was going to lose Grace forever. To spare me from the pain, another side poked its head out.

It was kind of thrilling. We were locked in a game that I couldn't escape, and my adrenaline promised to take away the dull pain that had been killing me since Leah had left. I'd been dead, struggling through each day to put my life back together. Letting go for one evening was exciting, being careless, not thinking about how it would affect the future. It was the very same mindset that had gotten me in trouble in the first place.

"You surprise me," Madeline said after the waitress left. "Since the day I first noticed I had a stalker, I pictured someone grimy hiding behind those tinted windows. A coward. Filth that would do anything for money, even harass a grieving mother. Yet you almost seem like a gentleman. You seem put together, willing to take a lady out somewhere nice, to back off when you realize you should. Or at least you seem conflicted about doing this to me. The two sides don't quite match. So, why are you doing this? What does Brian have on you?"

I wasn't sure if I should be flattered or insulted. I chose insulted, though I hid my wounded pride. I wasn't the gentleman she saw. I was the filth she'd initially thought I was. Her first impression had been spot-on.

"Brian and I were friends in college. You know how that goes. College buddies always have something on you."

She didn't answer for a moment. She didn't look amused. She beat me with those eyes, copper bars that left me bruised and bleeding. If half the allegations against Brian were true, I was shocked. I would never mess with a woman like her. She wouldn't deliver immediate consequences, but I wouldn't be surprised to find myself drinking arsenic as a result.

"It goes deeper than that, though, doesn't it, Declan?" She pondered my name, chewed on it, savored the taste. "Declan... sounds familiar. You two hung out from time to time, didn't you? Though we were never introduced."

"We were. That's how I knew what you looked like. It was a long time ago, though, back at Cole and Ryan's Super Bowl party."

"Right! After that, I declined to join Brian anymore. It was so boring. You were there with a girl..."

"Leah." The name still drew blood as it scraped over my tongue.

"Brilliant woman. Gorgeous and so sweet, if I remember correctly. I don't think she'd be impressed with you stalking me though. I'm guessing you aren't together anymore?"

"Doesn't matter," I snapped. "That's in the past. What matters is the situation we find ourselves in now."

The waitress came over with our drinks. I ordered an appetizer, the most expensive on the menu, excluding the caviar. I wasn't about to dish out quite that much, not even for Madeline, nor would I eat it. Then came the entrees.

Madeline ordered the salmon, one of the cheaper dishes on the menu, so I didn't feel bad ordering the halibut, which was also on the lower end. Still expensive, far more than I should be spending, but thankfully, she was finally showing me a bit of mercy. I hoped the distraction would get her off the topic of my past.

"It matters," she said the second the waitress was gone.

Of course she wouldn't let it go that easy. Women never did.

"Brian didn't talk much about you. He never talked about his friends in general, especially those from college. I didn't even know you were back in his life. I want to know about you, what he has over you, so I know how much I can trust you—which I suspect isn't much at all. However, I'm aware that if I keep pushing, you'll lie. So, for now, let's get to the business at hand. How did things go with Brian? Why are we here?"

I briefly explained what we discussed at the prison, omitting that I told Brian I would try to befriend her, betray her. Appetizers came out as I finished up.

"I can't believe him." She started on the oysters.

They weren't as unappealing as caviar but still didn't look great. I hated myself for every decision that had led me there.

"He really wants you to continue to snoop around, even though I found out?"

"Yup. Prison hasn't been good for him. He thought if I could hide better, you wouldn't notice."

"That seems like quite the risk."

"For the most part, though, I'd be the one taking it." That was a truth that hit a little too close to home, but when playing such games, it was good to sprinkle in a bit of truth. It made the other words taste a little sweeter. "Sure, you could blame him, but he could deny ever putting me up to it, and what does he have to lose anyway? He's already in prison for murdering your daughter. Can't get much worse for him. I'm the one who would suffer if you called the police, and he knows that. He's willing to risk it if he might get his answers, his freedom."

I braved the oysters because they were less uncomfortable than sitting in the aftermath of what I'd said. I was loyal to Brian. He was a great friend. But I wasn't blind. Brian didn't care if I got thrown in jail. He just wanted to get out. I was willing to help him, but I wouldn't go to prison for him. Neither of us would be willing to sacrifice that much for each other. It was a precarious balance.

The slimy texture of the oysters with halfway decent flavor was perfect for that night. I hated it. Loved it. They were easier to get through if I followed them with champagne. It was the sweetest drink I'd ever had, a good choice, though maybe not worth the price.

"He always was selfish," Madeline said. "For once, it'll work in my favor, though, because now you'll help me. Won't you? It's what you said you'd do, and you have no real reason to be loyal to him if he cares so little about you."

I'd said I would do a lot of things. What I would actually do, well, that was a mystery even to me most days. "I did say that, and it's what I intend to do. Brian's looking for a way to discredit you, perhaps get you declared mentally unstable so they won't believe he's abusive. Because the case against him largely rests on the fact that you and Brian were the only ones in the house that night and you accused him of abusing you. He's also exploring the option of painting you as a feasible suspect."

"What?" Red dusted her cheeks as she noticed the stares.

She was quiet with her anger, her fists opening and closing, her posture tensing. I could feel it in the air, though, as she sipped her champagne.

"I can't believe he would even think that I would kill my own daughter."

Of course, she was convinced he had killed their daughter. *Why would it be such a reach for him to come to the same conclusion?*

"He doesn't actually think that," I assured her. He wasn't sure who killed Abigail, though he was convinced it was an outsider. "And he knows you wouldn't be convicted of her murder. But if you were a suspect, that would indicate reasonable doubt, which would mean he couldn't be found guilty."

"But he is guilty!" Her emotion carried through in her words, though she kept them quieter.

She sounded almost sure of it, though I thought I caught a bit of hesitation. *Does she believe it? Should I care?*

"I'm sure he is, but the case is on rocky ground already. You need more to secure him a spot in prison. And I'm sure the police are looking for more, building a better case, but..." *Should I share this?* It would expose Brian a little. It might also gain her trust, or at least convince her she needed me. *Worth it? Justified?* "I've learned a couple of things of interest already."

Madeline's face paled. All traces of red were gone. All traces of color gone. "What things of interest?"

The waitress brought out the entrees. They looked delicious, almost worth the ridiculous prices. Madeline didn't even unclench her fists. She barely looked at the waitress as she set down the plates.

"Tell me right now, or I'm going to the police," she hissed once the waitress left.

Accepting the risk of infuriating her, I took a bite of food. It was the best thing I'd ever tasted. It was also the most expensive, and she might storm out after that. I might have to run after her. I wanted to enjoy at least one bite. I savored it. It paired wonderfully with the champagne.

"Brian and I found out you were diagnosed with postpartum depression," I confessed. "And that you've been taking meds for it for months."

I wouldn't disclose how we'd found that out, how I'd snuck into her house while she was gone. Twice. I'd almost gotten caught the second time, when her mother had shown up.

I also wouldn't disclose how shocked I was that Brian didn't already know about it. Before things between Leah and I got so strained, we told each other everything. We were close and open about our mental health issues, until mine took a turn for the absolute worst.

I couldn't imagine a husband not knowing about this deeper trauma. *Didn't he ever notice the pills? Didn't he notice the stress? How could he not tell something was seriously wrong?*

Madeline actually looked a bit relieved. She unclenched her fists and sat back a little. *Is there more? Something I hadn't found?* She also looked furious.

"That looks bad for you in many ways," I explained since she didn't seem to grasp the seriousness of the information. "It chips away at your credibility, as you're dealing with a mental illness, and many people don't actually understand how mental illnesses work. Besides, mothers with postpartum have killed their children before. Just look at Andrea Yates."

"Who?"

"A mother who killed her children during her struggle with postpartum depression." I waved it off. "It's a cheap shot but one Brian's not above using. He's already passed the information on to his attorney. He'll claim he knew about it all along, confess that he should've pushed you to get more intensive help but that he thought you were doing better. However, he'll claim he saw signs that things weren't quite right."

"That liar!" She fumed as she stabbed her salmon. "Of course he'll play it off like I'm crazy, like he's the victim. But plenty of mothers suffer from postpartum depression. My doctor told me that. They don't usually go on to murder their children, and I was treated for it. I got help, just like I should."

"And I commend you for that." I really did. I'd waited far too long to get help, and I regretted it every day. "But unfortunately, there's still a heavy bias against people with mental illness. Brian's in a great position to exploit that. Plus, there's been your behavior since Abigail's death."

"My what?"

"Your behavior."

She looked ready to punch me, but keeping my cool was easier when she was losing hers. It made me feel more in control.

"You've been out and about a few times since Abigail's death. You've looked pretty happy at times, like you've moved on already."

I'd taken pictures of those moments. She didn't need to know that though.

"How dare you!"

Tears threatened to ruin our meal. I took another bite so I wouldn't cave. *Cool and distant. Ignore what a jerk move that was.*

"I'm not over Abigail's death, but what am I supposed to do? I still have to live. Of course, it's difficult. Some days I don't want to carry on, but I take the moments I can to try rebuilding my life. Do you expect me to stay locked up in my house, crying every second, forever?"

"I don't," I said. "It's admirable that you're still coping, taking care of yourself, living. You're going through a lot, and all that would break many people. You've proven to be an incredibly strong person, and I don't see anything wrong with that. In fact, I think it's admirable.

"The jury, however, might not see it like that. If played up in the right way, they might see it as a sign that you don't care. Brian's attorney can twist it and play into the silent belief that after your child dies, nothing can make you even a little happy for at least five years. It's the same with widows. No matter how long they wait, the second they're with someone new, it's too soon. If you show any happiness while a murder investigation is underway, it's suspicious to some—to the most important people."

"That's so messed up."

"That's life, and if you want to stay ignorant of it, that's fine by me. But you'll get caught up in it eventually. I'm just trying to prepare you. That's what you wanted, isn't it?"

Madeline sipped her champagne, dried those few tears that couldn't be stopped, ate her food. Slowly. "You'll help me, won't you?" she asked a lifetime later. She batted those eyelashes. Pretty and smart, as manipulative as any of us. "I know Brian's got something on you, but I can help you too."

"You're helping me by keeping me out of prison." I didn't want to ask for more. I was tired of owing people, and I didn't want to start a transaction with anyone else.

"That won't be enough. I'll have to make up for whatever he has on you if you're to be truly loyal to me. For now, I have something on you. A bit. So, you'll help me?"

"Yeah." I sighed. "I'll help you."

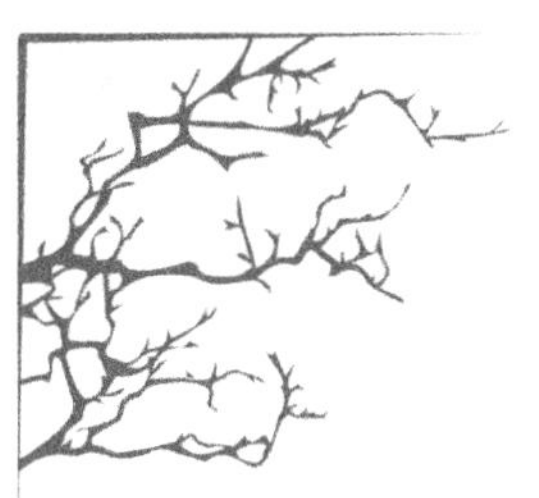

Chapter 17

"Can I get another round of whiskey over here?"

Justin cheered.

For the whiskey or the game? I didn't have time to care. *Am I going to help Madeline?* I would have to make a show of it, for the time at least. *But will I actually help her? No, but yes, I guess.* Helping Brian was my top priority. But the thing was I didn't want to ruin Madeline's life either. Not really. It was better to get to the truth of the matter, and I suspected I wasn't going to get the full truth from either of them.

Glasses clinked as two shots slid our way. It had to be Justin's sixth drink, and I couldn't even ask Brian to pay me back. He had given me money to cover that dinner, so I guessed it was fine. *Worth it?* Not yet.

Justin grabbed the shot closest to him and knocked it back. He didn't even grimace anymore as it went down his throat. He slammed it onto the table so hard I thought the glass would shatter. *That's what I get for taking a co-worker out for drinks. I just wish I hadn't chosen the most obnoxious one.*

"What a night, huh?" Justin glanced at the woman he'd been flirting with off and on all night.

Dark hair, curves for days, wrapped up in red, she was the perfect distraction. I couldn't be more thankful for her.

"Right? Too bad Brian can't join us," I replied.

"Brian?"

Did I get him too drunk? His eyes were glazed over, and his words had started slurring an hour ago. *He's still able to think, isn't he?* Suggestible but not completely useless. I did not want to have to do it again. I couldn't afford to.

"Riiiight," he said. "I forgot you guys were friends. It's so crazy, everything that's happening with him. I never saw it coming." He settled down a little as a commercial came on. The topic at hand was enough to grab his attention from that lovely lady—for the time.

"It really is." I nodded. "Do you think he did it?"

"What?"

Have I pushed too far? I wanted to root out any possible suspects besides Madeline. I hoped Justin could give me some answers, but that could backfire easily because it was the kind of thing Brian didn't know about. That was the kind of conversation he might be angry at me for having.

Justin leaned back. I thought he was going to fall, but he steadied himself.

"Nah." Justin shook his head. "Brian has always been a troublemaker, but he wouldn't kill his own kid. He talked about Abby all the time. He loved that little girl. Besides, he's not that kind of guy. His wife is probably just bitter because she found out about Katarina."

"Katarina?" Brian hadn't told me about Katarina. He seemed to really care about Madeline. Even after everything that had happened, he didn't think she had killed her daughter, which was more than she could say about him. *So, he wouldn't...*

"Yeah, that's what I'd guess. I told him he should be more careful. Having a side chick is one thing, but keeping one so close to home... that's just asking for trouble." He shook his head again. "The fucking neighbor! Ballsy guy. She's hot for sure. Probably not worth all this though. You know what they say about women."

"Hell hath no fury like a woman scorned," I said, still nursing the burns Leah left.

He looked at me like I had spoken French. Then he perked up. "Yeah!"

I pushed the second shot glass in front of him. He tipped it back and went off after his prize of the night. I paid my tab and left. Not like he would notice, and I couldn't be like those fools. I had work in the morning. Sometime tomorrow I would have to meet with Brian. *Or Madeline?* Both, but it was a struggle to know how much I would tell them.

Was Brian really having an affair with the neighbor? That didn't sound like him, but maybe I didn't know him well enough to know something like that. *Does it matter if he had an affair?* Maybe. It made me think a little less of him as a person, but that didn't mean he killed his daughter. It would give him motive perhaps. It would give Madeline motive as well.

Regardless of who did what, I had to be careful. I needed to see Grace again, and I wouldn't risk that for anyone. She was the only person I loved anymore, the only thing worth living for. I couldn't mess it up.

I MADE IT THROUGH ANOTHER blissfully boring morning at my job. Then, five days after I'd taken her out for dinner, I finally found that coffee shop Madeline had been talking about. I walked right in once I got there—I wasn't so worried about her bailing on me that time, and my lunch break wouldn't last forever.

The line would though. I stumbled into it right upon walking through the door. *Fantastic.* I craned my neck. The bitter smell of coffee grounds made everything worse. *How can she actually like this place?* A couple of teens sipped their drinks with one hand, carrying bagels in another. I wanted to reach out and grab them—the bagels of course. I was starving.

And Madeline wasn't even there. Of course. I'd never been there, but I already knew it wouldn't be great, not as great as the sushi my coworkers were ordering anyway. Plus, staying at the office would've allowed me to get extra work done. Or I could've used that time to look for a new apartment.

I didn't have a great history. I'd been evicted from the apartment I'd stayed in before the dumpster I currently called home. But Brian had contacted some people. A better apartment would give me a leg up during the custody hearing. I didn't even want custody. I just wanted to see my daughter, just visit. *Why is that so hard?*

The stupid hipsters walked around like they owned the world, enjoying their lunches, listening to coffeehouse music as soothing as the blenders' crunching sounds shattering the air. Mocha-colored walls assured me I had nothing better to do than sit there and drink coffee. Paintings and plants inspired writers who wanted to act like they were getting somewhere in life. The plants were probably fake.

The line moved forward an inch. Someone tapped my shoulder since I wasn't moving fast enough.

I turned to give them a piece of my mind. "Oh." Some of my anger dissipated into the dark tile at my feet. "Hi, Madeline."

"Hello." Madeline smiled, less put together than when I'd last seen her. Her long green shirt was wrinkled, and her black leggings were sprinkled with brown dust. Her hair fell around her face. *Is that mud on her cheek?*

"Sorry I'm late," she said. "I underestimated how long it would take to work on a vase."

"A vase?"

"Yeah, like for flowers."

"I know what a vase is," I snapped, the irritation already coming back, fed by my starvation. "Why were you working on one? What does that even mean?"

"Oh." She laughed. "I was at the pottery studio sculpting one for my friends, Cassandra and Allison. They're the most wonderful people you could ever meet."

That explained the mud on her face. Clay. The newfound knowledge made her kind of cute. Working on her passion. She seemed more like an actual person than she had the other night. *Except... Allison? Isn't that Brian's sister's name? It couldn't be...*

"So." She leaned closer to me. The smile went back into hiding. "What did you find? Why did you want to meet here?"

Is this the type of thing people told someone at a coffee shop? Should I even tell her? It was clear she and Brian weren't as madly in love as perhaps they had once been, but it might still hurt her, and she was already hurting so much. Besides, she looked happy right then, genuinely happy.

"Why don't we get our lunch first?" I suggested. It would give me a little more time to figure out what I should do. My moral judgment was rusty. It hadn't been used in a while. "So we don't have to talk about this in line."

She looked at the people in front of us, behind us. "That's probably best," she agreed. "I guess, while we're waiting, we can get to know each other a little more." She didn't want me to get to know her. She wanted to get to know me, to figure out what Brian had over me. "Where do you work?"

Should I lie? If I told her the truth, she would know Brian and I worked at the same place. *Does it even matter?*

Her eyes widened as I told her the truth. The line moved forward enough so I could see what the options were—fancy sandwiches mostly, or plain sandwiches disguised as something special. Madeline continued to probe me about my job, what department I worked for, when I started working there.

"Brian got me the job, okay?" I admitted right before we placed our orders.

She answered with a smug look. She'd suspected it from the start.

"So, he got you a job," Madeline said as we sat at a table dark enough to hide the coffee stains—almost.

That grating again. I was never coming back.

"That gives some insight as to what he has over you, but I doubt he could get you fired. He's in prison. His boss may like him, but he's going to hold a lot less power after this."

I hadn't even thought of that. Brian could possibly make me lose my job. *He would have less sway now that he's in prison, but what if he gets out? Is being here worth that risk? Is there a risk?*

Brian knew I would be spending time with Madeline, trying to convince her I was on her side. I would have to share some information to do so. *Would he think this is too far?* Most likely. In a weird way, I think he still cared about Madeline, and he wouldn't want me to do anything that could further upset the balance of their twisted relationship.

"You're right," I answered. "I never thought about that."

And I hadn't. I hadn't thought about my job being at risk, not until she mentioned it. She rested her chin on her fists like we were playing an innocent game—not one that could ruin lives. *But when she looks at me like that...* the adrenaline started in again. *Could I outsmart her? Could I outsmart them both?*

"There's more to it than that, though, isn't there?" she asked.

I found I couldn't answer. I couldn't easily lie my way out of it. She would know.

"I'll get it out of you eventually. This gives me something to work with though. See, I happen to be friends with Janet." The big boss's wife. "We go out for lunch from time to time. I could put in a good word for you. Tell her that you were friends with Brian but have really stepped up to help me during this trying time. Perhaps I could plant the idea for a raise, a promotion."

That was something. Climbing one more rung up the ladder so soon after I started my job would look great for me. It would show I was truly turning my life around, that I was worth something.

"What information do you have for me?" she asked.

That was the hard part. *I could make something up now, but what? What if this gets back to Brian? What if it hurts Madeline?* I'd hurt people all my life. I was so tired of doing that. I wanted to be a better man.

"You said you'd help me," she reminded me.

"I know, but what if I found something you wouldn't want to know? Something that'd be difficult to hear?"

"It can't be worse than Abigail dying. It can't be worse than my own husband painting me as an unstable person—or a murderer. He can't hurt me any worse than he already has."

Did Brian really abuse his wife? Am I helping an abuser? A murderer? Or is Madeline playing me like she played the cops? Brian wasn't a killer. I knew that. I suspected she did too.

"Do you know a woman named Katarina?" I asked just to think about something else.

I didn't need an answer. She slumped in her chair, her face paling. She bit her lip as she nodded.

"Declan!" the barista shouted.

I sat for just a second. Despite what she'd said, Madeline looked heartbroken. The joy she'd carried with her into the coffee shop had wandered off. She didn't look surprised though. Just an awful suspicion confirmed.

I'd seen that look on Leah's face after about the fourth lie, after realizing she would have to ask her parents for money for the second time. That look had become all too familiar to me until it was replaced by something much worse—freezing-cold indifference. Once that crossed Leah's face, I knew I had pushed her too far with no way of going back.

If I were in Madeline's shoes, I would want a moment alone—especially if I were with someone I barely knew, someone I had reason to dislike. So I got up and picked up our order.

Madeline didn't move as I set the food on the table. Her gaze didn't falter. I sipped my coffee because I had nothing else I could do. It was bitter, too hot. I picked at my sandwich but wasn't hungry anymore.

"He was sleeping with her, wasn't he?" Madeline asked.

It wasn't really a question. She knew. She'd already accepted it, even though she didn't want to. I hated him for doing that to her when they had a child together. *Was I ever that horrible to Leah?* No. I would never cheat on Leah, and I hated myself for telling Madeline about it when she was still mourning her child.

"I don't know for sure," I admitted. "But I went out with one of our coworkers, and he said Brian was having an affair with her. Nothing confirmed though."

"Just that he mentioned her name confirms it." Madeline sipped her chai. Anger brought her back to life. "I knew it, too, suspected it for a while. They jogged together from time to time. Her and him and that stupid dog of hers. He'd help her out with things every now and then. She's recently divorced, and he always said it was nothing—just being neighborly. But I knew. He's such a dreadful husband and a repulsive person."

"He is. But this could help you." I grimaced. I shouldn't say something like that, but there I was, my words revolting against my better judgment. "Think of how bad that will look for him. He abused his wife and slept with the neighbor. He had reason to want Abigail dead. He has the personality of someone people will believe capable of doing such a thing."

Whether he was capable or not. *Was he?* Absolutely not. *So, why am I making this worse for him?* I wasn't though. I assured myself I wasn't. It could make him look worse, but it also pointed to a reason for Madeline to kill Abigail. It even made Katarina a potential suspect. None of it would look good, but it would provide reasonable doubt. Brian's reputation would be ruined beyond repair, but he would be free. His parents' money would take care of the rest.

"You're right." Madeline took a bite of her sandwich.

I felt safe enough to try mine.

"But you found out by word of mouth. How will I prove it?"

"Well, you have an advantage Brian doesn't," I reasoned. "You have the cops on your side. Brian has to go through his attorney to investigate any suspicions. He puts it in his attorney's hands. You don't have to prove anything because you're not the one on trial. You could just slip the information to the police. Tell them that you think Brian was having an affair with Katarina. They'll find proof for you. You can give them his computers. They can seize the computers if you don't have them anymore. They can talk to Katarina about it. Most mistresses aren't exactly trustworthy."

"Why would she be loyal if he isn't?"

"Exactly!" I almost knocked over my coffee with enthusiasm. "She's not going to risk much for him. And who knows? Maybe they'll uncover more if they start talking to her. Either way, it'll make him look awful."

But it could keep him out of prison in the worst way. It would be a tradeoff for sure—hopefully one he was willing to make.

Her smile returned, slowly at first, but revenge was a powerful motivator. It was perhaps the only thing that could truly defeat heartbreak.

"Brilliant!" Madeline said. "This is great. It really is. I'll talk to Janet tonight and see if she wants to get together for brunch soon. I think you and I are going to do a lot of good for each other."

Or she would cost me my daughter. I was playing a dangerous game—thrilling until I thought about what I had to lose. But I would lose if I didn't play, so I might as well take the risk. Roll the dice again and hope for the best.

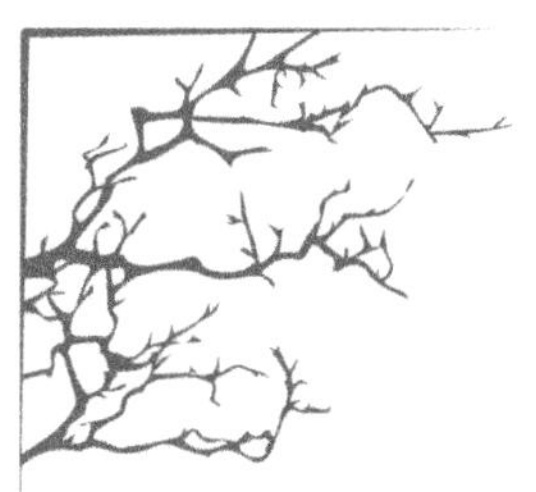

Chapter 18

"Fuck!" Brian's voice rang out with disregard to the guards, coloring the gray. Everyone looked over. "Fuck. Fuck. Fuck. Fuck." He banged the table.

A guard started walking over. Brian held up his hands in surrender. The guard leveled a glare at him but stepped back.

"You had to have known it would come out." I understood his frustration. Still, I was already losing patience with him. He was the one who had done something so cruel, so careless. If I got Leah back, I would never do something like that to her. "Something like that doesn't stay hidden under the scrutiny of a murder investigation."

"I wasn't thinking of that when we got together," Brian whined. Clearly, he hadn't been thinking much at all—ever. "I didn't think my affair would fall under the scrutiny of a murder investigation. I never thought my life would come to this."

"Maybe Madeline had an affair too," I suggested.

"Maybe." Not much conviction. "My attorney's been investigating it. No luck so far though. God, Katarina came in here just the other day too. I told her to stay away, but she came anyway. She assured me it'd be fine. She always was so fucking clingy. I knew I should've ended it earlier. I never should've started it in the first place."

I had looked up to Brian living the kind of life I dreamed of. Yet that was shockingly stupid, to have his mistress visit him in jail. With stunts like that, Brian would be locked up forever.

"How did Maddy even find out about it?"

"I guess she suspected it beforehand," I said.

He closed his eyes.

"And she mentioned those suspicions to the police."

"Of course she did. She always overanalyzes everything. She thought I was having an affair before I even touched Katarina. And maybe if she wasn't so cruel and cold all the time, she'd have no reason to be suspicious. I loved her. I still love her. Though I suppose she'd never be with me now. I wouldn't have cheated on her, but there's only so much a man can take."

He shook his head. "Can't this possibly work in my favor? I mean, yeah, it looks bad. But it also provides motive for Maddy too! She obviously knew about the affair, or at least she suspected it. Why else would she go to the police? And maybe that could've driven her to kill our daughter—so our shared grief would bring me back home. Or maybe she was so angry that she did it to frame me. Or maybe she didn't do it, but she named me as a suspect to get back at me for cheating on her. Maybe she accused me of assault because she was angry I cheated."

"You really think she'd do that?" I asked.

It seemed like a stretch, and Madeline wasn't at that level of crazy. She seemed dangerous in her own way—not like that, though, not a killer.

"Maybe? Probably not, but that doesn't matter. What matters is reasonable doubt. It could be enough to get the jury to doubt her, to doubt the case against me. It speaks to both her credibility and points her out as a possible suspect. The case is hanging by a thread anyway. At the very least, my lawyer could use it as leverage in a new bail hearing. With the help of my father's money..."

Ironic. Brian always complained about his father, about how his money allowed his brother to get away with things he should have been punished for, how his father used it to excuse all his bad behavior.

"It's something," I admitted. "A good way of handling it, but it could go either way."

"I'm aware. I'm just preparing myself to react. And it opens the possibility of bail. I can't stay here, Declan. It's atrocious. I'm miserable."

I wanted to tell him he shouldn't have been so stupid. They really didn't have much of a case against him for the murder of his daughter. It was his stupidity, the other awful things he'd done, that kept him in prison.

Brian slurped soda. It was much less pleasant than the meals I'd had with Madeline. I wished I were talking to her instead.

"What about Katarina?" I asked. I had no ties to Katarina, so it would be easier if she were involved. I wouldn't have to feel so bad. Of course, that was what I'd thought when I first started investigating Madeline too. Maybe none of it would be easy.

"Great point," Brian said. "I think, now that they know about it, they'll have to investigate Katarina, right?"

"I'd think so," I agreed. I paused. "Why didn't you tell them about Katarina before, Brian? Perhaps she would be here instead of you."

Brian scoffed. "Because by the time I realized I was playing that game, it was too late. I didn't know Maddy would point me out as someone she thought could kill Abigail. I wouldn't have done the same to her. I did as I've learned to do. I kept quiet." He shook his head. "Look where that got me. But honestly, I don't want to frame anyone for doing this, and I don't want Maddy or Katarina to go to prison over it. Maddy is the easier person to point to because I don't think she'd go to prison for it. But I wouldn't get either of them involved if it were up to me. Besides, then Maddy wouldn't know."

Brian looked away for a moment, but not before I glimpsed that look of desperation.

I was shocked as the pieces clicked into place. "You didn't want her to know because you were hoping to keep your family together." It was unfathomable, but I could tell it was true. She had him sent to prison, and he still wanted to be with her. I had never heard of a more toxic marriage.

"I love her," Brian said. "Maybe it doesn't seem like it sometimes, but I love my wife. I would do anything to keep our family together. We need each other, especially after what happened to Abigail. I was hoping we could apologize, admit to our wrongs, then get back together. But I'm not naive enough to rely solely on anything we have so far, and it looks like Maddy is never going to forgive me, so we might as well dig deep. That's why you're flying to Alabama, taking a trip to Maddy's hometown. Her mother already said you can stop by. I know you'll find something there that will secure my freedom."

"I know, I know." I'd put it off as long as I could. I didn't have time for that. Nor did I want to go snooping around Madeline's hometown. There had to be another way. "I'll fly out soon."

"You'll fly out next weekend."

"What?"

"You heard me. Gary's already booked the plane ticket and the hotel. I told him to pick out a nice one for you, no expenses spared."

"How do you get your attorney to do these things?"

"He's more than just my attorney," Brian explained. "He's an old buddy of my father's. And my father pays him enough that when I ask him to do something, he does it. Everything's taken care of. You leave at seven on Friday evening. You should be back around five Monday morning, so you won't have to take any more days off work."

"So considerate," I grumbled. That gave me an hour to get to the airport, and I had to be at work no later than nine on Monday. It was getting absurd.

"I try my best. If you stop by Gary's office, you can pick up the ticket, the hotel reservation information, and the keys to your new place."

"My what?"

"Apartment." Brian smiled. "This one has two bedrooms, a master and a kid's room—right by the park, safest neighborhood in Washington, and close to your job. It's suitable for raising a family, a small one anyway, certainly more than suitable for overnight visits. First three months' rent is already paid for."

Of course it was. That was my motivation to go on the trip, to dig up more information. I wanted to do it for him. I still did. But I began to see how he was pulling the strings. I should be more grateful, and I was. But I was also kind of angry. I couldn't turn down the new apartment, but it piled onto the debt I already owed Brian, and he seemed all too aware of that imbalance.

"That's..." I tried to come up with the words to express how I felt. Though I was frustrated, it would look good to the judge. It would help me get my daughter back. That was more important than anything else. "Great. Really, thank you, Brian. I can't even tell you how much I appreciate it, especially with the hearing coming up so soon."

"Thank you, Declan, for having my back. I really think I can get out of this, with your help of course. It's shocking how stupid Maddy can be sometimes. She's spent a ton of time with my sister and her wife since everything happened. Crazy."

So, I was right. *Allison and Cassandra. These two...* Madeline was more bearable than Brian sometimes, but they were both unfathomably stupid.

"That sucks."

"No." Brian smiled. "It's brilliant. If she really thinks I murdered our child, why is she spending so much time with my family?"

That was a good question. *Maybe she can separate the two?* Or maybe she didn't really believe it. I doubted I could spend time with anyone associated with someone who had murdered my daughter.

"I have so much on her. I'll be out on bail in no time. I don't know what you'll find in Alabama, but I know it will help. Maybe it'll be enough to get the charges dropped. Either way, I'll be proven innocent, and I can try to get on with my life."

"As long as nothing else comes up," I said. "Should we be worried about anything else?"

Brian sat back in his chair and crossed his arms over his chest. He tilted his head, just like Madeline did. "Should I really tell you that?" he asked. "You spend time with Maddy now."

"To help you out. I told you I was going to. You wanted me to."

"I know. But that means I have to be careful around you so nothing slips out in front of her. If she learns something, it needs to be controlled. Don't tell her about the trip to her hometown, okay?"

"Okay." I'd never intended to. That would make things way more complicated than they needed to be. Even though we were forming some kind of connection, Madeline wouldn't want me snooping around her hometown, no matter how I explained it. "What should I tell her? She'll want something."

"I don't know." Brian rummaged through the snacks again. "You could let slip a bit about my past. It's going to come out anyway. The police will find it as soon as they look me up. But my attorney will make sure it's not used against me in trial."

"And that is?"

Brian looked down at his snack, his shoulders hunched a little. He tried to look nonchalant, but he didn't want to share it with me. *Why?*

"This girl I was dating in high school, right before I left for college, filed a restraining order against me. The pending assault charges were dropped. The restraining order ran out, and she never renewed it. Nothing ever came from the whole ordeal. But I guess it could make Maddy's claim of domestic violence look credible. I'm sure she'd love to use that against me, though it happened forever ago."

I couldn't respond, not at first. It did make her claim look credible. *Why would a past girlfriend feel the need to get a restraining order against him?* Maybe a bitter ex. The charges were dropped. Except, she would be the second person who accused him of such violence. *Was he unlucky enough to have two vengeful women in his life? Or does this point to a pattern? Am I helping a monster?*

"Don't look at me like that," Brian snapped.

I hadn't realized my feelings showed. They were getting too loud to ignore. I had agreed to help because Brian had always helped me. I thought he was a good person, one of the best.

"The charges were dropped."

"Should they have been?" I shouldn't have asked. He'd gotten me an apartment. He was helping me get visitation with Grace. That was all that mattered. I couldn't help myself. "Did you... you know, did you hurt her?"

Brian clenched his fists as he looked straight at me. Guilt hardened his eyes. "I did not kill my daughter." Each word was direct, unwavering. "And that's what matters now. My past mistakes have nothing to do with this. I don't deserve to be punished for a murder I didn't commit. I love Abigail. I would never hurt my little girl."

But would he? If he abused his wife, if he hurt his ex, then why wouldn't he hurt his daughter? Why wouldn't his rage turn to murder? It wasn't all that uncommon. *That's why he was put in jail in the first place, isn't it?* They didn't have enough to pin him with Abigail's murder on its own merits. They were looking at the pattern, a pattern that painted a gruesome picture.

"I'm not a bad guy," Brian insisted. "I've made bad decisions, but I'm not a murderer. I shouldn't be in prison."

"I believe you. You shouldn't be in prison, and I'm going to help you get out."

Even if I'm helping free a monster? No. Brian did not do it. He was not a monster, and I could prove it.

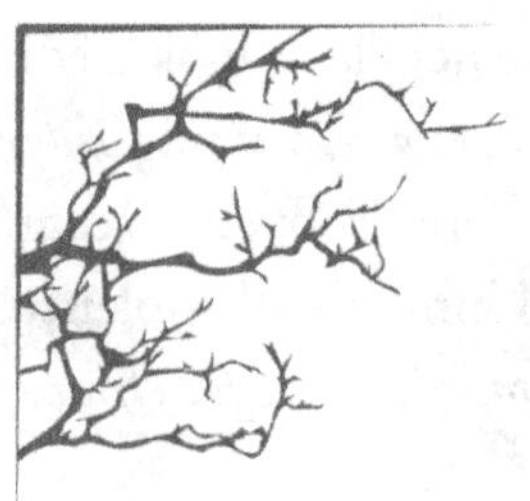

Chapter 19

I couldn't wait to bring Grace there again. It was her favorite place. We would fly kites when the sky was blue and the wind was cooperating. Those gray eyes would light right up. Her brown curls would get tangled, and Leah would complain, but she wouldn't mind, not really.

I would teach Grace how to ride her bike on the concrete path. She would be six in a couple of months, the perfect age to learn how to ride a bike. She would love the daisies, blue lilies, and purple chrysanthemums that grew around the base of the oak trees. I would help her pick the dandelions growing on the grassy hills, and we would give them to Leah. Maybe it would warm her heart a little. Even if Leah never loved me again, I wanted to do everything I could to make her life easier. She deserved that.

I would sit on the park bench and watch Grace as she played on the crayon-colored playground. We would sit under a guardian of green leaves and have a picnic. After, I would buy her any ice cream she wanted.

The warm sun gently reminded me why I was there. It urged me to remember all the little things I hadn't done when I'd had the chance, so maybe if I did get another chance, I would do better the next time.

Sure, I'd taken Grace to the park a few times when Leah and I were still together, not nearly as much as I should've though. Leah took her every single week, often more than once. I, on the other hand, was always in a rush. I kept looking toward the next thing, working hard to provide for my family, working all the overtime hours I could get. So I never saw them. Still, it was never enough. I was never enough.

I guessed I'd felt all that even back then. I had to work, but I'd noticed each day how much time I didn't spend with them. I agonized over all the little moments I missed and justified it. I had a family to provide for. That was what men were supposed to do. But the guilt got to me. I tried to fix it by fixing the finances. I messed everything up instead.

"It seems like we can't have this conversation here." Madeline stood so close to me that I could've reached out and strangled her if I wanted to. I could've taken her hand, which might have been something I kind of wanted to do. "The day is just too... gorgeous for such a dark topic."

It would've been better if Grace were there, if Leah were next to me. It would be perfect if Leah were still my wife, still in love with me, and we still lived together. Having my family back was what I wanted most in the world. It was the one thing I would probably never have.

But the day wasn't bad regardless. The sunset strap of Madeline's dress slipped over her shoulder, revealing skin blessed by the sun. The moment was lovely. I loved being there with her.

"Sometimes that makes it better," I said as I returned to how things were, not how they should be.

Dogs barked as their owners tripped over them. We slowed as a Frisbee zipped across our path, two children hot on its trail.

"It makes the difficult things seem a little less malicious when they're spoken about in the light of day. With plenty of other people around to let you know you're not alone. Lots of reminders of the wonderful things life has to offer."

Madeline smiled. A group of people set mats out under the sun and stretched in front of everyone.

"I got a job offer," Madeline said. "I started taking a yoga class last week. My instructor happens to be the owner of the studio, and she's looking to start another beginner's class. She needs someone to teach it. It's too soon right now, clearly. But she said the position is available whenever I'm ready."

"That's wonderful!"

And once again, I didn't want to burden her with bad news. She was starting to find happiness. I knew Brian hadn't killed Abigail, but I no longer questioned if Brian had abused Madeline. I knew he had. His reactions had said it all. She deserved to move on to better things.

"That'll be really good for you. I'm glad to hear it."

"Thank you. I miss Abigail, but—and this will sound bad..." The guilt crawled over every inch of her. "It's nice being away from Brian. I'm finding the person I used to be. I'm finding peace."

"That doesn't sound bad, honestly," I promised her. "It's great that some good came from this. I'm happy for you."

Madeline stopped and took a deep breath. She looked a little radiant. "Let's get it out there before we're so distracted by the day we're unable to talk about it. What did Brian say? What have you found out?"

"Well..." I had considered this whole conversation since I'd left the prison five days ago. I had already planned out what I would say, wouldn't say, and how I would say it. But that was more difficult when we talked like friends, when it felt like I might be starting to care about her. "Brian knows the police are investigating Katarina."

"Good. That means they're taking it seriously."

"They are. He's caught off guard by it, and while he was ranting, he mentioned something else he's been hiding."

Madeline's body tensed, bracing herself for the pain she suspected would follow. *Another affair? Another blow by the husband who ruined so much?* I suspected it wouldn't hurt her as much as she feared.

"Something to do with an ex."

"Oh." Her shoulders sagged a little. She was still on guard, though perhaps not as afraid. "How so?"

"I guess he's had issues in the past," I explained. "During his high school years. One of his girlfriends got a restraining order against him. Something bad must've happened between them, as charges of assault were pending. However, those charges were dropped."

"But someone else saw what I did." Madeline looked up at me. Her fear flew away to join the clouds. "I'm not crazy," she whispered.

"No, you're not. Others have seen exactly what you saw. They would believe you." I paused because lies came easily. *The truth?* That was tougher. "I believe you."

"Really?" She was opening herself up, allowing herself to believe my next words. That was so important, so much pressure.

"Really. That's why I'm helping."

"I appreciate it," she said.

Maybe I was getting caught up in Madeline's manipulation, but in that moment, I believed it.

"More than you could know."

"And why I should warn you..." I had to make up for snooping around her hometown somehow. "Brian plans to twist his affair around to incriminate you."

"What?" she fumed. "How is that even possible? He cheated on me! No way can he use that to his advantage."

"I thought that, too, but his lawyer is good—too good. I don't think Brian came up with it on his own at least. This goes way beyond him. They're going to claim you knew about the affair and that motived you to accuse Brian of abusing you, of killing Abigail. A way to get back at him for cheating on you. They even... they might even suggest you killed Abigail to get back at Brian for cheating—or killed her to refocus his attention on the family and toward a reunion."

She stopped. I hated how my words made her stop. All her happiness disappeared. And maybe I was overstepping my boundaries as I slowly reached out for her. She flinched as I touched her shoulder. My hand rested there a minute. She didn't pull away, so I gently took her hand and led her to a bench. We sat there together. Close.

I let go of her hand. I wanted to put my arm around her shoulders. I didn't want to make her uncomfortable though. I just wanted to offer her some form of comfort. It seemed life was out to destroy her, like I destroyed Leah.

"I can't believe it," she said. "I thought this would help me, not ruin my reputation. Could they use it to arrest me?"

"No," I assured her. "They won't. The police aren't looking at you. It's only the defense his lawyer might use, an excuse to get bail. Ultimately, it's a risky one because, if you did know, that would give Brian more motive to kill Abigail."

"How so?"

"Because her death would grant him a way out of his unhappy marriage. The life insurance money would anyway. And how could his marriage be happy if you knew about the affair? Besides, if you were upset over the death of your daughter, that would take the heat off him. It'd give him more time with his mistress. She's already visited him in prison."

"She has?"

"Yup."

"How could he be so stupid?" Madeline shook her head, but a bit of a smile returned. "How could she be so stupid? That's the worst thing she could do right now."

"Surely. It'll look bad for him. And the weight is already piling on with that past of his. You talk to his sister, right?"

"I do," she admitted. "It's been tough. People have asked why I still talk to her, knowing that her brother killed my daughter. But she and her wife are my only support. They're incredible and not at all like him."

"Honestly, though that could look bad, it can also work in your favor. It looks bad for Brian if his own sister is siding with you, if she thinks he did it. And that might give you a way to investigate his past, see if he dated anyone on the side before Katarina, look into any exes and what they might say about him. It could speak to a pattern of behavior—a pattern that doesn't look good for him."

That wasn't part of the deal. Brian said I could mention what the police already knew, not that I could give her ideas, help her out, side with her. She had talked to the boss's wife though. I'd gotten that raise, and she could do even more for me than he could.

If I were honest, though, I didn't care so much about that. I wanted to help her because it felt like the right thing to do. I was so tired of doing the wrong thing all the time, of being a bad guy.

I would still have to help Brian. I wanted my daughter back more than I wanted to be a good person, and I still didn't think he'd killed his daughter. But I could only find the truth by fully investing in both sides. And the truth mattered more to me now than what I did or didn't owe Brian.

"That's a great idea!" she said.

The song of an ice cream truck reinserted a taste of happiness to the day.

Madeline slumped a little. "But I can't betray them like that. I don't want to snoop."

"You don't have to necessarily fish for information." I'd said far more than I should've. "Just outright ask. If they're fully on your side, they might be willing to help you. If not, at least you tried."

"True. I think I will. Thank you for your help."

I stood as the ice cream truck came into view.

"How about some ice cream?" I asked.

"That sounds wonderful."

Each step she took bounced, like she could breathe since some of that weight had been lifted. I bought our ice creams, and we started back through the park.

Madeline licked hers like a child. Her eyes closed for a minute, and she smiled. Adorable, honestly.

"Aren't you going to eat yours?" she asked as we passed a pond with ducks floating in it.

"Of course." I laughed. I tried it, and it was heavenly, the perfect twist of creamy and sweet.

It wasn't quite as nice as seeing Madeline smile again though. She let every emotion play across her face, so it was much more satisfying making her happy. It was easier since I wasn't with her every day. She couldn't see the worst parts of me.

I wished I could go back and make Leah happy. The thought was a gray cloud I pushed away. It was like a new beginning, one Leah would never grant me. It was my chance to help a woman, to get my daughter back in my life, to prove I was worth something.

Just as we finished our ice creams—

"Daddy!"

The word broke me. I stopped. It couldn't really be. Madeline turned. I didn't dare. Tiny feet became louder as they grew closer. And if I turned and it wasn't her, my heart would break. If I didn't and it was, it might break her heart, and her heart was much more valuable than mine. I turned. She almost tripped as she ran toward me. Leah reached and stopped her from falling. Leah righted her, but she didn't stop Grace from running to me. Leah wouldn't look up at me. That was okay. Because there was Grace. I knelt to be right at her level. I welcomed her into my arms and hugged her like I'd dreamed of doing for months. I didn't even try to hide the tears. That was everything.

"Daddy!" She cried along with me. Even after everything, she missed me.

"Oh, sweetheart," I whispered as I held her. "Gracie, I've missed you so much."

"I've missed you too," she said as we allowed for a little space between us.

I wiped her tears. She wiped mine, and I almost broke right then and there.

"Where have you been? Why haven't you come to see me?"

Leah stood over us, not close but close enough, hands on her hips. The sun revealed the hints of red in her hair, of fire. Her gray eyes sparkled with concern, and I knew she regretted taking Grace to the park that day.

"I've wanted to," I told her.

Leah shifted.

"Believe me, I've wanted to see you every single day. I've missed you so much." *What can I tell her?* I couldn't tell her the truth. *What excuse would be good enough?* "I... I just... I love you very much. And I've been sick, sweetie. Very sick, and I didn't want to get you sick, too, so I had to go away for a little while. To get better."

"Are you still sick?" She took half a step back.

"A little bit," I said. "But I'm getting much better. I should be able to see you soon, okay?"

"Will you stay for a while today? Mommy and I are going to have dinner. Do you want to come with us?"

I wanted that more than anything in the world—just to have dinner with them, talk to them. Even sitting there and watching them eat would be a privilege. I didn't need to get anything myself. I would love to just buy them dinner, even if I couldn't stay. Anything to play the smallest part in their lives again.

I looked up at Leah, who was looking at Madeline—not with jealousy, only curiosity, which made it so much worse. *Why couldn't she be jealous?* Then I could assure her that Madeline and I were only friends, that the only one I wanted was her. Instead, she looked away from Madeline. She looked at me—no feelings.

"Not today, Grace." Leah touched her shoulder lightly. "We're meeting my friend, remember?"

"That's okay," Grace said. "You'd like Aaron, Daddy. He's really funny, and he's good at a lot of things. He's even teaching me how to ride my bike."

My body teetered. That was a punch to the face I needed, a reminder of why I was doing all this. That should be me. I should be taking them out to dinner. I should be teaching Grace how to ride her bike. I should be holding Leah at night.

Leah's face reddened. "We'll have dinner with Daddy another time," she said.

Hope resurrected me.

"You'll be able to see him again soon. But for now, we really should get going."

"But, Mommy!"

The strain on Leah was obvious in that moment. She looked just as worn out as Madeline had once looked. *Was I as bad as Brian?*

"I'm still sick, Grace," I told her. "A little bit. But once I'm better, I promise we'll go out for dinner. You can get anything you want, and we can do something special for the day. We'll go anywhere you want."

"Like the beach?" she asked.

"Even the beach." I hoped I hadn't made a promise I would have to break. I hugged her and hoped she felt how much I loved her through that touch. I awkwardly stood and faced Leah.

"I love you, Daddy," Grace said.

"I love you, too, Grace." And Leah. I loved Leah too.

"Keep working on feeling better." Leah finally met my eyes. "And maybe I'll talk to my lawyer. See what we can do."

"Thank you," I choked out between all the other emotions.

Madeline and I watched them go, devastated, ecstatic. We found our way back to our cars. I felt a little disappointed that we'd gotten back so soon. I could've stayed out there for much longer. I wanted to. I had so many things to work through, and it all seemed a bit more manageable when Madeline was around.

"We should get together again sometime soon," she said.

The sun began to die a bit behind her, one last show of brilliant colors. That was what this would be for me. It was my last chance to show everyone what I could do, my last shot before the darkness consumed me.

"We will," I promised. "I'll keep digging and—"

"I meant maybe some time we should get together just to get to know each other more, you know? Spend time together doing something fun. We're putting a lot of trust in each other, but so far, I only know you as a stalker. Or as someone who's stalking my husband for me. Maybe we could get to know each other as friends. I know it's not the ideal situation, but I have a lack of friends lately."

"I have a lack of friends myself," I admitted. I didn't have friends, not truly. "I'd like that."

"And thank you again for your help."

"Of course, it's the least I can do."

It was clearly time to part, to go back to my car. But she didn't move. It felt like she was waiting for something, like our time together hadn't quite come to an end. I was just too stupid to know what came next.

Madeline stepped toward me, then she wrapped her arms around me. I froze. *What is this?* Human contact that wasn't a handshake, that wasn't from Grace. It had been so long. *What do I do?* Before the moment could leave me, I hugged her back. She was so small, so warm. I hugged her like I wished I could hug Leah. Maybe we really could be friends.

Madeline kissed my cheek as the moment ended—short, warm, nice. "Thank you," she said.

And I wanted to thank her for everything—for not calling the police, for not saying anything about what had happened with Grace and Leah, for giving me a chance and wanting to spend time with me, for giving me a hug. Before I could find the words, she left. So, those words stayed with me.

I kicked off my shoes when I walked into my apartment. I kept on my socks. Kept on those words. I didn't have to stress when I turned on the lights. They revealed dark tile and light carpets with no stains, a fully stocked kitchen with stainless steel appliances, a living room with a black leather sofa, a big-screen TV, and a full toy box. Many more toys waited in Grace's bedroom with pretty pink-and-white touches. A comfortable bed in the master bedroom waited for me, a half-packed suitcase there. But the words didn't leave me. *So, could I still go?*

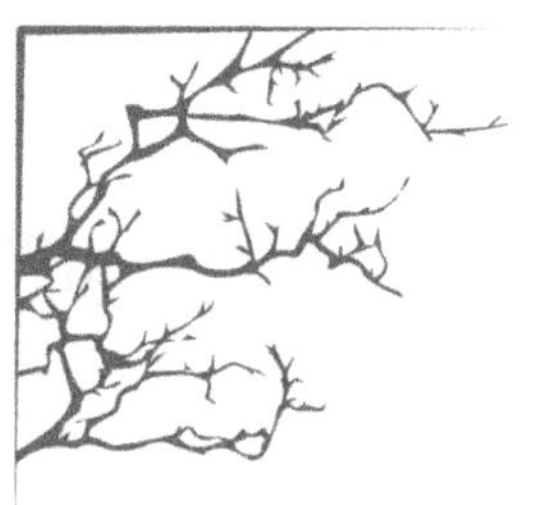

Chapter 20

I was surprised and a little disheartened as I arrived in Eufaula. Vibrant-green canopies kept the town safe. White farmhouses nestled between impressive, sprawling estates took me back to school, reminding me of videos of wealthy areas of the South way back when. Except there was no way back. Typical gas stations, cars, and cell phones in hands hinted that we were in the modern world. Brick storefronts and patches of land undisturbed by humans proved that if time hadn't stopped, it had at least slowed.

It was a small town in every sense of the word. And though I had never lived in a small town, thanks to various forms of media, I had some sense of what they were like. The loyalty between people might be stronger because they all knew each other. *Cared about each other?*

They also knew each other's secrets, and small towns were notorious for gossip. Surely the townsfolk knew plenty of secrets. *Will they be willing to share what they know? With a stranger?* Maybe. With everything going on in Madeline's life lately, I would probably be able to find someone anxious to talk about it all.

I would be better off finding the one person who wasn't a total stranger to talk to first though. She seemed more than willing to share her daughter's secrets. Even if it did feel like the biggest betrayal of Madeline that I'd committed so far. It was nothing compared to what I had done to Leah, and once it was all over, I would be a better man. I would be a good man. The very best.

It was hard to fight back that guilt, though, as I pulled up to the Southern-style mansion. It was upheld by stern white columns and surrounded by trees and Kool-Aid-colored flowers. A red barn was off in the distance, but even that looked tidy. The horses racing across the pasture added to the impression of wealth. Madeline had run from a luxurious life, one even better than the life she'd shared with Brian. *Why?*

At least I looked the part, like I could possibly belong there. I'd relearned how to look successful when Brian had started helping me out, when I'd started the climb up that muddy path to rebuild my life. No matter how many times I fell, the grime didn't coat the outer layer anymore. Despite that, I knew I didn't belong there. I never would. *Would Odette know?* I should turn back. But I couldn't turn back.

I started up the steps, one by one. I did it as much for myself as for Brian. I wanted my daughter back. I needed the things he provided for me, and I owed him everything. I was also personally invested, more than I'd ever been before.

I took deep breaths as I stood in front of the door. Brian wanted me to get answers. Some of the answers I'd found so far painted a dark picture of the kind of person he really was. He lied to Madeline about a lot of things. *Did he also lie about Odette wanting Brian to go see her? About Odette being open to sharing secrets? Was it all a farce just to get me to come here in the first place?*

I knew Brian would lie to get what he wanted, and I would look pretty stupid if he'd lied—going up to Odette's house like that, a stranger, expecting her to betray her daughter.

Yet even I had seen that ice between them at the funeral. I had been there when she gossiped about Madeline with Brian. I'd watched Odette barge right into her daughter's house while Madeline wasn't even there. Something lay between them. *Tension? Hatred?* Which was why I believed him in the first place. *It's possible, right?*

I felt instant regret as a knock traveled into the house, a sound I couldn't take back, yet desperately wanted to. I didn't ring the doorbell, so maybe she couldn't hear it. If she didn't answer the door, then my decision would be made for me. *Turn back.* I had to turn back. Yet, even as I turned around, I wasn't sure I was ready to leave. I wasn't sure I shouldn't ring the doorbell.

A slow creak brought me back around. It would look more suspicious if I got caught trying to leave. Odette stood at the door, blond hair in a bun. Her white slacks and loose coral shirt looked casual yet pricey, especially paired with all that gold jewelry.

"Hello," she said slowly, cautiously.

"Hello," I replied, awkward as ever. "Odette, right?"

"Yes." Her eyes narrowed. "Do I know you?"

"I'm Declan." I offered my hand. "Brian's friend."

"Oh!" The confusion faded, but the ice wall stood as strong as ever, even as she smiled like I was an old friend. "Brian mentioned you were coming over this weekend in his place. You were at the funeral, weren't you?" The smile faded. "Such tragic business." She looked away then at my still-extended hand. She shook it. "Declan. It's nice to formally meet you. Do come in."

It was too late to turn and run. I probably wouldn't have if presented the opportunity anyway. I needed to know more about Madeline. *Am I doing the wrong thing by helping her? Helping him? Who's manipulating who? Can either of them be trusted?*

My stomach twisted, appalled at the repulsive thing I was actively doing. My moral compass spun, begging me to go in the opposite direction, to be a good person for once. There was no turning back from this. It had been a long time since I'd listened to that though.

A sweeping marble staircase sprawled out directly beyond the entrance. The house followed an open design concept, so the floor above was visible, carpeted with wine, held back by a gold railing.

On our floor, the walls were white to provide contrast to the carefully chosen modern paintings. Gold chandeliers splashed the house with warm light. It was modern with a hint of classic vintage.

What kind of family did Madeline come from? Why did she end up with someone like Brian? How could she even consider being friends with someone like me?

"Would you like a drink?" Odette led me through the house. "I've been sipping a mimosa myself. Best way to start the morning. I can ask Evan to prepare us a snack. He's already working on lunch."

Evan? Madeline's father? Brother? Odette's boyfriend?

"I'm good, thank you. I just came to talk to you about Madeline. Brian told me you might have something to share, something that might help him out of his current predicament."

"That kind of talk." Odette sighed. "I assumed as much. We'll definitely need drinks for that."

I followed her into a small sitting room. A half-empty mimosa sat on an antique coffee table. Magazines were tossed about a light-blue couch. *Had Madeline ever lounged in here and thought about how she wanted more? Had she found that more? Or is she discovering it now?*

We walked right through it and into a huge kitchen.

Veggies sizzled on a pan, watched over by a middle-aged man in a chef's uniform. He set the pan down with a bang and turned to Odette. "Lunch will be done in twenty minutes."

"Wonderful! Could you bring out a couple of mimosas to the patio for me and my guest?"

"Of course. Anything else today, Ms. Talcott?"

"That'll be all, thank you."

Her personal chef. Evan was Odette's personal chef. I knew that was a thing, that some people had personal chefs come to their houses, but I'd never met anyone who actually had one. I was best at faking it though. Lying was my greatest skill, so I followed her outside like it was nothing. If she thought I was on the same level as her, she would be more comfortable opening up to me. Hopefully.

We sat at a vintage black table set upon a pattern of marble stones, a vase of white magnolias between us. The heat of the sun lulled me. The view of the trees, the sloping lawn, and the horses were an illusion. They hid my true purpose, promised nothing dark could happen there, nothing like snooping and betraying.

"So, have you met my dear daughter yet?" Odette leaned forward as if she were truly curious about my answer.

"I've talked to her a few times," I admitted. "She's a lovely woman. You should be proud."

"She wears a lovely mask anyway, much like her mother." She sighed. "She's far too much like me. She always loved her father, useless man that he was. But it's me she took after. Though she's not as blunt as I am, in many ways she's worse. I never would've done some of the things she has. She's always been particularly cruel."

"What do you mean?" I asked, though I hated her already, hated where she was going. *How could anyone talk about their only daughter like that? How could anyone talk about anyone like that?*

It was good though. She seemed open to sharing secrets, which was all I was after. I settled into my seat and sipped my mimosa to give the illusion that we were friends talking. It might be a long conversation.

"What do you want to know?" she countered, her eyes narrowing as she sipped her drink.

I sensed some reluctance but only some. I'd learned a lot about people as I tried to manipulate them. Odette seemed kind of lonely. She seemed like she was dying to talk to someone about what had happened, which was why she wanted Brian to come, but she also had to be careful, which was why she hadn't talked to him so far.

With wealth like that, I suspected there were some things she couldn't tell just anyone. But sharing secrets was always tempting. I just had to prove to her that I was the one she should share with.

"Everything," I said. "I want to know everything about Madeline. I've gotten to know her and Brian, and I want to understand what happened. I want to know what happened from your point of view, and I'm probably the best person to talk to."

"Oh, really?" she drew out her words like it was a game—a game I hated playing.

"Really." I smiled, hoping I was charming. "Since I know them both, I don't hold biases. I have no reason to share secrets, except to help Brian, of course. And I'm so far away from this town that it's not like I'll go and gossip to your neighbor. I'm a blank slate. Write your story. I'm here to listen."

Conflict played across her eyes. I could tell that with Odette, it would be all or nothing. Either she would tell me exactly what had happened, or she would make me leave right then and there. I tried not to get too tense as I waited on her decision, but it felt like everything was hanging on that decision, and she knew it.

"Well, she was a wild child, just like I was," Odette started.

Some of my tension lessened as relief swept in.

"We are so similar it's haunting. She is the very worst version of me. But motherhood never came naturally to me. Nannies mothered Madeline for the first few years of her life, only the best ones, mind you. And Sam adored her from the start. He was such a good parent, and I tried my best, but Madeline hated me."

"A shame," I said. "It sounds like she was so lucky."

Though it was awful to think of Madeline being raised by a cold, uncaring mother. I couldn't imagine Grace being raised that way. It made me thankful that Leah was the best mother I knew, even if she caused problems for me. It was only out of love for our daughter. *But at least Odette tried, right? She wasn't the worst parent ever by far, right?*

"She's always been so ungrateful." Odette sighed. "I failed her many times. Even I'll admit it. But she took it so hard, even though

I was struggling too. The crushing agony that followed Madeline's birth nearly destroyed me. They didn't have a name for it at the time. I had no help for it. Now it's known as postpartum depression. Hell to go through, but Madeline never saw how much I sacrificed for her.

"She turned against me. I was always trying to help her, guide her. I wanted her to have the best life, and she never listened to me. I always caught her doing the wrong thing, sneaking around—right there in the open, for everyone to see, talk about.

"Thankfully, though, she was an idiot in many ways. In others, she was incredibly smart. She got into a good school with the help of her father's money. She studied some useless subject. I can't even remember what it was now. But it wasn't important. College would help her find a suitable husband. I knew she was getting into trouble, but she was learning to keep it quiet. I had hope for her. Then she was stupid enough to get pregnant. Before marriage!"

That froze me. *Pregnant? Before marriage? That meant Abigail couldn't be her only child, right?* Brian hadn't told me about another child though. I'd always thought Abigail was their first, their only child. *So, where's this other kid?*

"Samuel and I liked Logan well enough," Odette continued, like she hadn't just dropped a huge bomb on the conversation. "His father also bred horses and was even more successful than Samuel. We saw the benefit in their marriage, but a baby before marriage? That caused quite the controversy. A stain on both families."

Logan. That made some sense. The baby must've been Logan and Madeline's. Brian had never mentioned an ex-husband though. Madeline never had. She'd never mentioned another child either. *Maybe she lost custody?* I knew the shame in that. *But what terrible thing could she have done to cause that?*

Maybe she chose to leave her child behind when she left her hometown. *But she wouldn't really do that, would she?* I realized in that moment that I couldn't assume anything about Madeline. I really hadn't known her for that long. She just had a way of making me feel like I had known her for longer. She had a way of making me trust. I started wondering if I should.

"Logan's parents sat down with us to see how we could remedy the situation," Odette explained. "We considered holding a wedding as soon as possible so no one would know Madeline got pregnant out of wedlock. But people would whisper when the baby came so soon after the wedding, and a shotgun wedding would be an even bigger disgrace to our families. So, we decided Madeline would finish out the semester then come home to live with us. As soon as she lost some of the baby weight, they would get married. We would help them buy their own house and be so successful that their scandalous beginnings would be forgotten.

"Madeline wasn't happy, but we were paying for her degree and for everything else. So, she agreed, and for a while, it looked like the baby would be a blessing. Madeline stopped acting like a child and focused on her studies for the rest of the semester. She was bitter when she and Logan first moved in with us. Her bitterness made her quiet, responsible. The daughter I'd always wanted.

"I became a better mother when Amelia was born. I loved being a grandmother. I didn't have to give birth to her, so I wasn't plagued by all the nasty stuff that comes after. I could just enjoy this sweet little girl, dress her up, show her off. She was a much better baby than Madeline had been, rarely fussy, always giggling. Truly the most gorgeous child I'd ever seen.

"Yet Madeline was cursed with the same darkness that had overtaken me, even though she didn't have reason to be. As I said, Amelia was a good baby. But for the first couple of weeks after she was born, Madeline didn't leave her bed. She moped, and she cried while Logan took care of Amelia. He was a great father, but he was in school. So, I hired a nanny to be there when Logan and I couldn't be.

"After a month, Madeline finally left her bed. She took care of her appearance and projected a good image of the perfect mother. Put together. Everyone gushed about how much good Amelia had done for Madeline, what a wonderful young lady my daughter turned out to be.

"Behind closed doors, Madeline didn't want anything to do with Amelia. She went back to her studies, spent time riding horses, doing yoga, working on getting that prepregnancy body back. It was like she'd had a child and put her up for adoption. So, I put my foot down."

Even after admitting to suffering from postpartum herself, Odette was going to judge her daughter. I regretted coming there, talking to that woman who was still a terrible mother. Yet I couldn't stop listening, even as I hated myself more with each word she said.

"Logan came to me, completely distraught over his fiancée's lack of interest in their daughter. So, I had a long talk with Madeline about her responsibilities as a mother. I warned her that she needed to take better care of Amelia, or she could kiss her education goodbye. She did so, very reluctantly. She was so harsh even with the smallest things. If Amelia fussed while eating, Madeline just gave up. She'd let that poor baby starve because she simply didn't want to deal with her. The worst was at night.

"Amelia didn't fuss much, but she wasn't flawless. Sometimes she'd still get up in the middle of the night, like every baby does. One night, after she cried and cried, I walked down to the nursery. Madeline was in there already, screaming at the baby, tears running down her cheeks. A picture frame shattered on the floor. Amelia was so close to that broken glass. I'd never seen such a wretched, frightful sight.

"I ushered Madeline out of the room and took care of Amelia myself. The next day, I hired another nanny to help with nights, as I was concerned about Madeline. The nanny was supposed to start at the beginning of the week, and I figured Logan and I could just get up with Amelia in the meantime." She paused, took a deep breath. Though she wasn't a pleasant person, I suspected she really did love her granddaughter. *Maybe her daughter too?* "But Amelia died three days before the nanny was due to start working."

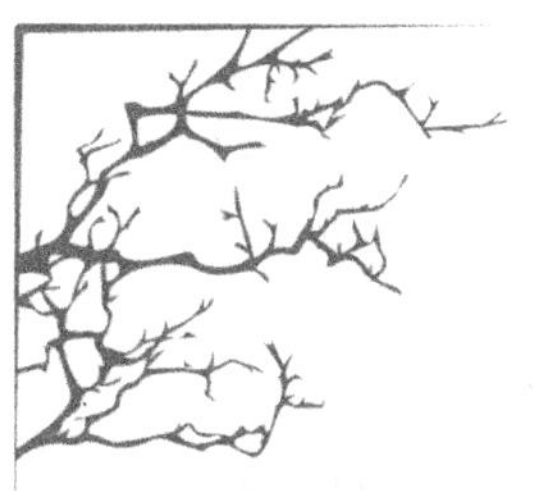

Chapter 21

The sun dimmed. We were two vulnerable people sitting around a campfire, telling ghost stories. But that one was so close to my own life that I wanted her to stop. It was too frightening. I didn't want to hear about the monster that ate children. I didn't want to see the real pain in her eyes, pain that no amount of money could soothe.

That was the worst part. Odette's agony was too bright for her to hide. She wasn't just spinning a tale to make Madeline look bad, though I suspected she had no qualms about making Madeline look bad. Madeline had a daughter, Amelia. And Amelia had died.

I wanted to question her. I wanted to ask if she was serious. I wanted to insist it couldn't be true. I wanted to confirm that I'd heard her right. "I'm so sorry," I said because, as much as I hated Odette, I didn't want to rub salt in her wound, and it was the only thing I knew to say that might be safe.

"Thank you."

We sat in silence as she traveled back to the past. I questioned the future. *Where would I go with all of this? How could I even start to process this? Does Brian know?* He hadn't mentioned it to me, and I doubted he did. That was the information I'd come to find for him. That was the golden secret that would make everyone question Madeline.

I started questioning Madeline. Two daughters had died under her care, and my heart broke for her. *How could anyone be tormented by such pain?* She was unfathomably strong to cope with something like that. Yet a small part of me wondered.

Evan came out, carrying two plates of food. Odette looked up, a true smile on her face. The hired chef, but maybe there really was something between them. He set the plates down along with more drinks.

"Thank you, Evan." She squeezed his hand for just a moment.

"You're welcome." A hint of a smile broke his stern face. "Can I get you anything else?"

"I'll need dessert after this," she said. "Disregard my diet, at least for today."

"My pleasure."

I wasn't hungry, but I tried the fish as he left. Odette started eating as well, washing it down with mimosas. I had to ask. I didn't want to. We were too busy eating. But that seemed like the perfect time—talking about the hardest stuff while distracted with food so we didn't have to face it head-on.

"How did Amelia die, Odette?"

Odette closed her eyes midsip. She opened them. Put her glass down. Continued eating like she hadn't heard me at all. *Would she answer? Was that too personal?* This was all too personal, but she matched my desperation.

I needed answers. She needed to tell someone about all her secrets, all the dark deeds that had haunted her life. She needed to confess her suspicions about her daughter, away from a community that would judge her for Madeline's actions. And maybe she knew that I was the perfect person to confess to—not because she believed the mask. Rather, maybe she saw past it and knew I had my own regrets.

"I don't know," she admitted. "I believe I woke up because Amelia was crying. It didn't happen often. She slept through the night most nights. Plus, the nursery was pretty far from my bedroom, so she had to be screaming for me to hear it. I can't be sure, because after I caught Madeline yelling at Amelia, I'd woken up in the middle of the night multiple times, startled out of sleep by nightmares. So, it could've been another nightmare. I don't know. I hope it was.

"Regardless, the following morning, I was woken by a scream. Of agony." She paused in the past. Tears gathered to remember with her. "I'd never heard such a sound in my life. Madeline's screams came close when she found her father dead in his office. But they weren't quite as awful as Logan's cries. I got up immediately and ran because they were so awful—and because they were coming from the nursery." Odette stopped.

I didn't press. I didn't deserve to hear those words, so I was grateful for whatever bits of information she decided to bestow upon me. I ate. She drank as she looked out at the horses. I never would've known by looking in from the outside, the dark secrets hidden in that house. I guessed it was the same with everyone's houses. I was trespassing on Madeline's property.

"Logan held Amelia to his chest, sobbing, rocking her. I tried to take her from him, and he batted me away. I demanded he give her to me, and the shock receded enough for him to hand her over. She..." Odette shook her head. "She was cold, so cold, even wrapped in her blanket. I leaned down and listened. No heartbeat. Her chest was still. Her cheeks blue. Eyes closed.

"Madeline was on the floor crying, brought in by Logan's screams. We called the ambulance, but of course, it was too late. They said Amelia had rolled over in her sleep and smothered herself on a stuffed animal kept in the crib.

"And I wondered—though I hated myself for doing so—I wondered if Amelia would've been alive if I'd hired that nanny sooner, if I hadn't pressed Madeline to get more involved. I wondered if Amelia would have lived if only I hadn't threatened to stop paying for that stupid degree Madeline never even got anyway.

"Madeline acted the part of a grieving mother, but she didn't cry for Amelia like she had for her father. And she was... different this time. She wouldn't hold Amelia. She didn't take part in planning the funeral. She stayed locked in her room for days in the dark.

"Then, when the funeral came, she screamed when she saw Amelia in the casket. She wailed more than she had that first night. It was an awful sound mixed with grief and something else, something stronger—incomprehensible to most people. She kept saying it was her fault, that if she had been a better mother, then it wouldn't have happened. Her words held so much guilt.

"Typical, I suppose. I felt guilty too. She left about a week later. It destroyed poor Logan, though he had done his best to be there for her. I knew it was for the best, so I didn't feel bad for her the way the others did. I did, however, wonder why she fled, if she meant something more with those words of grief. Then, I found out about Abigail."

Words faded away once more, replaced by chewing, slurping. I was extra cautious as I ate, drank. Each movement, each little sound was magnified.

Madeline seemed so nice. *My friend?* She couldn't have killed her daughter. Her mother was kind of awful. Odette had no qualms about making her daughter look bad. But I didn't know Madeline, not really, not like a mother would. A mother like that wouldn't know her daughter either though. *So, who is Madeline? Who is she really?*

"Do you think Brian killed Abigail?" I asked.

If she said yes, I would give it up for good. I would find another way to get visitation with Grace. I could keep my apartment on my own. I would talk to Leah, really talk to her. It might take more time, but she would see my improvement. She seemed to see it already at the park. She had to see how much Grace missed me, and she cared about Grace more than anything in the world. We both did. We could work something out. I could prove myself to her.

"I didn't see Madeline much once she left," Odette answered. "She didn't talk to me at all for the first two years, and after that, it was very sparingly. I know she didn't want to talk to me. She just felt obligated to, but it was all very surface level. Gifts and short phone calls on holidays and birthdays. Casual conversations that never went anywhere. I didn't even know she was pregnant until after she had Abigail.

"A month after Abigail was born, Madeline finally told me where she lived so I could visit. I stayed for as long as I could, unsure when I'd be allowed to come again. I stayed long enough to know that Abigail was no Amelia. She was feisty, fussy, excitable, joyful—a handful for any mother.

"But Madeline was also different. She was a little down when I visited. She spent time in her bedroom while Brian tended to their daughter. However, she was involved as well in a way that she hadn't been before.

"She played with Abigail, fed her, bathed her, changed her diapers, cuddled her. It seemed she'd grown fond of being a mother, and it was clear Abigail adored her. I thought maybe I'd exaggerated in my own mind what had happened in the past. Maybe I had been too dramatic.

"I ignored how frustrated she got in the middle of the night because what mother doesn't get frustrated? Exhausted. The darkness under her eyes is a makeup brand every young mother knows. It hurt to have her so far away from me, especially when I knew I could give all three of them a better life. But she was doing well for herself. Madeline had become the ideal wife and mother, even if she wasn't the ideal daughter."

Even if she'd become that way because Brian had beat it into her. No matter what Odette said, I knew Brian had a dark side. *Does Madeline?*

"Then, I got that phone call." She dabbed at the tears with a lace napkin. "Brian told me Abigail was dead, that someone had killed her. He said Madeline found her in the middle of the night, not breathing, just like Amelia. I don't know what happened that night, but you wouldn't be here if I thought Brian killed Abigail."

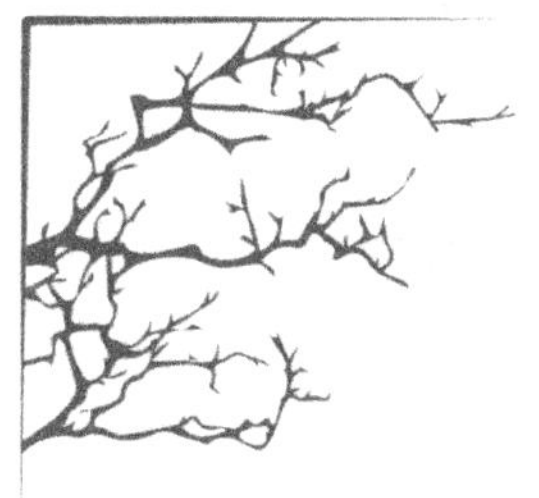

Part III
Brian

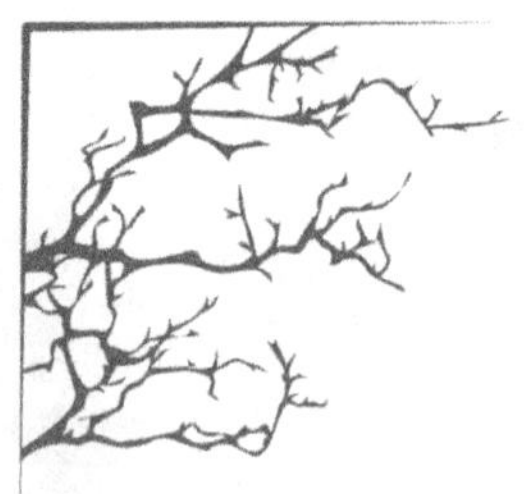

Chapter 22

"I didn't know," I said. The light shone through the skylight like a spotlight. An accusation. *How could I live with her and not know? How had I let her near my daughter? How did I have a daughter with her?* I'd been married to Madeline for almost six years. "I really didn't know."

I didn't. *Yet does that mean I'm innocent?* Maybe I should've investigated Madeline's past before I married her, certainly before we had a child together. She had always been reluctant to talk about her past, to have her mother over. I'd tried at first to get to know where she came from, what made her who she was. When I saw how uncomfortable she got, how angry it made her, I let it go. Who she used to be didn't seem as important as who she had become. That was clearly the worst mistake of my life—or at least, one of them.

How could this woman I loved, this woman I built a life with, have a whole life I didn't know about? How did I not know? Was I stupid? Selfish? Too busy building a life she didn't know about? Is she that manipulative? I couldn't remember anymore who was wrong and when, where, why. *How has my life become such a nightmare? Did she kill our daughter? Did Madeline kill our baby?*

I leaned back against the couch and took a swig of beer. Mom had left snickerdoodles on the table for us—like we were kids getting together to play video games, like her son wasn't going to be on trial for murder. I hated being stuck there like a kid again, living with my parents, with no way to escape, no room to breathe.

I also appreciated them for taking me in, for hiring a lawyer who had worked tirelessly until I was finally granted bail, for using something that looked awful and turning it into my freedom. I even appreciated them for the judge they'd surely paid off. I thought I would always resent that kind of money.

I thought I knew at least a little about prison from movies and buddies who had been there. But nothing could prepare me for being locked in a cage around men who had actually murdered people, who just might murder me. I had been unable to go anywhere, to make any choices for myself, and it had been unbearable. I still didn't understand how some people lived there for decades without losing their minds, because it wasn't really living. I would die. I'd spent much of my time in prison plotting how I could make it happen.

So, of course, I didn't take living at my parents' for granted. However, I needed to be outside, doing things, making things happen. My ankle monitor was a different kind of cage and an underserved one at that.

That was the most infuriating thing about the whole situation. I'd always thought that if I just didn't break the law and did everything I should, I wouldn't have to deal with that kind of thing. And I shouldn't have to.

I needed to break out of there and find answers for myself, free myself. Going through Declan was humiliating, and I'd started to wonder if I could really trust him—until then.

"I talked to Logan," Declan said.

My wife's ex. The man she'd had a baby with, lost a baby with. Maddy's image was slipping from me, and I mourned her almost as much as I mourned Abigail, though I'd lost Maddy long before—if we had ever truly been together. *How did I not know?*

"And?" I asked.

"Odette set up a meeting for me. I bought him dinner and a few beers to look like a friend, convince him to talk. He was dying to tell anyone who would listen. He was heartbroken over Madeline, still is. The conversation was... enlightening.

"He reiterated much of what Odette said about Madeline being distant regarding Amelia and frustrated at having to deal with her. He said that after Amelia was born, Madeline locked herself in their room and wouldn't allow light in. She cried all the time and often said she regretted having Amelia. She didn't want to be a mother, and she begged him to run away with her, leave Amelia with Odette.

"Of course, Logan refused. He didn't share her secrets, didn't want to cause more conflict between Odette and Madeline. He also didn't leave her alone with the baby much. He tried to be there as often as he could, but he was going to school and working a lot."

Declan started to get worked up, bringing back those suspicions. He cared about Madeline, more than I liked. He needed to remember that she was my wife.

"He thought that if they got out of Odette's house, things would be better. She was cruel to Madeline. I saw it when I was there. She'd made Madeline so unhappy, always putting her down, eroding her confidence, making her feel like she wasn't good enough. Odette wanted a daughter that Madeline just wasn't, and..."

"The baby," I said to get him back on track and because his anger was making me uncomfortable. *It's almost like he... almost like he loves my wife. My. Wife.* "What happened to the baby?"

"Oh." Declan shook his head. "Right. Logan said Amelia had been fussy that night. She was starting to teethe. He had gotten up with her a few times already, and Madeline was getting furious. As he got out of bed for the millionth time, she insisted she would take care of the baby. She couldn't go back to sleep anyway. She got up. A bit later, the baby stopped crying. She didn't cry for the rest of the night, and when Logan woke up, Amelia was dead."

"That's exactly what happened with Abigail!" It was so shocking I had to say it out loud. My wife killed our daughter. My wife killed our daughter. She wouldn't. "Maddy got up with Abigail and found her dead. I don't know, though... if she got up with her before that. I did once, I think. We were getting so tired, though, with Abigail crying all the time. A few weeks in, I stopped remembering exactly what happened throughout the night. It was brutal."

Declan's face shifted, changed, like he thought I killed Abigail. I didn't kill my daughter. I loved her. I wouldn't. My brain got a little fuzzy sometimes due to the exhaustion, but I still remembered the important things. I would remember if I had done something like that.

"What was Maddy like?" I asked. "After Amelia's death?"

"That was perhaps the most interesting part," Declan said. "Though Madeline wanted out of motherhood, Logan said that after Amelia died, she mourned more than anyone. She cried constantly, was inconsolable. But she was also weighed down by guilt. She kept saying that it was her fault, that she deserved to be dead, she wanted to die, she was an awful mother, and that was why Amelia was dead."

Maddy had said similar things right after Abigail died. I thought it normal. I felt guilty too. If I had been there, been a better father, woken up, done something, Abigail would still be alive. As a parent, it was my job to protect her. So, if she died, no matter how she died, it was my fault. I could've done better.

Was Maddy mirroring my feelings, or did she really kill Abigail? Was it truly her fault? Who killed Abigail? Did an accident happen in our barely awake haze? What happened to our daughter?

"Maybe that was because she wanted out of motherhood," Declan suggested, followed by a half-hopeful shrug. "Maybe she felt guilty because that wasn't how she wanted things to go, but she wanted out, so she felt bad that she was trying to escape Amelia in the first place."

I didn't know anything anymore. The whole thing was a nightmare. *Am I sleepwalking still?* I would give anything to wake up and get back to my old life. I would do everything better, everything differently. It was the worst feeling in the world. Death was something I couldn't fix.

The day Abigail was born had been the best day of my life. When I'd looked at her, I'd thought I would really make something of my life, be a great father, a better husband. It was a new start, and nothing mattered more than my family. Not since that day. And now, I didn't have a wife or a daughter. I wasn't a husband. Wasn't a father. *Where do I fit? Who killed Abigail?*

I bit into a snickerdoodle, far from hungry. The burst of cinnamon brought me back to the present, assured me it was all too real. I wasn't going to wake up, so I had to face it, fight my way out of the mess.

"Does Logan think Maddy killed Amelia?" I asked.

Declan grabbed a cookie for himself. Maybe we were still children, still playing games. He was my friend who came over to hang out because he was bored. Maybe I wasn't going to prison and he wouldn't answer me because none of it mattered.

"I don't know." His fingers drummed against the chair. "I didn't ask him."

He was lying. He made nervous movements when he lied. It was probably why he lost everything gambling. Because he thought he was a good liar, and he wasn't. He thought he was a badass, but he was just predictable.

Maybe that was my answer though. *Maybe my wife did kill my daughter, and that makes me guilty of murder, too, doesn't it?* I put my daughter in danger. I chose a murderer to be her mother. "And what do you think?" I asked.

Something had been off about him for a while, a shift that had started right around the time Maddy had caught onto him. I'd done everything for him. It was unimaginable that he would betray me, but I considered it a possibility. I wasn't about to get myself locked up due to naivete. The whole situation had taught me I really couldn't trust anybody.

"I wasn't there that night," Declan said. "I don't know what happened. I'm just telling you what I found out. It's not my job to judge. I have your back. That's my only thought on all this."

"Good." I wasn't fully convinced. Everyone judges everyone and everything. He just didn't want to share his judgments. I would have to keep an eye out. "The custody hearing is coming up soon, isn't it?"

"Yeah." Declan nodded. "In a week."

"Take some time to focus on that. I really appreciate all you've done. This will help me tremendously. I promise to return the favor."

"Thanks, man. You've helped me out too. I'm so close to seeing Grace. I can feel it. You've already returned the favor tenfold. Hopefully, we can be even after this."

"We already are." I didn't really care anymore.

Declan's life had become a fucking mess since I'd seen him. He'd found some measure of success, I guessed, right out of college. But gambling had gotten him, ruined his life. He'd squandered all his finances in an idiotic attempt to make things better and gotten arrested after a half-assed robbery attempt.

I'd never blamed Leah for leaving him, though I wouldn't tell him that. Declan almost lost them their house. She would share his debt forever. He was getting his stuff together, but he had been useless, a waste of space, a horrible husband, a horrible father. I'd helped him partly out of friendship, mostly out of pity. Grateful I was nothing like him.

I envied him now. He still had a chance to make his life right, fight for his daughter, rebuild after the mess he'd made. He had hope that he would see his daughter again. He probably would see his daughter again. That was something I would never have. All the success in the world didn't matter. Money was stupid, useless. Everything was. Nothing could bring Abigail back, and that pain was worse than any prison they could put me in.

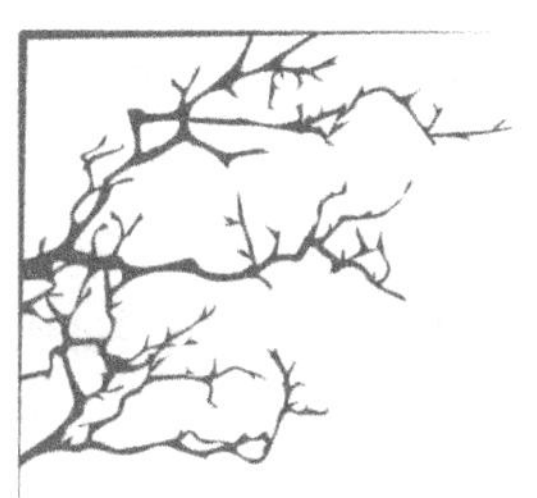

Chapter 23

I lay back on the couch as Declan left. I didn't walk him out, didn't have the energy to. It was brilliant, so stunning I couldn't think about anything else. That was the kind of information that would keep me out of prison. I didn't want Maddy to go to prison. I knew she didn't kill our daughter. She wouldn't. But that would make her look like a suspect. It would cause reasonable doubt.

So, why does it feel so crappy? Why do I feel worse than I have in weeks? Those secrets meant to cause doubt in the jury cultivated doubt in my mind. *Why didn't Madeline tell me about her past? About her baby. About Logan. Was it because I was that awful of a husband? So awful she thought she couldn't trust me with such things?* I didn't trust her with a lot of things, so maybe she was an awful wife too.

I wasn't that awful, though, right? I really wasn't. Sure, I regretted things, the times I'd lost my temper. I had never wanted to be that man. I'd tried to do better. Since Abigail was born, I hadn't been that man. I hadn't been that man since Madeline got pregnant. *Except there was that one time, wasn't there?* I closed my eyes. The image was even louder in the darkness.

Maddy had been so moody, unbearable for the whole week. And work was stressing me out. I just wanted to relax. I grabbed a beer from the fridge. I was drunk. That's a lie. I had half a beer. But I was so stressed, and when Madeline started interrogating me about why we didn't have as much money as we should, it got to me.

Maybe it was the beer—half a beer—the stress, the feeling that no matter what I did, it wasn't enough for her. I wasn't good enough for her. No matter how many hours I worked, it was never enough money, never enough time. I was never her ideal husband.

Maybe it was the guilt of knowing we didn't have as much money as we should've because I was spending it all on my fling with Katarina. She had a right to be suspicious, I supposed. I just wished she hadn't been.

I stood. She got in my face, so I just kind of pushed her out of the way, harder than I meant to. She fell and hit her head against the coffee table. I knelt beside her, anger gone. Worry became everything. Blood stained her beautiful hair.

"Baby, I'm so sorry," I said because I never wanted to be that man.

And it wasn't the first time I'd been that man. Each time, I swore I would never be that man again. *Would I be that man again if we were still together? Would we ever get back together?*

"Are you okay?" I asked.

She looked at me, wide-eyed. Her hand went to her head like I was a monster. I was a monster.

"I'm pregnant," she whispered.

Later, I learned that she had planned a surprise, a nice way to tell me. In that moment, the words had slipped out because she was only thinking about the baby, if I had killed our child. All I could think of was the baby, if I had killed our child.

"I... really?"

She nodded and sobbed. I was trapped in the moment as her tears fell, and I wanted to stop them, though I'd caused them. It became trickier to be the hero I wanted to be when I was already the monster. I couldn't save the damsel in distress from myself.

I took her in my arms, and she let me hold her, soothe her. She always let me back in, even when she shouldn't. I always promised myself I wouldn't take advantage of that, but it was so difficult once the boundaries were crossed.

"I'm so sorry," I had said over and over. "I'm so sorry."

"I'm sorry," I whispered as I opened my eyes. *An apology to Abigail? An apology to Madeline?* I'd failed them both.

"Dinner will be ready in about twenty minutes," Mom said, her voice ringing out. "We'd love it if you stayed, Dec—" She stopped inside the living room.

God, I needed to get out of my parents' house. I loved them, but it was getting ridiculous.

"Oh, sweetie. Did Declan leave already?"

"Yeah," I answered. *Clearly.* "He had things to do."

"That's too bad. I was going to invite him for dinner. Did he tell you anything useful?"

"Maybe we can have Gary over for dinner instead," I suggested.

"Of course! That would be fantastic. I've wanted to thank him for helping us out so much, for getting you back home with us. We can enjoy a nice dinner together and talk about the case."

"It's a private matter," I reminded her.

She laughed. "If you want privacy, then the two of you can discuss the case after dinner. I'll go call him now."

Of course she would. I was a teenager again, being taken care of by my mother. I couldn't go back to my house because my wife thought I was a murderer—unless Maddy killed Abigail. Then she knew I wasn't. Then I was a murderer because I married her.

To regain a bit of my life, I'd offered to work from home once I was released from prison. I had all the technology I would ever need there, and my parents would surely get me anything I might be missing. My boss had declined. I would probably be out of a job after that.

My whole life, so carefully crafted, was tumbling straight into a ditch. *Is this how Declan felt?* He deserved it though. I didn't. I should probably get a hobby, make some new goals.

I would probably be back in prison soon anyway. I looked at my phone and considered texting Katarina. I really wanted to call Maddy, but that would be an even bigger disaster. *What would I even say to her?* There were so many things I wanted to say.

"Do you need help, Ma?" I stood from the couch.

Maddy and I used to share the cooking as evenly as we could, but I hadn't done any cooking while I was at my parents'. I'd barely done anything at all. It had been great when I'd first gotten out of prison. I'd spent days eating good food, playing video games, catching up on my favorite shows. It was getting old though. I felt useless. I was useless.

"I don't know what to say, sweetheart." She looked up from the stove in surprise.

Her surprise broke my heart. My father never helped with things like that. He never helped with anything around the house, never really had anything to do with us kids. I was a good husband compared to him. *Was I a good husband?*

"I think I've got everything under control in here. Why don't you get some rest?"

"Mom, I've been resting for days now. I've done nothing but rest since I was released from prison, and I want to do something. I want to be useful."

"I know." She looked at me in that mom way, with that look of pity—no, empathy. "I wish you could get out more, but you know the rules. It's better to be trapped here than in prison."

"I know." Of course I knew. I would never forget. "I appreciate you guys letting me stay here. I can't leave, won't leave. So why don't I help you? That's useful. That's something. If anyone deserves rest, it's you."

She tilted her head and smiled a smile she kept for us kids. She never shared it with our father, though she loved him. She would never keep secrets from her husband like Maddy did.

"Thank you. I suppose I could use the extra help, and you do seem restless. It takes some getting used to, having someone else here, but I'll try."

"It shouldn't be too strange. We used to cook together all the time."

My father had shown me the kind of man I wanted to be, the kind of husband I didn't want to be. My mother had helped me learn to be better than him. She'd taught me how to care, cook, and clean. She'd taught me how to love, and I was better than him, even though I'd made mistakes. They weren't who I was. I wasn't a bad guy.

"I remember." She smiled. "Some of my favorite memories with you. Why don't you start on the salad?"

It wasn't much, but it was a start. As I cut up vegetables and made a vinaigrette, I felt a little less like a burden.

My cage was impressive. Three floors of rooms filled with different kinds of entertainment. I could go swimming, soak in the hot tub, play tennis, air hockey, or video games. I could watch movies on a theater-sized TV, read a library of books.

I had no real reason to complain. I really didn't. But I was tired of all that. I was tired of feeling like a child. I missed my old life. Cooking was a tiny step toward carving out a purpose, finding myself among the madness, making sense of it the best I could anyway.

My mind wandered to Maddie's past life as my knife went through the tomatoes. *Why didn't she tell me? Was I a horrible husband? Did that make me a horrible father? Was Maddy a reprehensible mother?*

"How have you been, Mom?" I asked to get my mind off those thoughts that would drive me crazy. Once I asked, though, I realized I wanted to know. My situation must've been tough on her.

"I've been good." She laughed. "How have you been?"

"You know how I've been," I scoffed. "But how have you been, really?"

"It's difficult." She sighed. "Losing a granddaughter, a daughter-in-law, and fearing I'll lose my son as well. It's a fear I know all too well. I've grown used to it after what happened with Cory, but the stakes are even higher this time, and I kind of... it wasn't surprising when it came to Cory. With you... plus, I just... I miss Abigail so much."

"Me too," I admitted.

She wiped away her tears. I held mine back and tried to ignore the sting of being compared to my older brother. He was always the fuckup, the kid I would never be like. I wasn't like him though. He'd actually committed the crimes he'd been accused of. He'd hurt all those women. He was a monster. I was a good guy.

"Have you talked to Alli at all?" I asked.

"Here and there. She sometimes answers if I call, stays on the phone for a few minutes. Never longer than that, and she's always too busy to get together. I know she'll come around eventually though. You can't be too tough on her. She's seen a lot, but she knows you. She loves her brother. She knows you didn't do this. We all do."

If Allison knew I didn't do it, then she would be around—no matter what. That hurt most. My little sister, one of my best friends growing up, thought I murdered my own daughter, abused my wife.

I abused my wife. *Abused?* Sometimes I crossed the line, but I would never kill my daughter. I never thought those secrets would get out. I was kind of glad Alli wasn't around. I didn't want her to look at me like I was a murderer.

"I'm sure the two of you will be close again soon," I assured her.

They would be. Alli was the most caring person. She would forgive my mother for supporting me. *Would she forgive me?* Only if she believed I didn't kill Abigail. *Would she ever believe me?*

"I've talked to Cory a lot lately though," she said. "He asks about you all the time. He's dating this new girl, and she sounds like the sweetest thing."

Does she know about his past? Probably not. Cory was the last person I wanted to talk about, think about, know about. But it made Mom happy, so I focused on my salad as she talked about the brother I was starting to look like. *Act like?*

No. It repulsed me that he was still considered part of the family after what he had done, what we all knew he had done. I stopped talking to him the second he was acquitted. Family or not, I wouldn't associate with a monster or condone his actions.

That was why, though it hurt, I couldn't blame Alli for her decision. We were the same like that. We wouldn't look past horrific crimes even if they were committed by family. I could be proud of her for that—especially when Dad came through the front door, Gary and his beautiful wife, Erica, at his heels. Her red curls bounced as she shook her head at the men who were laughing like old friends. Because they were.

Dad and Gary had grown up together, and he'd hired Gary for all legal matters, including defending my brother when Cory was charged with serial rape. They had worked together to free a rapist, and now they were helping me. Even I felt gross about it, uneasy.

"Brian!" Gary came into the kitchen as I helped Mom bring out the food, hot dish in hand.

I could've clocked him over the head with it. Instead, I set it down and turned to him.

"How are you holding up?"

"Doing good," I lied.

He reminded me so much of my father. Both had short gray hair and dressed like businessmen on the front of magazines. Their blue eyes looked nice enough. They held the arctic within them. I hated that I had my father's eyes.

"Thanks to your help, of course. I was dying in prison. Don't know what I'd do without you."

"Nor I without you." He casually grabbed the drink Mom poured him, didn't even thank her. He turned to my father. "This guy here has got to be the best client I've ever had. Somehow, he's got that friend of his to dig up gold. I've never seen someone try so hard to keep his ass out of jail, and it's paying off. No way the jury's going to convict him now. Hell, even I'm starting to believe he's innocent."

Gary and my father laughed. Mom and I did not.

"He is innocent," Mom insisted, and I was so grateful she believed me.

Truly. Even if she was the only one, she was the most important—she and Alli and Maddy. One out of three wasn't the worst, I guessed.

"Yeah, yeah." He chuckled. "I heard you have something new to add to your defense?"

"After dinner," Mom said.

She was the only reason I could stay there, I swore, my saving grace that kept me from punching Gary in the face.

"Let's at least have a nice meal together before we get into all that."

"I agree," Erica said. "It's always best for a family to focus on the good during such times. Those who obsess over the bad are the ones who fall apart, dissolve on the stand."

I wished Erica were defending me instead. She hadn't helped my brother go free after he raped all those women. She was much kinder than her husband. But I guessed her kindness meant she could never be a lawyer. She worked as an ad litem instead. Sometimes, I was still a kid who needed someone to look out for my best interests though.

"It looks delicious." Gary sat at the table and grabbed a piece of bread before anyone else sat down.

I didn't want to eat a single meal with the man, but he was the best. If anyone could keep me out of prison, it would be him. After all the guilty people he'd released into the world, helping an innocent man go free would be his penance—even if he didn't believe it.

I sat next to Mom, across from Erica. I couldn't quite bear to look Gary right in the face and still eat my meal. Mom insisted we pray, even though Gary had started eating. And though I'd lived a more secular life since leaving home, I was thankful for it, just to see his guilty look when he put down his food and took Erica's hand.

"It still shocks me that Madeline would turn on her husband like that," my father said about five minutes after the meal started, ignoring Mom's request to keep such talk away from the dinner table. "At the drop of a hat, throw him under the bus to save herself. Women these days, never loyal. I didn't trust her from the start."

That was a lie. My father had been excited when I'd started dating Maddy, especially when he'd realized how wealthy her family was. He'd only started to dislike her when he'd realized she wanted nothing to do with her family. But Mom had said not to talk about such things at the dinner table, and I could listen, unlike some people.

"After decades of working as a lawyer, I've learned you can't trust anyone," Gary warned. "I have this one client who came home one day to find his wife in bed with his brother. Shot him, of course. Most of the case is circumstantial, though, aside from the star witness—his wife."

My father shook his head in disgust—at the wife. Surely it was illegal for Gary to talk to us about cases. Privacy was never a strong suit for him, though, not around my father at least. That was one person he trusted.

Still, I couldn't help but picture him sitting at another dinner table, talking about Maddy and me in such a cavalier way. I ate some of the delicious food and resisted strangling the one man who could help me.

"I'll paint her as an unreliable witness, of course," he continued. "She was having an affair, and she clearly wanted her husband out of her life. But it won't be easy. All because he trusted the wrong woman."

As they went on and on about various cases and sneaky women, my mind went to Abigail and Madeline, like it always did when given time to escape. We never spent much time with my family for a reason. I felt bad for Mom, but I just couldn't stand my father.

Now I was stuck there, and my heart ached to get back to my family, desperate to get back to that point where I still had a choice. I was still shocked about how quickly everything had come crashing down. If I could go back, I would do better. I would be better. All I needed was that one chance to go back.

"All right," Gary said after the dinner plates were cleaned up and Mom brought out cherry pie, homemade ice cream, and dessert wine. "Dinner's over. Can we talk about the case now?"

"I don't know." Mom looked at me. "I think Brian wanted privacy."

"Privacy?" My father laughed. "He's been accused of killing his child and beating his wife. There is no such thing as privacy when you cross that line. The whole world will know soon enough, or at least whoever's at the trial. Do you expect us to wait until then? You know Gary will tell me anyway."

Gary laughed, but of course it was true. That was the price I paid for using a lawyer my father hired. He was embedded in my case as deeply as I was. There was no hiding from him. Mom looked between us, concern pulling at her features.

"It's all right." I smiled at her. "He's right. Everyone will find out anyway. And this will probably help my case a lot. I'm just honestly ashamed I didn't know about it before."

"Don't be," my father said. "We already know how sneaky Madeline was. Sure, you should've known better than to trust her, but we all do stupid things. Hopefully, you've learned your lesson."

"I have," I assured him. It was probably one of the nicest things he'd ever said to me, the most understanding.

I told them about sending Declan to Eufaula to snoop around. I told them about a past I should've already known about. I told them about Logan and Maddy and Amelia, a family so removed and yet so closely connected to mine. I felt like a shit as I told them and wished I could stop the torrent of words even as they scraped past my lips. But I told them.

For once, Gary and my father were quiet. Everyone was. Dessert forgotten, they looked at me as if expecting I would tell them it was all a lie, a joke. *Who would joke about such a thing?* They looked at each other.

"I can't even..." Mom shook her head. "I can't even believe that Madeline would hide such a thing. It's... too shocking."

"Damn right it is." My father sipped his wine. "I never trusted her, but I wasn't expecting something like that either. How did you not know?"

Exactly. How could I not know? How did Maddy keep something so huge from me? How do you hide your whole life? Who am I even married to? I couldn't defend myself. My lack of knowledge was indefensible.

"Some people are very good at manipulating others," Erica assured us. "And good partners don't typically snoop into their spouse's past. We believe what they tell us until they give us reason not to. It would be difficult to uncover a past life so carefully hidden."

Was it so carefully hidden? I hadn't taken much time to wander around Maddy's hometown, to get to know her past friends. I never pried into what growing up was like for her. She told me about her mother, how emotionally and mentally abusive she could be, about her father and how wonderful he was until he was killed at his office. When I probed further into her childhood, she shut down, and I respected that. Her past seemed traumatic, so it made sense at the time why she didn't want to go back, why she left it all behind. I wasn't comfortable talking about my past a whole lot, either, and I wanted to do anything to make her happy. I wanted to help her leave it all behind if that would make her happy. It had felt like we hadn't needed our pasts—we'd only needed each other.

Yet, if I had looked into it, even just a little, perhaps I could've uncovered it all. Perhaps I could've saved Abigail. *If I had known her last daughter died, would I have suspected our daughter would as well?*

"Difficult." Gary smiled a huge smile that tugged on my urge to punch him. He clasped his hands. "But it's incredible that you uncovered it. We should be celebrating! Sure, the woman's a snake, but now we have proof! A hidden life. A dead baby. A history of death and lies. And there's got to be more, right? I'll need to sit down with Declan, hash out the details, take a trip to her hometown myself, find proof, all that jazz. But for now, tell me exactly what he told you, everything you know. I've got to hear all about this."

How dare he talk about my wife like that? How dare he insist I share her secrets? And to celebrate them? Celebrate a baby who died? What kind of fucked-up sociopath does something like that? Thinks something like that?

Now that I knew about Maddy's past, all I wanted to do was sit down and talk with her, apologize to her for making her feel like she had to lie to me, ask her all the questions, mourn together, heal together. But I couldn't fix our marriage, not after all the damage that had been done. I'd blown through all my chances without even realizing it, without understanding there was a limit.

Would I want to know the answers to those questions anyway? What if they led to something darker? How could it get darker?

My life was on the line. They all waited for me to share Madeline's life, like it was some fun story, the latest entertainment, a dramatic movie. I despised them for not realizing it was real life, a real past. It was a real woman on the line, a real man, a real murderer being buried under things that didn't even matter.

I'd done so much wrong, and I wanted to do better, be better. I wanted to stop hurting people, stop manipulating, cheating, lying, sharing secrets that weren't mine. But all of that trapped me, and I would need to stoop even lower to get out of my mess alive. I would have to dig deep, ignore my morals.

Once I got out of my situation, I would be a better person. I would turn my life around. I just needed to secure my freedom more than I'd ever needed anything else. I needed to take advantage of anything I could get my hands on, no matter how bad that might be. Once I was safe, I would leave that path of destruction behind. I would be a better man, a better husband. For the time, I bulldozed ahead. I turned away from the person I wanted to be and shared Madeline's story.

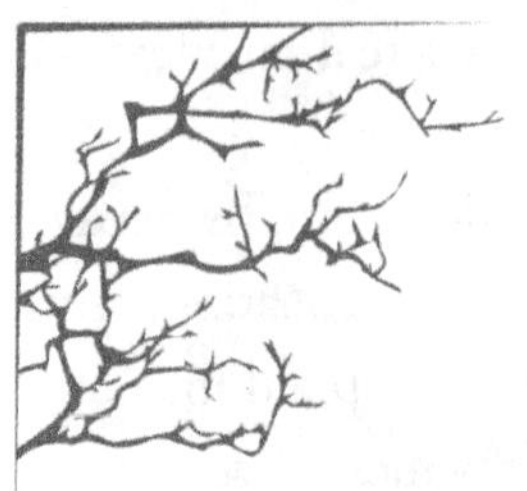

Chapter 24

Bacon sizzled. Omelets made with peppers, onions, and tomatoes added color to the morning. Blueberries oozed among the pancakes, casting their sweet scent into the air. Coffee brewed. As I made breakfast for my parents, my mind slipped back into the past.

I had been sleeping. I'd been working overtime, trying to save enough money for Christmas. It would be our first together, and I wanted to make it special for Maddy, for our families. I wanted to show them just how well-off we were, how we didn't need their help.

"Good morning, sweetheart." Maddy crawled onto our bed.

She woke me up, but I was still too groggy to be fully awake. I swore I didn't mean to. I never meant to. I didn't even know what I was doing. I bolted up, knocking her back with the back of my hand.

"What the fuck, Madeline!" I screamed.

When I fully woke and realized what I had done, I was horrified at myself, at the monster I was becoming. But if I admitted that, she would be horrified too. She would see that she should leave me, and I couldn't handle that. I didn't deserve to lose my wife to one mistake, so I had to commit, make her see that she was in the wrong, then change. I would never do it again. I just had to make sure she stayed.

"I was trying to sleep! Don't you know how hard I've been working?" I looked at the alarm clock. "I don't have to be up for another hour."

"I'm sorry," she whimpered as her hand went up to her red cheeks.

Her tears broke me. I couldn't let her see.

"I just thought we could spend the morning together."

"Well, maybe you should've mentioned that last night so I could've told you it was a fucking stupid idea. God, you're so inconsiderate sometimes." I moved to get out of bed.

She flinched, scurrying back like I might hurt her again. That killed. That was never the type of husband I wanted to be. It had never happened before, and we were shocked, horrified. I was terrified of myself, but I'd convinced her. She wouldn't leave. It would never happen again. I couldn't face it. I left our bedroom and headed for the kitchen to get a cup of coffee so I wouldn't have to look at the damage I had done. Coffee made everything better.

Except, right before I reached the kitchen, a familiar smell taunted me—coffee, maple syrup, bacon. I slowed my steps, but still, I reached the kitchen. Coffee sat on the table along with a plate of bacon, toast—homemade strawberry pancakes shaped like hearts. I had been a monster.

My mind returned to the breakfast I should've been making for Maddy but was cooking for my parents instead. I flipped the blueberry pancakes onto a plate. Bruises, the berries looked like bruises. I was told that Maddy had shown the cops her bruises to convince them I abused her.

The thing was I never physically harmed her after that time when she was pregnant, never once after Abigail was born. Those bruises weren't from me. I didn't know where they came from, but I'd hurt her so many times in the past. My hands had left bruises that I had never been held accountable for, so I couldn't even say the bruises weren't from me. I never told anyone they weren't. That punishment felt a little deserved.

Mom came into the kitchen, followed by my father, bringing me out of those memories. For the time, anyway. They would never truly go away. Maybe I didn't deserve for them to.

"Oh, sweetie!" Mom hugged me while my father poured coffee. "Thank you so much. This is wonderful."

"I wanted to show you how much I appreciate all you've done for me," I said. That was part of it. Also, maybe by doing that, I could start to make up for all the other bad stuff I'd done. Be a good son to make up for being a terrible husband. Maybe if I could remember how to be a good man, I could become a good husband. I always said I would change. When it was too late, I was changing. "So, thank you."

"You know, it really is nice having you around." My father leaned against the granite counter and drank his coffee. "Next time, you'll have to marry someone who lets you visit us. In the meantime, feel free to stay as long as you want."

I didn't want to stay for a second longer, and Maddy had always let me visit them—just as much as I'd wanted to, anyway. I still saw them more than I ever wanted to.

"Thanks." He was paying for my lawyer. "Why don't you guys sit down? I'll bring everything out."

That little bit of alone time allowed me to transition from a man haunted by his past to one unfazed by everything—doing his best to stay out of prison, innocent, blameless.

"You would not believe the stuff they're finding out about Madeline." My father started in on the bacon.

It had been four days since I'd shared Maddy's secrets with Gary. It was helping my case tremendously. but sometimes I wondered if I had done the right thing. I used to be so sure of myself. Anymore, I spent every minute regretting something.

"I can't even believe they're still having a trial after all this," he continued. "The woman is clearly mentally unstable, and it looks like that was brought on by that baby who died. Some depression or something. Can you believe having a child could make a woman unhappy?"

"Unhappy?" Mom asked. "I thought Madeline loved being a mom."

"She did." I shouldn't speak in her defense, but I knew what he was talking about.

He didn't know what he was talking about. It was one thing for Gary to talk about it, to use it to keep me out of jail—unfortunately necessary. But my parents shouldn't talk about it like it was the truth.

"Madeline loved Abigail. She just dealt with postpartum depression. It's not her fault. It's a chemical imbalance. She was getting treated for it, and she was a great mom. She loved Abigail. We both did."

"Great mom!" he scoffed. "If she loved Abigail, then she wouldn't have killed her. I've known it from the start, and thankfully, now everyone will see. This depression stuff will turn the jury against her. Even before that, she got into plenty of trouble. Busted for underage drinking, possession of marijuana, was arrested at some hippie protest. It all stopped before she had her first child, but it proves motive. She wanted freedom. Abigail's death would grant her that.

"And that other baby, they never found out what happened to her, but she died in her sleep, just like Abigail. I can't believe they didn't arrest her in the first place, instead of you. Useless investigators. Gary tells me that something like that wouldn't have been reported, that it'd be easy for Amelia's death to fly under the radar, but I think that's bullshit. I'm telling you she killed our granddaughter, and I hope she rots in prison for it."

"I'm not trying to put her in prison," I said.

I wanted to save myself, and I wanted revenge on Maddy if she did kill our daughter. But I also didn't know if she had killed our daughter. She couldn't have killed our daughter. There had to be some other explanation. And it still made me uncomfortable to hear them talk about my wife like that, especially considering I didn't believe she had killed Abigail. No matter how I'd treated her throughout our marriage, I'd never let anyone talk about her like that.

"I don't think she killed Abigail. I just want to escape prison myself."

"I know, honey," Mom said. "But this will help you. Whether Madeline did it or not, convincing the jury that she did will help you. And after all this, I agree with your father. As difficult as it is to accept, it sounds like she just might've done it."

"Might have?" my father asked. "Obviously, she did. She just has you both so blinded that you can't see it. She was the only other person in that house. Her baby died before. She wanted freedom. She didn't want to be a mother. Madeline killed Abigail, and I don't care what kind of mask she presented. She deserves to go to jail for that. Our granddaughter is dead because of her!"

I wanted to argue with him, but he was right. I didn't kill Abigail. I had been sleeping. I wouldn't have killed our daughter. The only other person in that house had been Madeline. She'd gotten up with Abigail in the middle of the night, soothed her, crawled back into bed. Abigail had never cried again. Madeline had killed our daughter. And anyone who harmed my daughter in the slightest deserved to suffer. The person who killed her deserved death, torture, the worst the world had to offer. The least Madeline deserved was prison time. It would save me from prison. *So why is it so hard to accept?*

"She does need to be punished," Mom agreed. "It's just so difficult to think of someone we know doing something like that—someone who was part of our family. Losing Abigail is difficult enough as it is. I can't accept that her own mother..."

When will this horrible grief end? Hopefully never. If I was a good father, it would be never.

My father took Mom's hand. "I know," he said. "It's hard for me too. I loved that little girl. That's why we need to get justice for her. Even if it's difficult, it's what Abigail deserves."

"But first, we'll get freedom for our son," Mom said. "We can't bring Abigail back, though I know we all wish we could. Brian's alive though." She looked at me with love. "You're our focus right now."

That broke through all the doubt, confusion, and mixed-up feelings I had toward Madeline. I could be sent back to prison real soon. I couldn't go back there. I didn't deserve to go back there. So, I tried to be more grateful for my freedom over the next couple of weeks.

But grief had me caged, and their house was getting tiny. I swam laps around the pool, played video games, worked on building a computer, helped Mom out when I could. I got lost in thoughts of my old life every time.

I made myself some lunch and brought it up to my room, then out onto my balcony. I kicked off my shoes so I could feel the warm sandstone under my feet and threw off my shirt because, man, did that California sunshine feel good. Though I agonized over being stuck there, prison wouldn't offer such easy access to sunlight. Prison was a million times worse. I wouldn't naively say my parents' home was a prison. *Right?*

I put on my sunglasses and sat on my black lounge chair. It just about scorched my skin right off, but I loved the burn. It made me feel alive. I sipped on a fruity drink I would never order if I weren't alone then tried the lamb. It was an over-the-top lunch, but faced with the threat of prison food, I ate the best things I could think of for every single meal.

I kind of wanted to jump off the balcony and get away from it all, fly away to find my old life—or just end it. Anything had to be better than my present, better than what might await me.

Yet I had hope even still that what awaited could be better than the purgatory where I was stuck. Maybe I would jump off the balcony headfirst another day, when I was sure I was going to prison. Right then, I might have a chance to escape that fate.

A door slammed. Heavy footsteps came toward me. I savored that bite of lamb then fully sat up. I took off my glasses and faced Declan. "Sit." I motioned to the chair next to mine.

"I'm good," he said as he paced.

Not good. Something was wrong. *Why is he here?* He never came over anymore unless he had information to help me out about my case or news regarding Maddy. Any friendship we had before had been crumpled and tossed to make room for something else.

"What's up?" I asked so I could be oblivious for a little longer. I could not handle any more bad news right then. "How are things?"

"I don't know. You tell me," he snapped. "What the fuck did you do?"

I hadn't done anything since I'd gotten out on bail. I had no clue what he was talking about. All my secrets had been exposed.

"Jacklyn?" he asked.

Right. All my secrets had been exposed except for that one.

"I guess I assumed Madeline wasn't the only one you hurt. But what you did to Jacklyn..." He shook his head. "I can't believe I ever helped you! Please tell me it's not true."

As if the things I'd done in the past affected who he was, affected who I was now. After all I'd done for him, he was appalled at me. Unfair. He had reached a low before too. He wasn't perfect either—far from it. *Could anyone still claim to be a good person if all their darkest secrets got dug up like this? Strung out for everyone to see?*

"I didn't judge you," I reminded him. "When we met at the bar that day. You were a mess, and I still welcomed you as a friend. Your life had fallen apart completely, and I was there to help you clean it up."

"As if!" His eyes blazed in a way I'd never seen them, radiating pure fury. He always kept his cool, except in the small ways. "You judged me the whole time. It was in every word you spoke. You couldn't believe I let myself fall so far, and I felt it. I ignored it because you weren't wrong, and your silent judgments were worth the mask of support. Or so I thought. The only reason you ever helped me was so I'd owe you. Or at least that's why you gave me the illusion that you were helping me. You never actually helped me clean up my life. You just dragged me down further!"

"That is not true!" I didn't help him so I could use him. I helped him because he was my friend, because I could make things better for him. I thought I could be a good man, somehow, when I was failing at that in my own home.

But then why was he the first person to come to mind when I needed someone? He offered to help me, but I did reach out. Perhaps I had done some heavy hinting. I hadn't helped him to use him, but I had been well aware of just how much he owed me. He would have done the same thing to me.

"I didn't drag you down. You did that all on your own. All I've ever done is help you. The only reason you have visitation with Grace now is because of me. You should be grateful for that instead of believing every bad thing you hear about me. What happened between Jacklyn and me is none of your business."

"You made it my business when you dragged me into this! Everyone's going to know when the trial starts. You know the prosecutor is going to use it against you. What are you going to say then? How will you defend yourself against that?"

I was baffled. I didn't know what to say because I didn't know where it was coming from. I didn't know how he even knew about it.

Declan shook his head with impatience triggered by my confusion. He brought up his phone, punched in the password, and pulled up a video. He handed it to me, making sure not a single part of his skin touched mine.

A familiar face came back to haunt me. Jacklyn had always been a gorgeous woman. She was from a good family with strong moral values, so she tried to hide it sometimes. She was incredibly insecure.

But her beauty shone through. Her long dark hair fell in soft waves over her tan shoulders. Her big brown eyes brimmed with tears. Her blue dress hid some of her curves, but they couldn't all be tucked away. She looked truly distraught, even after all that time. *Could it have stuck with her after all this time?*

"I don't even know where to start." She looked away from the camera as a blush dusted her cheeks. "I... I've never done anything like this before, and I wouldn't, but I want Madeline to know she's not alone. I know Brian will paint her as a liar. He'll try to gaslight her like he does everyone else, like he did to me. But I know he hurt her because he also hurt me."

I didn't though, not really. Okay, maybe a little, but we were both toxic. She was mentally unstable. I heard later on that she'd been diagnosed with borderline personality disorder, making her emotions erratic. She was cruel with her words sometimes, yet she never wanted me to leave her. In that moment, I just wanted her to leave me alone.

"Our relationship started out in the most loving way," she said. "It really did. Brian was a great guy. I still believe that deep down, perhaps a part of him is good. He's just..." She paused as she shook her head. "I don't know. I really don't know. He had trouble controlling his anger, I guess. His family... he comes from a family with a lot of issues. A family that always gets away with everything, and I think that worked against him. I really do. I think he tried to do better than them. Be better than them. But you can't escape your past. You have to make real changes to have a chance at a real future. Brian was never able to do that."

Her words stung like bees attacking me all at once. *Is it true?* Maybe a little. *But is it really true?* I tried to make changes. I tried to be a better person. *I'm not a bad person, am I?*

"We fought," she continued. "A lot. Sometimes it was my fault. Sometimes it was his fault. Something about our personalities clashed. Something about us shouldn't have been together, but we couldn't seem to stay apart from each other until..."

Until. I wanted to close my eyes and shut my ears. I wanted to run away and start over, truly start over. I knew if I could just start over, I could do better the next time. I wouldn't keep making the same mistakes. I would truly change.

"Until one day, one fight got out of control. I guess they were all out of control. Their severity increased over time. But one night..." She stopped and wiped away the tears that fell on her cheeks. "He grabbed my throat. He grabbed my throat, but he didn't suffocate me. He didn't. He grabbed my throat, and he froze as if he couldn'

I didn't. I wasn't sure I ever truly loved her, but I cared enough to get out of the situation. I cared enough to want to put her out of harm's way. I thought it would be different if I were with someone else, someone who didn't trigger me as much, someone who was a better match.

I handed Declan his phone.

"I didn't kill Abigail," I said. That was the truth I clung to because it was the truth, and I had nothing else left. "I know how this looks, but I didn't kill my daughter."

Suddenly, I was exhausted, drained one hundred percent. I was so tired of everyone looking at me like I was guilty, the same way Declan looked at me right then. I was fed up with people accusing me of killing my daughter. I would never do such a thing. I would give my own life to have her back.

"And all that other stuff they've accused you of?" he asked. "Did you do that? Did you suffocate Jacklyn?"

"I didn't suffocate Jacklyn." I knew where that line of thinking led. If I suffocated Jacklyn, that meant I could suffocate Abigail. But even Jacklyn said I didn't suffocate her.

"Fine." He crossed his arms over his chest. "Did you grab her throat?"

How am I supposed to answer that? I didn't do everything they accused me of, and he needed the context behind the things I had done, or he would never understand. My explanation would make me not a monster. He wouldn't listen to it though. I had no time to explain. Maybe I had no real explanation.

"I've made mistakes," I admitted. "I'm not proud of who I was, who I am sometimes. But I didn't kill Abigail. I never would. I loved my daughter. I would never hurt her."

It was the truth, plain, simple, stripped-down honesty. But Declan was so disgusted by the other things I'd done, I doubted I could ever convince him I hadn't killed Abigail, never fully. I'd suspected he was turning against me a while ago. Now, I knew.

"What kind of fucked-up shit did you drag me into?" He uncrossed his arms and shook his head, like he was better than me.

"You only helped me because you owe me," I reminded him. "Because you've done some pretty fucked-up shit yourself."

"Never this bad," he insisted.

"I didn't murder my daughter!"

"Either way, I'm out. I don't care what you did or didn't do anymore. I can't help you. I won't. Do what you want to me. Take everything away. Nothing you've given me, nothing you could ever give me, would justify this. I want to be a better man, and I can never truly be one if I'm tangled up in your mess. I've done enough for you. I don't owe you anything else." Declan slammed the door behind him.

I didn't bother trying to stop him. I had given him a lot. He had helped me out a great deal. I couldn't tell anymore if he still owed me, if I owed him. I didn't really care. It probably never really mattered.

I wouldn't help him any further. I couldn't see why I would after all that. I wouldn't mess up his life either. He had his job, and he deserved it. The custody case was over. The apartment was paid up for a couple of months. I couldn't withdraw the deposit if I wanted to.

And actually, I didn't want to. Like him, I wanted to be a better man. I wasn't about to go out on a limb for someone who'd turned against me. But as far as I knew, Declan hadn't betrayed me. I wouldn't betray him. Maybe he could get his daughter back full-time, maybe even his wife. If I couldn't have that, someone else could.

I sat back down. It would all have to be dealt with. I would have to talk to my lawyer, though it was likely he'd already heard about it. We would have to figure out something. First, I would eat my lunch.

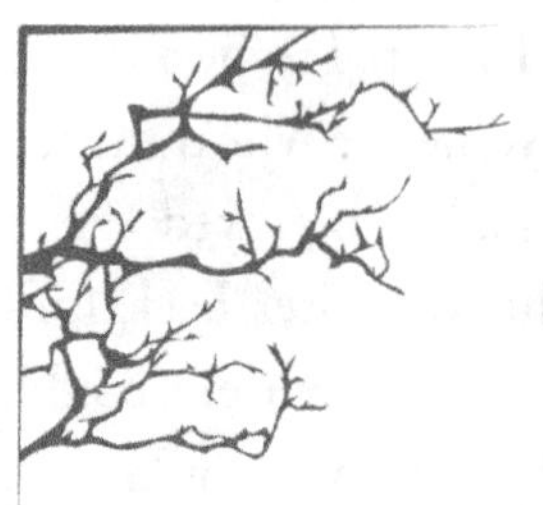

Chapter 25

"I've missed you so much!" Katarina leaped into my arms, far too loud. I couldn't protest, not right away. It was too nice to hold her against me, to hold a woman that tight. I needed to get laid. I needed the stress relief. But that wasn't the only reason I'd asked her to come over.

I clung to her because I also needed comfort. I needed to be around someone who didn't know all my secrets, who didn't care to know. I needed someone who still saw me as the strong, successful man I was instead of what I'd been reduced to. I needed a reminder that there was life beyond the present. Someday I would live it again.

"I've been so worried." Tears made her words unsteady, a bit louder.

Getting hysterical? Why would she think I'd want to be reminded of that?

"Shhh, I know." I ran my hand down her back, slowly over her curves. Her dark hair fell in waves over my touch. "But we've got to be quiet, okay? At least until we get to my room."

"Are they still awake?" She looked around the living room. Shadows lounged against the couch, crouched behind my father's chair. Embers refused to die in the fireplace.

"They aren't."

I wouldn't have invited her over if they were. They would kill me if they knew. Even if I were acquitted, there was no universe in which they would accept her.

"That's why I don't want to wake them. My bedroom is about as far away from theirs as we can get, though, so we'll be fine once we're there. It's the getting there we have to be careful about."

"Okay." She followed after me, tiptoeing, which was unnecessary, annoying. "This is kind of exciting. It reminds me of when I was in high school, sneaking a boyfriend in."

It reminded me of that, too, but I didn't find it very exciting, and I didn't appreciate her bringing it up. She always said stupid shit like that. I felt like a kid again, instead of a man with his own house, a man who could have women over whenever he wanted. Someone who could have an affair with the neighbor and get away with it. A husband who never really had to worry about sneaking around before because it was so easy. Too easy.

It had all been just a bit too easy. That was the biggest red flag I'd ever ignored. I should've known nothing was ever like that. That peace was the creepy quiet in a horror movie right before the monster struck. I should've known it would all come back to haunt me. Now I knew. If I did something wrong, I would feel the consequences, even if not right away. The moments of peace were facades, entertainment to rack up the tension. It would come back to get me every time. Everything would. No one could get away with anything, not truly. Even sneaking Katarina in would come back to haunt me. I would definitely regret it eventually.

But I hadn't called my lawyer that day, even though I'd intended to, even though I should've. I didn't tell my parents, didn't share my secret with anyone. They would find out. I wasn't naive enough to hope they wouldn't. They had access to the internet. They'd avoided hearing things about my case, but that was unavoidable.

I just wanted one more night before being told I was screwed, one more moment of fun before I accepted that I was going to prison. I wanted to spend that night with Katarina before she thought I was a monster, like everyone else did.

She giggled as we crept up the carpeted stairs. It was the most unsexy thing I'd ever heard. It made me want to send her back out the door, right then and there. God, she pissed me off sometimes. But she was hot, and it probably wouldn't have mattered. Because she was the only one who would sleep with me, and I needed that—in both ways, all ways. I ignored the giggle and focused on her ass as we reached the top floor. I led her to my room and finally got her behind that door. Safe.

It was demeaning, sneaking around, living in my parents' house in general. But when I turned around, all was forgotten. I took her in my arms and kissed her with all that frustration, desire, desperation. And I was grateful she was there. Almost.

I tried to get out of my head as my hands traveled under her red dress. She dressed up for me. I needed to focus on the person in front of me, the body in front of me. I wanted her, more than I'd ever wanted her. But I didn't. Not really.

I pulled her toward me like I wanted her. I stripped away her clothes like I desired her. She was just a replacement for what I really wanted though—a spot that any woman could fill right then but could never really fill, never quite fit. I wanted Madeline. I needed Madeline. More than I'd ever needed her. More than I'd ever needed any other woman in my entire life.

I kept the lights off as I pushed Katarina onto the bed. I couldn't look at her when every thought was of Madeline. I tried to push her out of my head. It was impossible. I was obsessed with Madeline when we first met. She was everything I ever wanted and all the things I didn't know I wanted—brilliant, gorgeous, funny, adventurous, a free spirit. She was at peace with herself in a way I longed to be. At the time, I swore I would do anything to have her, keep her.

In time, something changed. She changed. I changed. I changed her. She changed me. Our marriage twisted into something awful, something ruined, and neither of us knew how to fix it.

Katarina was the first and only woman I'd slept with aside from Madeline since I started dating Madeline. She was far from the first woman I'd desired since then though. I hadn't even thought of straying when we first got together, but after about a year or so, others became so tempting.

Once Maddy and I started fighting, it didn't stop. There were days, of course, weeks, months, moments when everything was okay. Our life was better than okay. It was amazing. That was the thing about our relationship though. When things were good, they were incredible. I would break it off with Katarina. I would fall back in love with Madeline. Hope would explode for our marriage.

When things were bad...

We always made up, forgave each other. But each thing stacked up, built up into resentment, into uncontrollable rage. Hate. Love. God, I loved her. And I couldn't stand her. I couldn't leave, but I wanted to be with someone else. Anyone else to get me through those awful times, to distract me.

And now? I'd spent so much time wanting someone else, getting someone else, fantasizing about being with someone else. And now I never had to see Madeline again. I could have someone else forever, someone who ignored the awful things I was accused of, the awful things I'd done, someone who wasn't as stubborn, as cruel, as obnoxious. All I wanted was Madeline. All I needed was my wife.

So, I kept the room dark as I touched Katarina and tried to pretend she was Madeline. But I knew them both too well to even come close to fooling myself. So, I opened my eyes and used her, enjoyed her. I convinced myself that she was using me for some unknown reason.

Once we were worn out, once that base desire was satisfied, the walls fell. So, I could really be close to someone. Maybe part of me had actually grown to care about Katarina after all the time we'd spent together. Maybe I just needed that comfort from someone, anyone.

I held her close, and it felt like I cared. I buried my face in her hair, a protector once again. I was someone who would take care of her, a real man. She could relax around me, and it was so good to touch another body, to have someone after all those nights alone.

We fell asleep, and I didn't think of Madeline—not until that exact moment right before I slipped into the darkness. But that thought brought so much longing, so much agony, that it was as if I'd been thinking of her for at least one eternity.

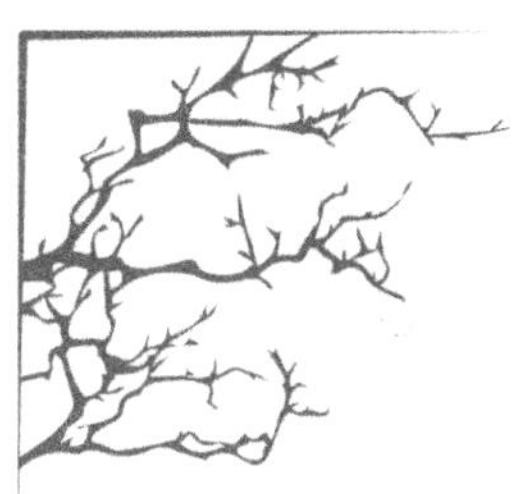

Chapter 26

Bangs slammed me out of sleep. Katarina and I sat up at the same time. She looked at me, her brown eyes wide, and that pleased me for a moment. She looked to me for answers, to protect her. And I wasn't a kid anymore. I was a man.

"Brian!" my father yelled as he pounded on the door. "We need to talk."

That tone. I may be a man everywhere else, but there I was a kid. And the kid in me always responded badly to that tone. Something had happened, something bad.

"You need to go." I turned to Katarina.

Confusion colored her face.

"They won't be happy you're here. You shouldn't be here. I'm under investigation for murdering my daughter. I shouldn't be spending time with my mistress, the very same woman I cheated on my wife with. You have no idea how much trouble you're getting me into."

"Me?" she squealed as my father hollered.

The mess of my life collided. The worst part was, I knew it would happen. *Was it worth it?*

"You're the one who called me! You wanted me to come over!"

"And now I want you to leave. Go hide in the bathroom or something. I'll get you when it's safe."

"Is someone in there with you?" my father asked. "I swear to God there better not be anyone in there!"

"Go!" I shooed her as I scrambled up.

Katarina jolted out of the bed, almost tripping herself on the way up. She grabbed her dress as I threw on my shirt and dug around for a pair of shorts. The scramble of a teenager, it was repulsive.

"Give me a minute!" I yelled. "I just got up. Let me find some damn clothes."

"You have five seconds!"

Perhaps being a murderer wouldn't be so bad. Most everyone already thought I was one anyway, and my father deserved it. After what had happened with Jacklyn got out, I would be found guilty for sure. If I was going to jail, I might as well be locked up for something I actually did, something that would make it worthwhile. I didn't have a wife anyway, didn't have a child. I didn't have anything worth living for.

Katarina disappeared into the bathroom, leaving no witnesses. I opened the door just as my father raised his fist. When he saw me, his face changed. He wanted to punch me. I had somehow done something so awful that he wanted to pummel my face.

For a split moment, I thought he would actually punch me in the face—harder than he had when I was a teenager. I wanted him to. I would claim self-defense. Maybe I would even get away with it. Maybe I wouldn't. It would give me a reason to kill him anyway.

He lowered his fist. His face was bright red. Maybe I wouldn't have to kill him. Maybe he would have a heart attack right there. *Does he even have a heart?* He took a deep breath.

"We need to talk," he said as if I hadn't heard him screaming at the door.

"How about over breakfast?" I smiled despite my inner panic.

He must've found out about Jacklyn. I'd been waiting for him to find out. If he found out about Katarina, though, it would only make everything worse. If I could get him away from my room, then Katarina could slip out. And I would never have her come over again. I would never see her again, talk to her again. It had been stupid to have her there in the first place. I promised karma I had learned my lesson.

"I mean..." He was angry but hungry. "I guess that will work. Your mother's already... is that...?"

I followed his eyes to my floor. Nestled among blankets was a red-and-black bra. Sexy. I barely noticed it in my need to forget last night.

"Are you serious? How stupid are you?" He pushed past me.

I was so distracted by my anger at Katarina that I didn't even think to stop him. *How could she be so careless? How could I be so careless? Is she trying to get me killed? Am I trying to get myself killed?*

"Where is she?" he demanded as he looked around the room.

I didn't know what to say. I couldn't even deny it at that point. It really wasn't his business anyway. It was pretty stupid though. It wasn't his problem, but I did deserve it. I acted like an ignorant child, even then.

"Who do you have in here?" He pounded on the bathroom door.

Katarina shrieked.

"Dad, stop." I put my hand on his shoulder.

He swung his fist as he turned.

I dared him to punch me, to give me that reason. After all that time, I had plenty of resentment, anger. "You're scaring her."

"You're the one who should be scared!" He shook as he lowered his fist once again. "You're facing prison time, and you're still running around with some woman? What will that look like? You can't afford to be doing stupid shit like this. She could be in cahoots with Madeline."

"I doubt it." I sighed. "Katarina, you can come out."

We backed away from the door and waited. Slowly, it opened. Katrina's hair was a mess, her cheeks streaked with tears. The poor thing was shaking.

Her fear shamed my father into better behavior. He deflated as he ran his hand through his hair. "Katarina?"

She nodded.

"I'm sorry for scaring you, but you need to get out of my house. Right now." She nodded again. He turned to me, a silent threat that everyone could hear. "Meet me downstairs."

I didn't answer. It wasn't a request or a question. Finally, he left my room and closed my door.

Katarina broke into tears. I watched her for a moment without much sympathy. It was her stupidity that got me caught. She would leave my house and go on with her life anyway. She would recover. *Will I?* Then, I did the right thing. I hugged her extra tightly because it would be the last time I would ever hug her. I felt something almost like sadness as I comforted her, helped her find her things, walked her to the door. Sadness because I would miss her. Sadness because I wanted to leave with her, leave that place—forever. But I stood there as the door closed behind her. Whatever once existed between us had ended, for real, for good that time.

"Katarina?" my father asked the second I sat at the table, before I could even butter my toast. "The whore you cheated on Madeline with?"

"Wow, Dad. I have no words. Honestly."

He'd cheated on Mom before, plenty of times. We all knew it. And she wasn't nearly as obnoxious as Madeline could be. But if I said that out loud, it would only hurt my mother. I still had some sort of broken morals, and I'd always cared about my mother, so I kept my mouth shut.

"Don't use that tone with me! You know you shouldn't even be talking to that woman, let alone seeing her! She's already caused you so many problems."

Mom continued eating breakfast like nothing was going on. She turned a blind eye like she always did.

"And you can't afford problems, especially with what's going on now. I don't know how to keep you out of prison anymore, if there's even a chance. You were supposed to tell Gary everything so he could prepare a proper defense for you!"

"I told him everything he needed to know," I said. Of course, saying so would only make my father angrier. It was nice to fight with someone though, a good distraction.

"Oh really? What about Jacklyn?"

Mom stopped at that—so dramatic. It happened in college. *Why is everyone making such a big deal out of it now?* It had nothing to do with Abigail or even Madeline. None of it did. But the case wasn't built on the truth of what happened that night, or they wouldn't have anything on me. It seemed nobody cared about what actually happened to my daughter.

"What about her?" I asked. "We dated in college. I think I brought her here once. I broke up with her and moved on quickly with Maddy. I guess she was angry at me, so now she's making all this up."

I knew I sounded like an asshole lying about it like that, but I would have to lie or I would end up in prison. And the thing was, I could accept getting punished for grabbing her throat. But I didn't kill Abigail, and I simply couldn't accept going to prison for something I didn't do. *Lying to save someone who's innocent isn't that bad, is it?*

"Then you knew she was a risk! You should've told Gary about it so we could have squashed any possibility of this happening!"

Mom went back to eating as my father went back to raging.

"We could've found her, paid her off, prepared a defense, done something!"

"I don't see why we'd need to pay anyone off when I didn't kill Abigail! Doesn't that matter? Doesn't the truth matter?"

"Not to the jury," he said. "Not to the judge. What matters is who presents a story that's most believable. She's presenting the idea that you grabbed her throat, when you're accused of suffocating your daughter. How do you think that'll look for you?"

"It doesn't have anything to do with this though! I didn't kill Abigail."

That was the truth. Maybe if I said it enough times, someone would believe me. The thing was, I didn't want anyone to bribe Jacklyn. I didn't want to have to trick people or work up a defense. I wished I didn't have to lie about it. That sounded too much like what my brother had done—bribed and tricked and called in favors. He'd cheated the system.

Our situations were strikingly similar, but he was a rapist. I wasn't a murderer. *How could an innocent man be put in prison?* That wasn't how our justice system was supposed to work. It was a nightmare, but the truth would set me free. It had to. *So, why am I not telling the truth?*

"Then use your head, why don't you!"

I knew all too well the sound of my father's anger. Something aside from the anger lingered in his voice. *True concern?*

"If you really didn't kill your daughter, that gives you more reason to get yourself out of this. Prove you didn't do it so they can find whoever did. Get justice for your daughter.

"I'm well aware that your past doesn't mean you killed Abigail, even if it is true, even if you did those things. But people associate one action with another that isn't even related, and all of that is going to land you in prison for a crime you didn't commit. It's going to allow a killer to go free. It happens all the time. Do you really think you're so special that it can't happen to you?

"Take one moment to think about how this looks for you. Madeline accused you of abusing her. Now, Jacklyn is accusing you of grabbing her throat. The prosecutor will claim that you lost your temper or something, that it's not such a leap you'd go on to suffocate Abigail—it was only a matter of time. They're going to argue that you wanted a new life with Katarina. And now, with your baby dead and Madeline estranged from you, you're getting together with Katarina. If you heard the story on the news, what would you think?"

Guilty. If I were an outsider looking in, I would think I was guilty, a murderer. And he made it sound like I was guilty too—maybe not of murdering Abigail, but of other things, awful things. *Am I?*

"Madeline's past makes her look just as guilty as I do," I protested. "If not more so. Her baby died. That's so suspicious." It was suspicious enough to make even me uncomfortable. It was enough to make me wonder if I was involved in Abigail's death through negligence alone. *Can it be considered murder if you choose the wrong woman to be your child's mother?*

"And that would've been enough to get you off," he said. "You two were the only ones in that house, and if it weren't for all this other stuff, she would've probably been charged instead of you. But you were the one charged, so they're going to look at you closer than they would her. She's also a mother. No one wants to believe a mother would kill her own daughter. You have so much stacked against you. Madeline's past was enough to evoke reasonable doubt. You were going to be acquitted. You might still be, but this puts you at risk, huge risk. It makes you look guilty when you already looked pretty awful. And it all could've been avoided. But now... now Gary doesn't know if you'll be convicted or not. That's just not acceptable." He finally stopped talking and looked at me. He waited for a response.

I couldn't say or do anything though. I was stupid. Everything was a mess, and I didn't care enough to clean it up. "I'm sorry." I didn't even know who I was apologizing to anymore. I was remorseful though. Regret and the horrible agony of losing my whole family were the only feelings I felt anymore. "I didn't know this would all come out. I didn't even think of it. I haven't thought about Jacklyn in a long time. And I know I was stupid, but I am sorry." Sorry sounded silly, though, stupid. Nothing I could say would make this better.

"It's okay, sweetie," Mom said. "We're just worried about you. That's all. But we'll fix this, okay? No one's going to prison. This will all be okay. We'll find a way to fix it."

My father shook his head and started eating. It was something he wasn't sure he could fix, and I'd never seen him like that—unsure if he could fix something. I wasn't sure I could fix it either, so we let it go. We enjoyed breakfast while we still could and made plans to meet with Gary in an hour so he could tell me I was screwed too.

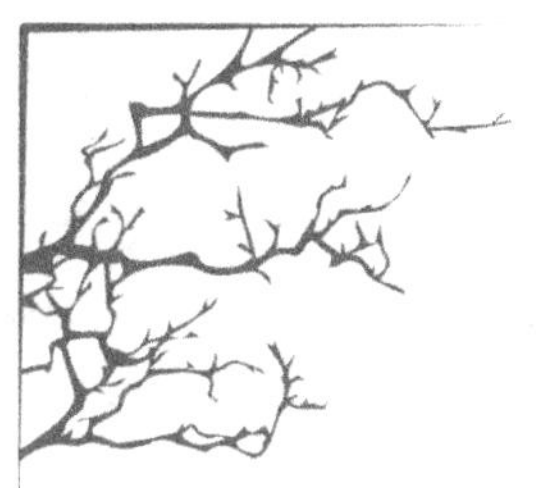

Chapter 27

I picked a blue tie to go with my black shirt. It looked strange, wrong. I'd worn black every day since Abigail died. I looked in the mirror. Wrapped the tie around my neck like a noose. Guilty. They would all think I was guilty. Everyone thought I killed Abigail. They thought I murdered my daughter, that I was a monster.

Even if I were acquitted, everyone would wonder, speculate. Even if they thought it was possible Madeline killed Abigail, they would also think it was possible that I did. There was no escaping it.

But we would plan my escape. I tossed the tie to the floor. It was proper to look nice when meeting with my lawyer to discuss my case, but it wasn't a normal situation.

Gary wouldn't be dressed too professionally, and he certainly wouldn't act the part. He would joke around with my father, share a drink with him. Then, when he was good and ready, he would scold me, as my father had, for not telling him in the first place.

He would complain about how screwed I was, how difficult it made his job, just like he did when he found out about Katarina and my past girlfriends. Then he would tell me what he would do to fix it, how we would make Madeline look bad to save me.

And the thrill it all held for him would be crystal clear. He would pace, get a determined look in his eyes. He would talk fast with more hand movements—not because he was stressed, but because he thrived under the pressure. He was happiest when the stakes were higher. He wasn't playing with his life, so he enjoyed it. He loved it.

He didn't care if I was guilty. He probably thought I was, probably thought that I was just like my brother. That wouldn't faze him though. All he cared about was winning, securing that precious not-guilty verdict. That was his mission. That was what made him great. That was why I couldn't stand him.

Shatter! Followed by excruciating pain. Blood, real, hot, something I could embrace. A physical pain I could deal with—had dealt with since I was little. My father's words were always worse than his blows.

I withdrew my fist from the mirror. Shards of glass stuck to my skin. It didn't seem like it was my fist, like my actions had caused it. I watched someone else do it, and he was a moron. He was spiraling. I was watching him ruin his life, unable to stop him. Maybe he deserved it too.

He didn't kill his daughter, but he did abuse his wife. He cheated on her, hurt her, and he never wanted to. He had become the very same man he'

He always did it again, though, so I guessed the guilt wasn't enough. It wasn't that bad, because he always pushed the edge, always, because he was never actually punished for it, not truly. And perhaps he thought he never would be.

Now he was really being punished. He was facing the repercussions of all he had done, and I couldn't say he didn't deserve it, at least to some degree. *But I'll never do it again! Never!* If I could just get out of my situation, I would never hurt Madeline again. I would never sleep with Katarina. I would never cheat on anyone. I would be a great husband, a great father. Except my daughter was dead.

Crash! The man who looked like me, who lived my life but wasn't me, knocked all my things off the bathroom counter. I watched in horror as bottles and brushes and soaps fell to the floor. His hand still bled, staining the white sink, the white tile. Mom would be so worried if she saw.

He picked the glass out of his skin. It didn't look like he felt it. I didn't feel it because I wasn't him anymore. He wasn't me. We just happened to inhabit the same body. I always fought him. I realized that then. I had fought him my whole life as I tried to build the life I wanted, be the man I wanted to be. He always tried to ruin that for me. We always battled for control.

I watched helplessly as he tossed the bloody shards into the sink, grabbed a towel, and wrapped it around his hand—white too. He was kind of an asshole like that.

He avoided looking in the mirror. He didn't want to see the mess he'd become. He already knew. He did look at his shirt though. It was blood splattered, bringing color to the black for the first time since Abigail had died.

How could he talk to his lawyer like this? He laughed, and that scared me. Everyone already thought he was a murderer. *What would they think if he showed up like this? Would they be surprised? Is it expected from someone like him?* He couldn't see them like that. He couldn't stay there.

I had tried to avoid that truth for weeks. He embraced it though. He couldn't stay there. *Where could he go?* He couldn't leave. He looked down at the plastic cuff around his ankle. It tracked his every move. If he left his parents' house, the police would come for him. They would find him.

I packed my things in a frenzy. I didn't even know what I was thinking, planning. There wasn't much there I cared about. I didn't know that until I lost the things I actually cared about.

I grabbed a few T-shirts, a pair of jeans, Abigail's pink teddy bear, a poem Madeline had written for me way back when—before I'd ruined her, before she'd ruined me—a picture of the three of us, some food I'd stashed, a few cans of soda. I zipped it all up and threw it on my bed. *Why?*

He dug through my drawers for something else, different things, the sharpest things. He grabbed a knife, a rope cutter, a dagger. He didn't throw those into his backpack though. He picked up his backpack, threw it over his shoulder, and left. Just like that.

He had some thought though. He took the long way round, farthest from where he guessed his parents would be waiting for Gary. Gary wouldn't show up for another twenty minutes or so. He had time, no time at all really. Time had become such an odd thing he didn't have time to puzzle over.

He paused by the door. A key ring hung off the coatrack, spare keys for various things. He picked out a small silver key with a black ring around it. He hoped his father would still care enough to keep his mouth shut.

His father would be furious to see that he had left—with his father's car. It would be better to take his own car, but he was past caring about doing the right thing. He had never cared. That was the problem. He had no way to redeem himself anyway, no way but down from there for us both.

He walked to the garage that held the castaway cars no one cared about—or at least, older luxury cars his father no longer fancied. He chose the black Lexus. His father had upgraded to a new model recently. The older one had remained untouched since then. He threw his backpack onto the shotgun side and slid into the driver's side.

It was so nice to be behind the wheel again, to feel in control of his life. Yet not in control. He was fucking stupid. He was ruining everything, every chance at any shot of redemption.

That didn't faze him. He tossed his morals in the back seat then got to work on that ankle bracelet. It took longer than he wanted it to, yet it wasn't as difficult as he feared it would be. He left it sounding off alarms on the floor, in a place no one would hear it—for the time being.

Then, he drove out of the garage, his better sense in the back seat. He didn't care about the future. He couldn't care about how his behavior would look. He needed to get away, and he couldn't think about anything else if he was going to do it. He had to do it.

He drove without looking back to see if his father was watching, to see if his mother was watching. He could face his father and all his anger. He couldn't face his mother. His flight would break her heart, but he didn't care about that. He couldn't, or he wouldn't be able to leave. And Gary would arrive soon. Time was running out—always sprinting away.

He drove away from his parents' house, which thankfully was secluded among wineries and trees, gorgeous views sinners could hide behind. Secrets nestled in a tangle of nature. He didn't feel safe until all he could see were trees.

I didn't know where he was going. I didn't know where his mind was. The maniac had taken me hostage, taken control of my life. I had lost the lifelong fight, and I didn't know what he would do next, but I did know that no matter what he did, I was screwed. The police would come after me. There would be no bail. I would sit in jail until I was convicted. If I'd ever had a chance of true freedom, I'd tossed it out with that ankle bracelet.

Not even a small part of me thought I could escape the police forever. But I did think I could've possibly gone free if I'd stayed. Maybe Gary would have figured out something. He'd worked wonders before. Maybe he would've made Madeline look guilty enough. Maybe my father could have paid off the right person. I was screwed, but if I stayed, I at least would have had a chance. I would at least have more time before getting locked away again.

I had no chance anymore. He had chosen a path for me, and there was no going back, no apologies, nothing regret could fix. I watched him destroy everything, and I couldn't do anything to stop him. So I watched in equal parts fascination and horror to see what he would do next.

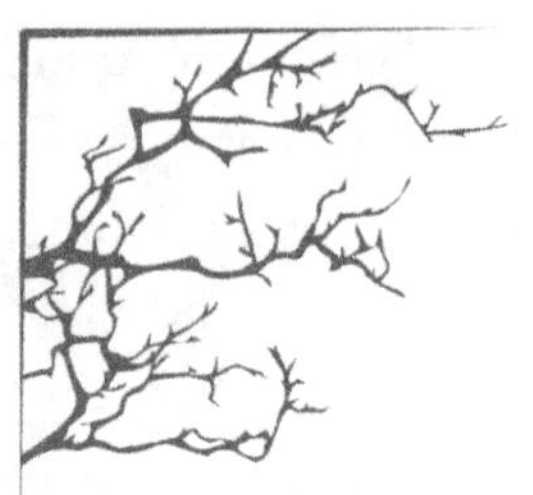

Chapter 28

He drove, and he kept driving. Aside from a quick pause for gas, he didn't stop until he found a hotel a good ten or eleven hours away from his parents' house, one of those expensive ones where they didn't ask questions. They didn't ask questions when people had enough money anyway. He had enough money, and he was far from the only criminal they'd ever kept safe.

He was safer in the dark, so he only turned on one lamp, light enough to not walk into something. Tinted windows protected his secrets. He was safe enough to throw his backpack on the bed, take off his shoes.

He paced, started the water in the shower, turned it off. No time for that, not yet. He only had time for dinner. He was starving, after all. Being on the run made people feel all sorts of things. Starving was one of them.

He ate dinner in the hotel restaurant, a huge meal of lobster, vegetables, and cheesecake—mostly lobster and cheesecake—a bit of wine, but not too much. He couldn't drink too much because, once he finished, he went back to his car and drove again.

That time when he stopped to buy gas, he got one of those cheap bouquets they sometimes sold at gas stations. He wished he could get something better, but he picked out the prettiest one they had—white and pink roses that were only a little wilted. Like they could bribe the police officer who arrested him. It wasn't until that wrought iron fence came into sight that I knew where I was going. It was unmistakable. I'd only been there once, but it was burned in my mind forever.

When I went that first time, I noticed how much the fence looked like those creepy gothic ones in horror movies, dark with pointed tips. The gate was a flourish of haunting decoration, like they tried to keep people out—or spirits in. It reminded me of those haunted mansions that were home to a whole family of ghosts. If any ghost wanted to do some haunting, that graveyard would be the perfect place.

The gate would be locked at that time of night. I was thankful for that. It would keep my baby safe from those nasty folks who would desecrate her grave, intruders who would creep in for the cheap thrill of being in a graveyard at night, ignoring the fact that real people lay there—people who others loved, gone but not forgotten. They would be messing with others' lives.

I didn't want to do that. I wasn't like them. I just wanted to see her, be near her. I needed to. I would never see her again, but I was as close as I could get aside from breaking into my house, being in her room again.

I'd thought about it. I wanted to more than anything. I needed to be back in our home. I hoped that maybe, if I went back to her room, she would still be there, that it had all been a mistake. I would wake up and realize it was all a nightmare, and I could do everything right. I would fix everything.

I wasn't that ballsy, though, or that delusional. And I didn't want to scare Madeline. Even if she did kill our daughter. I still hoped she didn't kill our daughter.

I kept driving until I found a back road to park my car alongside. It was almost two o'clock in the morning, so I didn't think anyone would see it. If they did, that would be okay, too, though. I would be caught eventually. Time was running faster, closing in on me. And if I got caught, it would be worth it. Nothing else could make getting caught worth it.

Walking alongside the road back to the cemetery would be the quickest way there. But though the trip would be worth getting caught for, I didn't want to get caught until after I'd seen my daughter. I didn't want to get caught at all if I could help it, so I decided to navigate through the woods. The fence didn't stretch all the way around the cemetery. It didn't protect the graves from intruders that came through the woods, and my parking spot wasn't far from the cemetery. I wouldn't get lost. Hopefully.

The moon shone brightly enough to allow me some idea of my footsteps, a sign from Abigail that she wanted to see me. She always loved the night, the moon. She trusted it. *Why didn't it protect her that night?*

Creaky trees with their obnoxious branches reached out for me as I tried to puzzle out the answer. *Why did Abigail die that night?* No one seemed to care anymore, but I did. *How could the moon let that happen?*

I stumbled over a stone hidden under leaves, caught myself. I caught a possibility. Maybe the moon was watching over her that night. But it was so far away, it couldn't get there quickly enough to save her. Instead, it sent its light to beam her up, welcoming her to its home. Maybe she was playing among the stars. Maybe she would grow up in the shadows, sleep under the warmth of the sun.

I pictured her like that as I walked to her, got closer to her. I tried not to think about the possibility that I was lost, walking in circles, that I would never find the cemetery—at least not before they caught me.

The first place they'd suspect a grieving father to go is to his child's grave, right? Probably. Except they didn't think I was a grieving father. They thought I was a murderer.

I imagined I was walking to Abigail, that the moon held her so she could see her father. Maybe the moon would take pity on me, take me up to her. Even the night couldn't take care of her like I could. Even the moon couldn't love her like I did. They had to know she needed me, that I needed to be with my daughter. At least one of the stars had to see that.

I kept walking, but I became less desperate to reach her grave. I was already reaching out to her. I heard her in the rustle beneath the trees, in the hoot of the owl. I smelled her in the chill of the night, the leaves dampened with dew. I felt her as the tree limbs reached out for me, as my feet became more aware of the ground beneath them. I saw her sleeping among the stars, her eyes flickering in the darkness.

I found the break in the trees. No fence to protect it. I walked over and stayed in the quiet for a moment longer. Now that I was there, I wasn't sure I wanted to be. I wasn't sure I would find her there. *What if I don't find her here?* That would destroy me completely, and I was already so fragile.

But I couldn't leave because I might be where I belonged. *What if Abigail is here? What if my family is still counting on me? Where else would I go anyway? Does breaking really matter anymore?*

I took a deep breath, closed my eyes, and pretended Abigail was still there for a moment, still with me. I had taken her outside to show her the stars. My precious daughter was right there in my arms. I would protect her from anything, everything.

I opened my eyes and kept walking, past the monuments of all those loved ones whose bones were kept safe in the ground, a carefully chosen stone at the head to remind their families they did exist, even when the world inevitably forgot about them. Their grief was real, but so were those sweet memories.

I remembered Abigail's weight in my arms—so little, especially when I first held her—wailing with the force of the night. She steadily grew a bit heavier each day. She calmed down as she recognized us, realized we were there to love and protect her, that we were her safe place in the world. She found her favorite spot in my arms, in the crook that was now empty.

I died as my knees hit the wet ground in front of a white marble gravestone. The stars and moon carved into it looked over a little angel with a teddy bear in her arms. I couldn't cuddle stone, though, so my arms would always be empty. I laid the roses in front of the grave. Other flowers still marked it, a whole garden of them.

Which flower would be her favorite when she grew up? There was so much white and pink. *Would she even like the color pink? What would she be like when she became her own person? Did we get it all wrong? If the moon reached out and strangled me now, would I be able to see her grow up? Would I find all the answers no one cared to know anymore?*

I sobbed as my heart broke over the flowers, bled, and stained the petals. Since I'd been arrested, I hadn't had the proper time to breathe, the privacy and space I'd needed to cry, grieve.

Madeline was the only one who understood what I was going through, really understood. Yet she was gone. Forever. I didn't want to cry with anyone else. But I could cry with the moon, with the stars. I fell against Abigail's gravestone. She wasn't there. She was up with the bright souls of the night. Her body wasn't trapped deep within the earth, alone, cold, buried so far down that I could never reach her, never see her again.

Why didn't I protect her?

As I cried, I released all the guilt. My body clenched under the pressure of the worst agony. They were all right. I didn't kill her, but I didn't protect her. I was guilty. I was sleeping in that house, rooms away, when my daughter was murdered. She would've looked for her parents, for me. She was scared, unaware of what was happening, no way to stop it. And I wasn't there to save her.

The guilt, the sadness, was too heavy to bear, too painful to live through. It would kill me, and I embraced that. I looked forward to the day when I wouldn't have to wake up to the reality.

A touch on my back saved me. A hand, cool and small, assured me I wasn't alone, that someone was there. They would help me get through this. *Abigail?* I closed my eyes, focused on that touch, that hand. *Is it a living human? A hallucination?* It was cold but solid, getting warmer as it touched me. It was too big to be Abigail's hand, even if she had grown since she died. The hand was small but not tiny, not like a baby's.

It was a person, then, who was there with me. *A cop here to arrest me?* Possibly. At least I'd made it there. And the comfort of that touch was so great I didn't care. I continued crying, curled up. The hand stayed. The person, the hallucination, the touch helped guide me out of the crushing pain—made it almost bearable.

As my sobs subsided, a body fell to the ground next to me. The hand became a full arm around me, and I didn't want to look. Because I knew that feeling, that particular weight. But it didn't make sense, and if I looked, she might fade away. I enjoyed that moment when I pretended it was her. Time was running out. I deserved moments like that, even after what I had done, because time was running out.

Curiosity tempted me cruelly. No longer able to resist, I looked. It was her.

"Madeline?" I whispered. If I talked too loudly, I might scare her away—like I already had.

"Hi, Brian." She smiled a small smile that was filled with more sadness than happiness.

I wanted to make it better, but I was the one who'd created that sadness in the first place. So, I couldn't. I knew that now. I could never fix it.

"How did you know I'd be here?" I asked.

She couldn't have known. She came on her own, and fate brought us together. It was meant to be. We were meant to be. Even after all of it. Always.

"Why are you here at this time of night?"

"Because I knew you'd be here," she said.

How?

"The police came by to warn me that you were on the run. They told me you cut the ankle monitor and took off. They suspected your parents gave you money and arranged for your escape. They didn't think you'd stick around the area. They figured you'd already flown to some other country by now. They wanted me to know anyway. To be safe."

I hadn't thought of that. Now I did. My parents probably would've arranged for an escape if they truly thought I would be found guilty. They might even arrange for one still if I went home, when the police weren't there, if I just called them, found a way to reach out to them somehow. They would be furious, but there still might be a way out of my situation.

"It made sense to me at first," she continued. "Your parents could easily send you off, and things were starting to look pretty bad for you. It'd make sense for you to escape. But then I thought that if you were in the area, you'd come here. Even if you were going to leave, you'd come here first. I didn't say anything to the police because I wanted to talk to you. And I don't think they'll suspect it on their own. I think we're safe here, at least until the sun comes up."

"Aren't you scared to be with me?" I looked into those eyes.

Her everything was washed in moonlight, faded shades of black and gray, touches of white, except for her eyes. They were still warmed with brown, like hot chocolate on the coldest day of my life. Their point of view was the only thing that mattered.

"Everyone sees me as a murderer. How do you see me?"

She took my hand. It was so nice to hold her hand after all that time. So stupid that I hadn't appreciated her fully until right then. I didn't realize how much I loved her until then—or I did, way back when. I'd cherished her but lost sight of that, forgot what was most important. Until then. Until she would soon be gone from my life forever. Too late. *Why am I always too late lately?*

"I see you as a monster," she said.

I would rather she'd shot me in the face.

"I see you as the person who has hurt me like no other, the husband I hate, the villain who trapped me—not with threats. You never did threaten me if I left you. What you did was much worse.

"You trapped me with my love for you because I did love you. I do love you with more than just my heart. I love you with my entire soul. You have every piece of me, and I'm still learning how to take these shards you left to rebuild even a fragment of myself. But I know, I know, that pieces of me will always be embedded in you. We're locked together in such a way that we could never part without breaking. And I watched it happen. I didn't even mind at first.

"You were wonderful in the beginning, and you sprinkled those amazing moments throughout. You tore me down until I was ready to leave then rebuilt that cage with enchanting words, loving gestures, stunning gifts, and romantic getaways. Abigail was the final lock, ensuring I could never escape—bars no one could see.

"You made my life a nightmare and a fairy tale, and I think I resent you more for the fairy-tale parts because they made it so difficult to leave, impossible. Losing that fairy tale was the silent threat that bound me to you. Regardless, that incredible love has twisted to breathtaking hate, and I know you hate me too. You hate me and love me just as much as I hate and love you."

Do I? I hated her, and I loved her. Because I wasn't the only one who made our life a nightmare and a fairy tale. Madeline broke me down, sliced me in half with her words, her cold actions. She was cruel, so much so that sometimes, it was hard to see her as human, as anyone I could possibly love.

The next day she would be the most loving, amazing, intriguing woman I'd ever met. One moment, I would feel justified in cheating on her, saying the things I did because she was awful, the worst. Then she would make me feel guilty because I'd hurt someone so incredible, who did so much for me, who was so romantic, so lovely.

Except I crossed the line in a way she couldn't. I physically hurt her, harmed her. And that made everything else meaningless. No matter what she did, I would be the monster every time. Maybe not in her eyes though. Yes, she said it herself. I was the monster. But it seemed maybe she saw it was we, not just me. We were monsters, and that was what kept us together. We loved and hated and lived in the chaos we created.

"But I've always believed you were a great father."

She was wrong about that. I couldn't be a great father if I hurt our daughter's mother. I couldn't see it then, but I could no longer escape the truth.

"You always loved Abigail in a way you never loved me. That was another reason I stayed. I never believed our daughter was in danger. I knew you'd never hurt her. She needed her father. She deserved to have you around. I still know that. I don't believe you're a murderer, not in the way everyone thinks you are. I know you didn't suffocate our daughter. I know that because I did. I suffocated Abigail."

I turned on her, drew up my fist, ready to kill her, destroy her. *She killed my daughter!* She was no longer the wife I loved. Hated. *She's a monster! No mother. She's the person who killed Abigail!* I needed to get justice for Abigail. No one else would. No one would believe me, especially not anymore. I'd ruined any chance of that.

How could she? Madeline was Abigail's mother. She knew her in a way no one else did. She was there for all the moments I'd seen, for all the moments that would make it impossible for me to ever think about harming her. *How does a mother kill their daughter? Why? How? Why?*

It didn't matter. She was dead. And the knowledge ripped through my body like nothing else I'd ever felt, agony that would burn my veins forever. My wife killed my daughter. She needed to pay for that. Someone needed to pay for Abigail's death. If I was going to jail anyway, I might as well kill her there and then, do what the justice system never would. They could arrest me after. My whole family would be destroyed. It didn't matter.

The moonlight caught the angel on the gravestone, reminding me it was Abigail's resting place. *What if she's watching right now?* I felt her presence so strongly before. Probably just in my head. *But what if it wasn't?* She would be frightened to see me like that, horrified to watch me kill her mother. She wouldn't understand what was going on. She would see me as a monster, just like everyone else did. I couldn't kill Madeline there. I couldn't stain our daughter's gravestone with her mother's blood. The restraint made my wrists bleed. It was the worst kind of agony, frustration, rage.

I would kill her elsewhere, anywhere. I would make her pay. I would get revenge, then I would accept my punishment gladly. Because I finally would have gotten justice for Abigail. I would finally make up for not protecting her that night. *But would I? Would that make up for it? Could I make up for it?*

"Don't look at me like that," Madeline said as I settled down, lowered my fist. "I suffocated Abigail, but we both killed her. We're both guilty."

"You killed your own daughter," I hissed, revolted at the sight of her, disgusted. I thought I hated her before, but I hadn't even scratched the surface of how deeply I could feel toward her. "You murdered our daughter! I didn't. I would never hurt Abigail like that. I'd never hurt her at all. This is all on you!"

"You know that's not true." She glared at me, and some of that color returned to her cheeks.

Old sparks heated between us, aflame like never before. And I hated her for what she had done, despised her for what she was saying.

"You made my life so unbearable that I was forced to find an escape! You knew I was vulnerable. You knew I was struggling. I told you how much I was hurting. Yet you were always putting me down, tearing me down. You slept with Katarina even after I broke myself to give you a daughter. You set me up for all of this. You hurt me, destroyed me. So of course I would snap under the slightest pressure, let alone the pressure of having a child. You never cared about that.

"You wanted me to have a child because you wanted her. You never considered that after all you had done to me, I couldn't handle it, couldn't be a mother. You never helped me handle it. You turned me into a murderer. You set the stage for our daughter to be killed!"

"It wasn't all me!" I screamed. Her words ripped through me, and only proving her wrong would stop the bleeding. She had to take it back. "You killed Abigail! You made my life miserable! You trapped me just as I trapped you in a never-ending cycle of love and pain. Your words were daggers too. You never appreciated anything I did for you, until after I did something wrong—just in time to make me feel guilty. And, God, how I've always loved you, Maddy. Loved you so fucking much that it hurts.

"But I've hated you too. Hated you and loved you so fucking intensely that I couldn't leave you, even though I wanted to just as much as you wanted to leave me. So I slept with Katarina. I did awful things, and I am a monster. But so are you, Madeline. You killed our daughter! Nothing you say justifies that. You sound crazy trying to do so."

"I'm not trying to justify it." She touched my shoulder carefully.

I wanted to break her hand so she could never touch me again. Vile filth. Her touch made my skin crawl. It also calmed me.

"What I did was awful, unforgivable. I killed our daughter, our sweet, innocent baby."

Tears came, and I almost cried with her, almost forgot she was the killer.

"I am a monster. I have issues that need to be fixed but can't be. I always have. All I'm saying is I didn't do this alone. You said it wasn't all you, but that means it wasn't all me. I may be a monster, but so are you. We're both guilty. We'

Her words cut straight to my heart, incinerated the remaining pieces. I'd been burdened by intense guilt since Abigail died, guilt for not protecting her, for not knowing Maddy better, not being the kind of husband she could confide in. Not seeing it before it happened.

After being accused out loud, I couldn't quite accept it. I wanted everyone to assure me it wasn't my fault. I didn't suffocate Abigail, so I wasn't the one who killed her. I'd done all I could to protect her.

Except that isn't true, is it? I could've been a better father, a better husband. Maybe I could've saved Abigail if I were. I could've saved Abigail if I were a better father, a better husband—not perfect, it never required that. But halfway decent, and my baby wouldn't be dead.

Maddy knew that. She was making me face the truth, and I didn't want to. Yet it was so bright, so painfully stunning, that I couldn't look away, even as it melted my eyes.

"I love Abigail." Tears blurred my words, watered them down so even I could see their insignificance. My love for Abigail had nothing to do with the conversation we were having, but I desperately wanted it to. It had to mean something. The fact that I didn't actually kill her had to be worth something.

"I do too," Madeline said.

The crickets chirped an answer as I tried to think of the right things to say, to somehow make sense of the situation. But I'd never learned how to speak cricket, so I couldn't lean on them for help. I was on my own. Maybe I didn't have to be though.

"I love you too." I looked at Madeline. Somewhere beneath all the hate, a twisted kind of love remained. "I've always loved you, Maddy."

"And I love you, Brian."

That moment under the moon taught me I could love someone more than anything and still hurt them, even if I never wanted to. I could destroy someone most precious to me. I could. I had. I killed Abigail. I killed our daughter.

But I don't have to be alone in this, remember? The weight was far too heavy for any one person to take on. I certainly wasn't strong enough. I couldn't carry the burden on my own. Maddy couldn't carry it on her own. But we weren't on our own. We didn't have to be anyway. We could get through it together. That was the only way we might not shatter.

If only I could accept the truth—that I had played a part in it, even if I didn't want to. I'd done what I did, not realizing where my actions would lead. Yet my actions led to it. I couldn't take them back after realizing the consequences. I could only take responsibility so I wouldn't have to be alone, so maybe it would stop hurting so much.

"I loved Abigail," I repeated. "I still do. But I killed her. We killed her."

Madeline nodded, slowly, like her head was too heavy for her neck. She wasn't relieved by my revelation. I wasn't as hurt by it as I thought I would be. The words were awful to say out loud—the worst things I'd ever said, and I'd said a lot of awful things in my life. I didn't want to face that I killed my daughter, the one person I loved more than anything or anyone. I never thought I would have to, never thought I would hurt her.

But I knew, the day they said she was murdered, that this was my fault. It sounded like a horrible truth. It wasn't an enlightening moment. I was just finally sharing it with someone, the only person who could understand.

"We're monsters," she whispered.

"Yeah."

Silent tears fell from her eyes. She was just as hurt by the things she had done as I was. I was just as hurt by the things I had done as she was. I never thought I would hurt my wife. But I did, and in doing so, I killed my daughter. We'd made such a mess of everything. Our actions had horrific consequences.

I hated her, but I wrapped my arms around her, and she fell against me, against the wet grass. We held each other in front of the gravestone that screamed our sins loud enough for the whole world to hear. And I hated her, but not as much as I hated myself. I cried for us as I held her in the way I always should've—the only person who could ever understand—precious, treasured.

I wanted to take back all I'd done. I never thought the consequences would be so brutal. I never would've done it if I had known. Never ever. It wouldn't have been worth it if only I'd known where it would lead. I regretted it. I regretted everything so much it hurt. It hurt in the most unbearable way possible. It hurt so much that I would give up everything and anything just to go back and do better. All I wanted was that chance to do better.

I had that chance so many times though. *I just never thought...* I never thought. That was the problem. We never thought—until it was too late.

"I'm sorry." I kissed the top of her head. Tears mingled, sealing us together once more, as if we could ever really be separated. "If I could take it all back, I would. I'd be a better husband, a better father. I'm so sorry."

"I know you would," she replied, her words watered down with tears and overwhelming regret. "I wish we could start over because I know you'd do better. I'd do better. I'd be a perfect wife, a perfect mother. We'd be better. We'd be perfect. And this time, maybe Abigail would survive. We'd love each other. Never kill our daughter.

We'd be the perfect family, the absolute best. We'd have all we ever wanted, the things that really matter anyway. We'd... we'd be so happy." She cried, her chest heaving as she tried to grab enough breath to say what needed to be said. "I'm sorry."

We held each other tighter as we embraced our sins in a final bid for forgiveness. We knew what we had done, how awful it all was. And if we could go back, we would do better. We would change everything.

But it was too late. We had committed too many unforgivable acts. The damage was irreparable. It was too difficult to even know who had done what anymore. The only truth was that we had destroyed everything together. We'd created a nightmare we couldn't wake up from. So, we held each other and cried under the protection of the night.

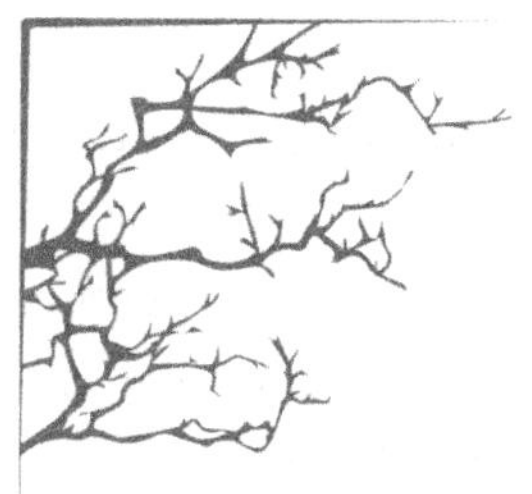

Chapter 29

By the time the sun blessed us with safe shades of pink, blue, and purple, I thought I had a good idea of what Abigail's favorite colors would be. The sunrise would be painted across her bedroom walls, watching her as she slept, wrapped up in the gentle warmth of the sun. Maybe she'd always felt safer during the day, under the protection of the sun. Maybe that was why she slept in the daylight, because she loved the moon and the stars, but somehow she knew what would happen to her one awful night.

I wanted to stay there with Madeline forever—or at least until the earth took us, brought us to our daughter, allowing us another chance to be the parents we knew we could be, the family we always wanted to be.

But Maddy wouldn't stay. I would never ask her to. She had to get on with her life, be free in a way I had never let her be, do better next time. She had a chance to survive everything, and I wanted her to.

I couldn't go with her, though I wanted to. I wanted to be in our house again, our bed. I wanted to go home again, but I would trap her again. Or I wouldn't, but I would be taken away, and that might be harder for her.

After fleeing the police, I would be found guilty if I didn't keep running—unless she confessed to them too. Then, she would go to prison instead, and that would be even harder for me.

Once upon a time, we had been soul mates. We still were. That wouldn't change. But once upon a time, we'd had a real chance to be together. We'd had a beautiful life ahead of us. We'd had so many dreams, and we could've made them all come true, but we chose a different path. We chose the worst path. And we no longer had room to walk beside each other.

In our own fucked-up way, we'd tried so hard to stay together. We'd destroyed ourselves just so we could knit our pieces into one bloody canvas. But we could no longer ignore the fairy tale we had ruined beyond repair. There were no words left except the one we never wanted to say.

So, we kissed. Her lips were cold against mine, a bit damp. Still, it was amazing to have her body pressed against mine. For the first time, I appreciated it as much as I should've all along. I held her as tightly as I could without hurting her. I kissed her as long as I could before the sun nudged us, warned us we should leave.

"I love you," I said as our lips hovered inches apart.

"I love you too," she whispered.

And the hate was still there, but we had already talked about that. No need to bring it up again. We knew. Love was more important anyway. We left it at that, at the love. I kissed her forehead, and we didn't say that one word we never could say to each other.

I heard it in each crunch of the leaves, though, when I walked back to my car. Goodbye. Goodbye. Goodbye. *For now.* Until we all met again and got back to raising our family. We would do better then. We had learned how too late. We wouldn't be too late sometime, somewhere. That wouldn't be the end of us. For people like us, there was no end.

It was a jolt to see my car again. I'd walked so slowly, hoping to get lost and never find my way out of the woods. I almost turned back to stay at Abigail's grave for as long as I could. Until they finally found me.

But I had one thing left to do, and I knew it even then, so I got back in the car. I turned the heat up as high as it could go and started the long drive back to the hotel. I thought about Maddy and Abigail every mile.

How could I have done such awful things to them? How could I kill my own daughter? All I wanted to do was take it back, be with them. It was so cliché but so crazy how people didn't realize the importance of the time they had with someone until that person was gone.

I was surprised when I reached the hotel and police cars hadn't surrounded it. The tall black building was a fortress for the wealthy. Yet I never quite trusted it to hide my secrets, not when they were so loud, so big, so brilliantly bright that it shocked me the whole world couldn't see.

What if the police are in unmarked cars? I listened to my favorite song one last time, enjoyed my last moments of freedom. It didn't feel so much like freedom. I didn't care about it so much anymore anyway. I turned the car off the moment the song ended and opened the door. No one rushed out to apprehend me, so I stepped out, shut the door, and took another step. Each one was slow, deliberate.

I tried to avoid looking suspicious, but I was waiting for someone to grab me, and I wanted to be steady. Maybe they would realize they didn't have to knock me to the ground. If I was knocked to the ground, I would shatter into millions of pieces, all over the parking lot. I wanted to go my way. I didn't want to break completely, not yet, not in some gross, impersonal parking lot.

It took me longer than necessary to reach the door, but I did reach it. I paused before opening it. They were probably waiting inside. Dark windows kept me from seeing in. They would jump out and tackle me. And maybe I would turn to dust before I reached the ground. That wouldn't be so bad.

I opened the door and walked inside. Unfortunately, no one waited there to tackle me. The young man at the front desk looked up, recognized me, smiled, and went back to work.

Cool teal walls welcomed me into my room. My bed with its white satin sheets was made up. Fluffy pillows and a fluffier comforter tempted me. I could get some sleep before I did what came next. No one was after me. I had time. I was exhausted. *I deserved it?*

Yet that exhaustion drove me. If I left my sleep-deprived state, I might not be able to do it. And I wanted to. I needed to do it. I didn't want to change my mind. The consequences would be too great, and I'd learned I couldn't get out of paying them. I ignored the bed, undressed, threw my muddy, stick-strewn clothes on the white carpet.

The bathroom resisted my grime a little more. Everything there was black and gold, aside from the white towels. I washed my filth off in a shower that was heaven, worth every cent I paid for the room. But I wasn't clean. I could never convince myself I was. My soul was stained, permanently.

I brushed my hair, put on a nice black button-down shirt and black dress pants. I looked at myself in the mirror and saw the face of a monster. I was a monster. We were monsters. I dug through the backpack that looked so out of place there and sat on the bed. Let myself linger on the edge of temptation as I looked at Madeline and Abigail. The photo was small in my hands. I had to be careful not to crumple it, drop it.

When my hands were big and strong and the people around me were tiny and fragile, it was far too easy to crumple my whole family, whether or not I meant to. My grip could get a little too tight. I could convince myself I could close my fists just a little bit more. Then it would all be ruined, and I would have to live with the knowledge that I had ruined it, the one thing most precious to me.

Madeline was lovely in the photo, so pretty. Her hair played in the wind, danced around her face. Abigail sat on her lap, smiling. My arm was around Madeline's shoulder as I looked down at our baby—the best thing we ever did, the worst thing we would ever do. A tree stretched out above us. Ducks floated on the pond behind us.

An elderly couple had offered to take the picture, and after giving them a quick lesson on how to use our phone, it had come out perfectly.

If I went to sleep right then, I might be able to go back to that. Maybe I would dream about them. I'd been plagued with nightmares since Abigail died, but every now and then, I dreamed about them. Maybe if I held the photo as I slept, I would go back to that place where everything was still perfect.

And maybe when I woke up, I would change my mind. I wouldn't have the nerve to do what needed to be done. Maybe I would crumple the picture in my sleep. Maybe I wouldn't go back to them at all. I laid the photo on the nightstand, put on my wedding ring and my shoes, then went downstairs for an extremely early dinner.

Two men sat in the corner talking over drinks. A young couple toward the center of the room tried to keep their children under control. The children looked to be about seven, maybe a bit younger. The couple held each other's hands as they watched their children, a shaky facade. They were tense, waiting for one of the children to ruin the meal.

I sat in the corner opposite the other men. It was barely lunch, so I wasn't surprised it was much less busy than it had been the evening before. I was grateful for it. Candles still flickered on the tables, next to the vases with single red roses. The shades kept it dark, the lighting kept low. If I ignored the clock, I could pretend it was night.

I had to pretend a lot of things just to keep going, still living in a world that didn't exist anymore. I grasped onto the sweet illusions, desperate. But time was running out.

I slid into the black leather booth. It was comfortable for restaurant seating, and the day was all about comfort. I looked over the fancy black script that made up the lunch menu.

A young woman with red hair that fell all the way down to her ass, hugged by that black dress of hers, walked over to take my order. Those green eyes were dangerous, especially with that red lipstick. But she wasn't what I wanted. So, for once, I wasn't tempted. I ordered a bottle of champagne.

"Is there any way I can look at the dinner menu?" I threw a few hundreds on the table.

"Of course." She stared at the money as if it might disappear if she looked away. "I'll get that for you right away."

I smiled to hide the monster I was. *Could she see beyond the mask?* Since I could see who I really was, it baffled me that everyone else didn't. Maybe everyone did, but the need to be polite kept them from mentioning it.

I glanced over the dinner menu as she poured me a glass of champagne. I could've saved her the trouble and drank right out of the bottle. I intended to drink the whole bottle. But I hadn't lost my grip on reality that much, and I didn't want to add any undue attention to myself.

"Can I get you an appetizer while you look over the dinner menu?"

There were some great options. All of it sounded delicious, and I was in the mood to eat as much as I could—the best that I could get. "Can I get a plate of buffalo wings?"

She blinked, looking taken back. I wanted to start my meal off with comfort food. Nothing sounded better to me than wings right then.

"Buffalo wings?" she repeated.

"Yes, please."

She nodded and didn't even write it down before turning to leave. I turned to the menu at hand.

I never realized how much effort I could put into things when I had nothing else to do. I was always distracted by something, looking forward to that next thing, hoping that once I reached that thing, I would be happy. And I would celebrate, for a moment, before going after that next goal, that next moment when I could breathe.

That list was dwindling. I wanted to do a few things, and those things had to be done perfectly. Under such pressure, I expected it would take me forever to decide. But I made up my mind quicker than normal, without so many other things to cloud it. Everything was much clearer.

I ordered lobster, steak, salmon, fettuccini alfredo, scallops, and shrimp scampi. The waitress looked reluctant as she wrote each new thing, like she impatiently wondered when I would stop. It made the hundreds of dollars on the table diminish, but I would add more to it—after I watched her fume. The day could use a touch of entertainment. *Everyone likes to watch people suffer a little bit, don't they?* That was why people laughed when something small went wrong, why a story never quite captured someone's attention without conflict.

The spicy smell of wings rewarded me. Since I had nothing better to do, I picked up on the scent the second they entered the dining room. I watched as the waitress brought them closer. My mouth watered with sweet anticipation.

I barely acknowledged the waitress as I dug into the perfect mix of barbeque and spicy cooled down with creamy ranch. I still tried not to draw attention to myself, but not many people were there anyway, so I dug into the wings without caring about the mess. It was heaven.

I didn't plan to eat them all so I could save room for the other courses. I didn't quite eat them all. Two were left by the time I pushed the plate away. I would have to slow down if I wanted to make it through everything. I wasn't in a rush.

I went slower through the other plates. They added up, brought out one after the other. I picked through them for over two hours.

Diners there before me left, replaced by new people, then they left too.

Once I was satisfied with dinner, I spent another two hours eating a sundae, cheesecake, creme brûlée, lava cake, and tiramisu. I couldn't eat all of it, of course. But I enjoyed bits of everything and stuffed myself more than I ever had before. I savored each bite, each taste, and ordered another bottle of champagne. I watched more people come and go.

The waitress looked equal parts stressed and awed when she brought out the last dessert. She knew there wasn't a whole lot left to tip her with if anything, and she looked shocked at how much one person had ordered, how much one person could eat. But I hadn't eaten since the day before, and I wanted to enjoy as much as I could.

So, I took my time. And when the waitress finally brought the bill, with a look of horror on her face, I pulled out my wallet again and gave her the kind of tip she had expected when I first asked for the dinner menu. Then, I bought a bottle of wine and a box of chocolate to bring up to my room.

I tossed the chocolates on the little black table for two in the corner of the room. I was far too full to eat anything right then. I bought them just in case. I had no idea how long my task would take.

I pulled off my shoes, threw them in the corner, then went into the bathroom, where a massive whirlpool tub sat. It could fit multiple people. I wished Maddy were there with me. It would be too difficult for her, too much, especially after all I'd put her through. I couldn't put her through that. But, God, would it all be better if Maddy were there.

I closed my eyes and went back to that night at the graveyard a lifetime ago. I opened my eyes, turned the water to the hottest setting, and dumped some bubbles under it. I turned on the TV, an actual TV in the bathroom, and found a relaxing music station. Enough to calm me.

It urged me to turn off the water, crawl into bed, think about my plan after a good night's rest. I wasn't in my right mind. *Had I ever been?*

I left the bathroom and those seductive voices, poured myself a glass of red wine, and sat on the bed as I held Maddy and Abigail. How I wished I could hold Maddy and Abigail one last time. I would hold them and never let go.

But I had been gifted that time with Madeline already, that last time. And I'd known it even at the time. That was why I had cherished every second, even as our limbs had cooled on the ground. I'd memorized every part of her, knowing it would be the last time I could do so. I was greedy. I still wanted more, though I was thankful for that last moment. It would get me through my last moment. I only wished I had that time with Abigail.

Though I did, didn't I? I'd held her that night—her last night. I had rocked her to sleep, fed her, cuddled her. I hadn't known it would be the last time I would hold her, though, or I would've held her longer, protected her.

I had learned I could never know how life would change, what consequences would follow my actions. Even after I was sure what the damage would be, sure I was willing to pay it, I had no idea. I had lived my whole life with the illusion that I could see what was coming, but I had been blind, careless. How I wished I could go back more than anything, cherish those last moments with my daughter, love my wife, be a good husband and father.

There was no turning back though. Not anymore. I had made too many careless missteps, caused too much destruction. I could only move forward.

I carried the photo with me into the bathroom and set it by the tub, within arm's reach but far enough away so it wouldn't fall into the water. I brought Abigail's bear into the bathroom as well, the bottle of wine, the glass, the chocolates. I turned off the water. That music was haunting, creepy. It scared me as it reminded me too much of what had to be done.

I switched the TV to a comedy channel, to lighten the mood, so I could get through what had to be done. Then I would turn it back so everything could be perfect. I was still stuffed. I was also nervous, so I ate a chocolate as I watched the steaming water waiting for me.

It was far too hot to get in. I should just drain it. I walked back into the bedroom to get away from the doubt. I grabbed a few stray pieces of paper. The only person I wanted to talk to was Madeline, but we'd said all we needed to say to each other. Anything else would just hurt more. I wrote a quick letter to Mom because it would hurt her most. In her letter, I referenced my father because she would want me to. She deserved the world, but that was all I could give her, so it had to be perfect.

I also wrote a letter to Allison. I wanted her to know that I loved her, that I wasn't angry at her for choosing Madeline's side. I was thankful she was so supportive of my wife, a great aunt to my daughter. She had always been my best friend even when I forgot. I wanted her to remember that.

I thought about leaving a note for my brother, but I had nothing to say to him that I hadn't already said. Maybe my actions would inspire him to follow in my footsteps, at least take responsibility for his. I didn't hold out hope for that though. I'd given up on him. I wouldn't be like him. I would prove that tonight.

I finished my glass of wine then laid my letters out on the bed in a poetic manner. I dug through my backpack and brought out the dagger I'd sawed my ankle bracelet off with, then took the glass and the dagger into the bathroom.

The water was still hot but bearable maybe. It was difficult to really tell until I was in it, so I slowly stripped off my clothes. I wished I could call Madeline. *Would that be wrong? Would she answer? Would she want to talk to me?* I needed to hear her voice one last time. I already heard her voice one last time though. That had to be enough. I was grateful for even that. I almost didn't get that chance.

I held Abigail's bear to my chest. The baby smell hadn't worn off quite yet. I looked down at the photograph of Maddy and Abigail and me. Happy. That was how I wanted to remember us, the place I needed to get back to, desperately.

I hated myself because we would still be there if I hadn't ruined us. If we hadn't ruined us. But I didn't need to hate myself. Not anymore. Holding onto that hate made no sense anymore. So, I let it go. I laid the photo a little closer to the bathtub, the teddy bear a little closer to the water, ate another chocolate, though my stomach begged me not to, drank some more wine.

The water scorched my feet, my ankles, my shins. It was a shock through the exhaustion. *Am I really doing this?* I couldn't—wouldn't. There had to be another way.

Laughter drew my attention to the television. Some stupid joke about life with kids, and I laughed, though I shouldn't be able to. It calmed me. This wasn't so serious. Life was never so serious. It was mine to do with as I pleased, and that was the only thing I wanted to do. It was the only thing I could do.

I eased my body into the water and embraced the burn. It thawed me after that time spent in the graveyard. I felt comfort in the pain, a distraction from the harder stuff, from the guilt. The heat burned it all away, leaving just me, my true intentions, my life, and the good memories. Love. With so little time, it wasn't selfish to think of them.

The ring of the tub felt cool as I rested my head against it. My back arched then lowered slowly. My muscles protested then loosed. The heat was good for all the stress. I closed my eyes as I let go of everything. Guilt. Fear. Pain. Leaving only happiness, only hope.

That drove me forward, the hope that my choice would lead to something better. I didn't know what would come next. I was walking into it blindly. I couldn't even imagine what to expect, and that horrified me. *But it has to be better than this, right?* Reaching for something new was my only option. I could not live like this. I wouldn't.

I dried my hands on the towel and picked up the dagger. I could sink under the water once it was done, get my hair wet. I could have another piece of chocolate. I could have all the wine I wanted.

Maybe I could see my daughter.

I lowered the tip to my skin. Not as bad as I thought it would be, just a needle prick—probably because I hadn't really dug it in as deeply as I would need to be effective. A drop of blood pooled around the tip of the blade.

If only that was it. If only I could push a button, offer up a small amount of pain, a tiny blood price. If only someone were with me, someone who would do it for me—or just someone who could comfort me, tell me it would all be okay. It would be okay. I could do it slowly, savor the pain, the blood. Maybe it wouldn't be such a shock that way. Maybe I could get through it better, easier, get used to the pain like people got used to a minor burn after a while.

I laughed, not at the TV. That was not the kind of pain someone could get used to. It would take strength, nerve, and a lot of force to get through something like that. Determination to actually do it. I would have to be careful to do it right. There were no second chances. If I did it too slowly, I would never do it.

This is so fucked up! I couldn't do it. Wouldn't. Couldn't.

I reapplied the pressure methodically. It was the last thing I had to do ever, the only thing. It had to be perfect. I couldn't take it back once I started. Ruining it would ruin everything. I had to keep my shit together just a little longer.

My lungs ran out of breath. No matter how quickly I breathed, I couldn't drag enough air in. My hands shook. I didn't let go of the knife, afraid I would never pick it up again if I did. The room grew blurry. My mission blurred. I grabbed the teddy bear with my free hand and brought it to my face, breathing in that baby scent.

If I went through with it, maybe I could see her again, hold her again. Maybe I could raise her among those stars. I could take care of her so she wouldn't have to be alone, wondering where her daddy was. Maybe, eventually, Madeline would forgive me, and eventually, in her own time, she would join us and complete our family. We could be the family we were always meant to be.

And if I don't? Madeline and Abigail stared up at me. If I didn't do it, I would have to face a world without them—live in it knowing I deserved to die, deserved to be punished. I would be arrested, thrown in prison, caged. My life would be no life. And even if I didn't get to see Abigail again, at least I would have a better chance than if I lived.

My hands steadied as my breathing evened out. Abigail. I was doing this for her—maybe even for Maddy someday, if she could ever forgive me, if I could ever forgive her.

Imagine the pain. Imagine the reunion. Hope for something better. Hope.

I moaned as the knife dug into my skin as deep as I was physically able to plunge it without being completely crippled by the pain. My survival instinct tried to talk me out of it. I dug the knife in deeper, traced it down my arm. *My veins?* Hopefully. Everything was madness. I couldn't stop.

If I stopped, I would have to go to the hospital or keep dealing with the never-ending pain for all eternity—or until someone found me. I would suffer more than I was currently suffering. Prolonged torture.

But fuck! That pain. The knife ripped through my veins as blood gushed out into the water, into the bubbles. It was all I could do to keep going. Every part of me screamed to stop. So, I dug into the pain, into my skin. I let the adrenaline drive me, the only part I could afford to listen to.

I intended to go straight to the crook of my elbow, but the room started spinning. I plowed through, screamed, and hoped the walls were soundproof as I let out that last, triumphant roar. Not close to the crook of my elbow. *Close enough?*

I longed to put the knife down. Blood poured out of my arm. Pain shook my whole body. It had to be enough. I couldn't do it anymore—couldn't do it again. *How the fuck does anyone do this? Go through with this?* I would bleed out. *What if I didn't?*

I cut my right arm first because I knew if I cut the left first, I wouldn't have the strength to cut through the right one. I had no more strength left, no grit, no determination. It hurt like a bitch—worse than anything else. I didn't have the strength to cut through the left one.

I roared like the monster I was as I held my arm to my chest. But it wasn't worse than everything else. It didn't hurt worse than losing my wife. It didn't hurt worse than losing my daughter. Didn't hurt nearly as much as realizing I was partly to blame for her death. *Does it hurt worse than living without them? Living with guilt? Living with regret?*

I didn't know—did not know. I could not do this. There was nothing left. *Madeline and Abigail.* I looked at their picture like they could save me. They could save me. I could hold it, hold her, if I just finished. But I didn't have much time. Time was running out too fast.

My right hand was my strongest, but with so much pain, so much blood loss, it would still be useless soon. *What would happen if I didn't cut my left arm too?* If I left those veins untouched, I might not see Abigail again—or at least not anytime soon. I would never be left near anything that could be seen as a weapon again.

I picked up the knife that had fallen on the rim of the tub. There was nothing left. Nothing but a sliver of hope, which meant it was more than anything. It was everything. I sobbed as I held the knife over my arm. My hand shook. There would be no care in this. I had to get it done—no time for perfection. It was nothing like how I thought it would be.

I didn't want to do it. I did not want to do this.

In between heartbeats, I found a split second of courage. I used that tiny moment to bear down into my skin. If I stopped, I would never continue. I screamed so loud surely the whole building could hear me as I leaned into myself with everything I had. I gave myself everything I had. My veins ripped open, adding to the bloody mess. But I was doing it.

Agony punished me for my sins. They were so great, I deserved it. Though I didn't think about that at the time. I didn't think about anything but pain. Subconsciously, I think that helped me get through it. It was my redemption, and I embraced it, screamed into it.

The knife clattered onto the floor as I sobbed. The line stopped just a bit above where I had ripped through my right arm. I gave my all, but it wasn't quite as deep as the first one, not quite as bloody.

Enough? I thought it was—hoped it was. I was already woozy, dizzy. Pain colored everything in shocking shades. Energy left me as I remembered I was supposed to change the channel. I was supposed to die to the sound of music.

I couldn't get up though. I had no strength left. There would be no chocolate reward, no wine. I couldn't look at my tattered arms as I held the photo in one hand, Abigail's bear in the other.

Maddy smiled. Abigail looked at me like I was her hero. I sobbed. My arms burned but not as badly as my heart. I turned the whirlpool on with my toes and sank deeper in the water as I looked at them, loving them with everything I ever was.

"Oh, Abigail," I cried. "Madeline. I love you both. I know I didn't always show it, but I always loved you both."

I clutched them for comfort as I lay dying. I never thought I would be so aware of dying, but I felt myself racing toward death each second. I saw the sand running out. And I didn't know if I was happy about that or regretful. I was scared. Frightened. Horrified. Terrified.

It was a new level of fear that words could never fully explain. I'd done things I was uncomfortable with before, but I'd never faced such a daunting unknown—where I had no frame of reference, only hope and pain.

Why did I fuck things up so much? Why did it have to come to this? This was never my intention. Why did I rip everything apart?

As it became more difficult to hold up my arms, the photo and bear dipped dangerously close to the water. They would be ruined, disintegrated, the last things I had. I wouldn't need them soon.

"We love you."

I turned to the whisper. Madeline stood there, just out of reach, Abigail in her arms. They both wore white dresses, white flowers in their hair. I no longer needed hope. I cried because it was incredible to see them again, to be together again. It was worth every bit of agony.

My arms dragged me back down as I tried to sit up to get to them. The pain of any pressure on them was unbearable, but I needed to hold them. *What if I scare Abigail with all this blood?*

"It's okay." Madeline stepped closer. She touched my cheek. "It'll all be okay."

The photo slipped into the water. The bear floated on top, fur stained with blood. We would buy Abigail a new bear though. We would take a new photo. Everything else could be fixed, solved, as long as we were together. That was what we should've realized all along.

"I love you," I said as the world faded into shadows.

Madeline and Abigail grew brighter in a glow of gold-and-white light. Everything—we became everything, the only things left. The only thing that had ever mattered.

"I love you too," Madeline whispered.

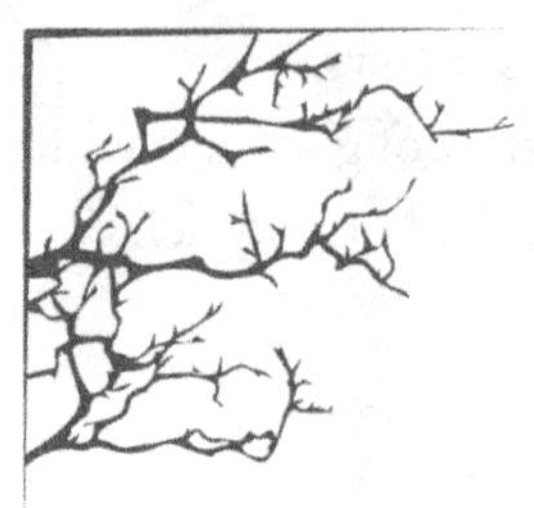

Part IV
Odette

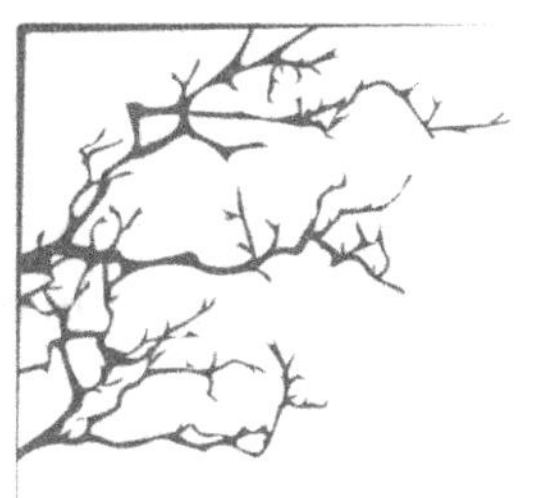

Chapter 30

The new house wasn't half as bad as I thought it would be, one of those where vines crawled up the dark brick to a pointed roof. A little guesthouse stood off to the side. The whole property was sheltered by tall trees with colorful gardens underneath. I guessed Madeline tended to it herself, or at least she had. I was sure that had changed recently. It was smaller than their old house. I walked up a cute stone path with my suitcase and two silver bags.

Cute. That was how it could best be described. I could give her a much better life if only she moved back home. Cute would shift to luxurious. She was silly to reject the offer. I had room enough in my mansion for multiple families, and I would be a lot more comfortable if she were in my sight, especially after Amelia, after Abigail.

At least she'd given me the address, soon after she moved, if I was told the truth. As if Madeline could ever be trusted to tell the truth. Aiden was only a couple of weeks old. I even knew about him before he was born. She told me when she was about six months pregnant.

We were making progress, and I hoped that meant something—beyond just her and me. I hoped that meant she would be a better mother. Maybe it would be easier for her if she had a son instead of a daughter.

I heard his cries even before she opened the door. Sweet boy, I wished he would just stop, be a good boy, especially for the first few years. I was certain that if he could make it through the first year or two, his future would be bright. *Doesn't he know he's in danger?* If I could convince him to settle down, I could give him the best chance to survive. *Is having my daughter as a mother a risk?* Of course. Obviously. She was a bigger threat than those strangers on the street people always warned about. She killed my grandchildren. We both knew it.

And the future didn't look good for the new one. Madeline tried to put her greasy hair up, but it fell in front of her sickly pale face. Bits of spit stuck to the tangled strands. She wore baggy sweatpants, an even baggier shirt. Aiden's face was red from screaming. He wailed as she rocked him. The bags under her eyes were darker than I'd ever seen them. She looked like she was two seconds from crying, like maybe she had been crying but had stopped to open the door. She knew exactly what I would be thinking.

"Hey, Mom."

She never called me Mom unless she wanted something. I'd been Odette to her since she was a teenager. But she didn't need to speak in such a way to get me to help her. I saw her desperation, and I wanted to lock her away and do everything, take control so maybe things wouldn't go so terribly wrong.

I took Aiden out of her arms. She handed him over without hesitation. Her body sank as I held her son. She breathed a sigh of relief. She looked drained, ruined. She had been for years, honestly.

"Where's that guy you've been seeing?" I stepped inside.

She closed the door behind me.

"Declan?"

Something was off about him. I'd sensed it when he first came to visit. But someone needed to know the truth, and Madeline needed someone. He was someone. He wasn't even the worst someone she could have, not by far.

She'd told me a while back that he had a daughter. He didn't have full custody, though, only visitation every other weekend. The girl was old enough to be out of danger. I hoped.

"I stopped seeing him when I moved to Oregon," she said.

My hope dwindled.

"I wanted to cut ties with that life. I would've moved farther away, but I wanted to be close to Allison and Cassandra. They're the best aunts, and I wouldn't have made it through this without their support."

I believed her. She was already barely making it through. I wished she had moved closer. To me. To them. To anyone.

"Isn't Declan Aiden's father?"

I hoped. Maybe Declan would come and take Aiden, or at least have visitation. Maybe that would be enough to save him. Maybe I could convince him to fight for more. Madeline could be trusted for weekend visits. I suspected that would suit her perfectly.

"No." Her footsteps were slow and heavy before she crashed onto the couch. The room was lovely, in lilac, gold, and white. The open concept allowed lots of light. She didn't belong in it. "Brian is Aidan's father. I got pregnant right before Abigail..." She buried her face in a gold pillow and cried.

I pretended I couldn't hear her tears as I brought Aiden into the kitchen, away from the stress of his mother. He was my main focus. I couldn't do much about Madeline, and I couldn't bring myself to care about her sadness. I couldn't be bothered to care about her at all anymore. She deserved all the unhappiness the world could give her.

Aiden calmed a little just by being taken away from the stress. His diaper was dry, so I opened the fridge. No bottles were prepared. No bother. I reached into one of the silver bags. It had toys, a little mobile, clothes, a blanket. It also held a few essentials, like specialty, overpriced formula. The formula was touted as the best. It mixed up just like the others though.

I rocked Aiden as I prepared it. As Madeline cried on the couch. *What should I do? About Aiden? About Madeline?* I wouldn't let her kill another of my grandchildren. I wanted the chance to do better. I'd messed up with her, but I'd learned my lesson. Yet she kept murdering my shots at redemption. *What kind of monster had I given birth to? Does it mean I was a monster to create such a child?*

I stripped Aiden of his blanket, stained with milk and some other crusty substance I didn't want to know the origin of, and took out the fluffy light-blue blanket I'd bought him. He cried and cried but started to settle once he was swaddled properly. I eased the bottle into his mouth and hoped he would accept it. I needed him to give us some quiet so I could figure out this mess. And he did, sweet boy. He drank, allowing room for Madeline's cries.

She stopped crying after a few minutes too. She kept the light low, but it was still bright enough to see the sink full of dishes—baby bottles mostly and coffee cups, far too many coffee cups. The floor hadn't been swept. Garbage piled up in the trash can and all over the counters.

Madeline had struggled with each pregnancy she'd ever been cursed with, but she'd always had someone there with her before to attempt to pick up all her pieces. She'd barely managed even then.

"How long will you be here?" She poked her head up over the couch. There was hope in that, hope that I would stay for a while, and resentment because she never liked having me around, which was fine. I didn't particularly like being around her either.

"A couple of weeks," I said. "You should come back with me. You know I have plenty of room. You and Aiden are more than welcome. I could help you with him. We can get you back on your feet."

"I am on my feet." The fire in her voice might've convinced me if she didn't look like such a mess. "I'm in the process of opening my own yoga studio here while I'm working at the one down the street. I've made friends. I have this house. I have plenty of money to maintain my lifestyle."

"People can struggle in other ways," I reminded her. As if she didn't already know.

"I'm not struggling," she insisted. "I'm just tired. Having a newborn isn't easy for anyone, especially a single mom."

"No." I sat down with Aiden in the cozy white rocking chair, a horrible color for a child. Madeline never used her head. "It isn't. But not everyone has a history of murdering their children."

"What are you saying?" Madeline's voice rose as she sat up straighter, death in her eyes. "Are you really accusing me of killing my babies?"

"Settle down," I nearly whispered, stern though. "Aiden's starting to fall asleep, and you don't want to wake him, do you?"

She looked at her son. *With…fear?* His eyelids flickered as he ate. He hadn't been crying because he was hungry. He was just exhausted, always kept on edge by his mother's emotions.

"And I'm not accusing you of anything. I'm stating a fact. We both know what you did. We need to make sure it doesn't happen again."

"I didn't kill them." The fire was gone from her words.

If only I could convince her to admit to it, face it, maybe we could get somewhere. She could go to therapy or something. She could let me take Aiden. I could raise him and love him like she never could. Nothing would change, though, if she didn't realize there was a problem. Aiden would end up just like his older sisters. She had to know by then that there was a problem.

Aiden looked so peaceful, though, his little hands curled up. His tiny eyelashes flickered slowly. He was a gift, truly, a third chance we didn't deserve—fourth for me. He was so warm, so tiny. We couldn't fight, not there, not in front of him. He deserved all the peace the world could offer him. No matter what happened, from that moment forward, his life wouldn't be easy.

I rocked him and remembered Abigail, how precious she was with the spirit of a dragon. I'd only seen her during that one visit. One visit had been enough to fall in love. Though if I were honest, my heart ached more over Amelia, the little angel I'd helped raise. She was supposed to be my redemption. Instead, she'd been another way I'd failed. I couldn't get out of the trap I'd created with Madeline. I couldn't make up for all the wrong I'd done in raising her.

She was miserable. She made everyone around her miserable. And perhaps I could've saved her if I'd loved her the way a mother should. I couldn't, especially not now. I couldn't bring myself to care for a murderer, even if that might stop the murders. My ties to her died the day she killed my first granddaughter. She knew it too.

She watched me, watched Aiden with jealousy as I dealt with him in the tender way I could never quite tap into when she was little, when everything was overwhelmingly dark for me. I kissed the top of his forehead as the bottle slipped from his hands.

Would Madeline have the ability to love a baby that didn't set off her depression? Would she love her grandchildren like I loved mine when she got older? Would any of her children make it long enough to have children?

I got up without saying a word and carried Aiden into his nursery. She'd done a wonderful job with it. Clouds floated across light-blue walls. A skylight allowed the night in. The silver crib was perfection in a way the rest of the house wasn't. I laid him in it.

"Sleep well, darling," I whispered.

I spent a moment longer just watching him, trying to figure out the right thing to do. I always tried to do the right thing, even when it turned out I didn't. We all did I supposed. *Does Madeline really think she's doing the right thing through all this?*

Madeline still lay on the couch when I came back out. Good. She would do less damage that way. If only she would stay asleep forever. It was already past seven. I was starving. Surely she was too. She never took care of herself when she got that way.

The cabinets were pretty much bare. The refrigerator was in an even more desperate state. But thankfully, she still had some food, probably left over from when she wasn't so down—a box of pasta, a jar of spaghetti sauce, frozen vegetables, some grated parmesan cheese. I found a couple of pans and got to work.

Though I'd hired a personal chef for myself, I'd always enjoyed cooking for my family. We hadn't had a personal chef when I still had a family. And though it was foreign to me at first, I got back into it quickly. It was like a long-lost friend, whom at first I was awkward around but then remembered all the times we'd shared and reconnected naturally. It was a good distraction from the mess of emotions I couldn't afford to feel right then.

Madeline and I didn't talk. She didn't even look over. So, as dinner cooked, I opened my purse and took out the vial of arsenic. I'd used it before, back when less testing was done in autopsies, but boy, how he'd suffered.

Madeline would suffer. Aiden would be safe. I held it. Then I returned it to my purse. I despised her, but I couldn't see her like that. She was still my daughter, and I felt something for her.

I set the table with the only clean dishes left. I took out the bottle of wine I brought with me as a gift to her. It was transported from Italy, one of the best there was. My mouth watered at the glimmery red, a perfect gem. I didn't need it, not then. Maybe later. I would need my mind fully clear, so I didn't do something I would later regret.

She probably hadn't drunk enough water lately anyway. All my friends talked about how important drinking water was. So, I got us both a glass of water and served dinner. Madeline still didn't look up.

"It's dinnertime." I sat at the table.

She didn't stir. *Is she sleeping?* She could probably use the sleep.

"Madeline, you can rest after, but you need to eat."

Still nothing. *Did she do the world a favor and die right there on the couch?*

"Madeline!"

"I'm coming," she grumbled as she got up. Right back to how she was with Amelia. "I guess I am hungry."

She didn't so much sit at the table as she did ooze onto her seat. She'd gotten pretty bad when Amelia was born, but never like that. It was as if each child had taken more out of her, brought her into an irreparable state of ruin. She should've known better. She was my only child for a reason. I knew I wasn't up to the task, so I never had more. She shouldn't have had more. She should've been extra safe, never been so selfish.

Finally, some light came into her eyes as she took the first bite. I followed suit, but the pasta didn't quite sit right with me. My stomach was twisted, starving.

"You need to let me take Aiden home with me," I said.

She paused then continued eating.

"It's up to you if you want to come back. I don't care either way. But Aiden is going back home with me. Period."

She chased her food with half a cup of water. Then Madeline looked straight at me. "No," she said, as if she had a say in the matter. "Aiden is my son. He's staying with me."

Fury rose to the tip of my tongue. She didn't want her son. She just wanted to hold him over me. Selfish. She was always so selfish.

"You killed your daughters," I said. "I will not allow you to kill him too."

"I didn't kill them!" She slammed her fists on the table. Another sign of how unfit she was to be a mother. She didn't think about the child sleeping in the nursery. She didn't think about anyone but herself. "And you have a lot of nerve thinking you could be a better mother than me. Look what you turned me into!"

"I've gotten better," I pointed out. "Why can't you see that? The wave of darkness that haunted me after your birth is long gone, while yours is still settling in. Maybe someday you'll get better too. For now, you need to think about what's best for your son."

"I am! I'm what's best for my son."

"You'll murder him! You think I was so awful, but at least I didn't kill you."

"I wish you had," she said, her eyes steady on mine.

It was the first glimpse of rationality I'd seen from her in a long time. She wasn't driven by emotion. It was a simple fact.

"You made my life miserable. You destroyed me when I was so young, so vulnerable. It would've been better if you'd killed me. Better than living with a mother who didn't want me, didn't love me, who gave me the world yet still broke my heart. You were cruel to me."

Tears slipped out at that, though her face remained calm. I saw all the pain I'd caused her, how much I'd hurt her. It was my deepest regret. I did love her, in my own way, even if I couldn't find the right way to show it, the right words to say. I did love my daughter.

"I'm so sorry." For the first time, I found words for my biggest failure. "I should've been a better mother. And I am truly sorry."

Madeline blinked. She was shocked I didn't fight her. I had no reason to fight anymore. I wouldn't win. No one would. We all lost in the messed-up game we'd created but no one wanted to play.

She looked down at her plate and began eating again. I watched her in silence. We would never get through it because real life wasn't like that. I could feel as sorry as possible, true regret, but there would be no redeeming moment. Some things could never be taken back. She finished eating then stood in a daze. She left the plate there and walked away.

I closed my eyes. I knew what I had to do, but it would be the most awful thing I'd done yet, the most painful. It would be so painful I wasn't sure I could live through it. I wasn't sure I could do it. But I had to, so I would.

I went back to my purse and pulled on a pair of white satin gloves. I'd brought one other thing with me. It was Madeline's from long ago. She didn't even like it, but her father had. So she'd joined him. That was how much she loved him—a stark contrast to how much she'd never loved me.

Madeline's gun was cold in my hands. Her prints were already all over it. She had already been diagnosed with postpartum depression. She'd lost her husband and two children. No one would be shocked.

My heart didn't race as I walked to her bedroom. I had no fear that I wouldn't get away with it. I would. I had enough money to ensure that, plus the best lawyer. I only felt deep sorrow, agonizing regret.

She lay in her bed, lights off. She slept in the same shadows she killed her children in. I never thought I would be the kind of mother to kill her own child. No matter how I suffered, I never even considered it. But it wasn't the result of my depression. It was my desperation to save my grandson, to stop the trail of damage. It had to be done.

And yet... I reconsidered it, as I stood in the doorway. She looked so peaceful. Maybe I could just take Aiden right then and run home. Maybe she would be so relieved she wouldn't fight for him. Maybe she would though. Maybe her hatred for me would drive her to reclaim him, kill him, just because she could—because she was stubborn like that.

Even if she didn't, she would have another child. There always would be more children until she got caught, and time was running out.

The new carpet caught the sound of my footsteps and didn't let them go. It was a sign I was doing the right thing. It was everything. I mapped out the perfect angle then waited by the side of her bed for her to wake up. I couldn't do it if she turned her head, looked at me. She didn't.

"Forgive me," I whispered.

In the next breath, a bullet barreled straight through her head. She didn't scream. Thankfully, there was no time for that. No pain. She was gone in an instant—one loud noise, one second.

I stood there and looked down at my daughter, my greatest failure. I leaned down and kissed her head, not a moment too soon, because then blood poured out of it. "I love you," I whispered.

I'd already perfected my act, but the tears were real as I called the police.

Acknowledgements

First and foremost, all my gratitude and love goes to my husband, Tyler, who believed in me in the most incredible way, supporting me through every step of this journey: reading my work so many times over the years, getting me through college, encouraging me to write when I wanted to give up, discussing my work with me like my characters and worlds were real, and being my muse. This success is ours to share, and though he has since left this world for another one, the echoes of our love will follow me through every story.

I'm also so grateful for my sister Sarah, who has also eagerly read through each manuscript, nagging me to write more and hyping me up, even when I was still just starting out and didn't really know what I was doing. Knowing I'll always have a reader helps me be a better writer.

And to my sister Helen, who has inspired me in so many ways: I love you so much, no matter what. We'll always be writing our stories together, wherever life takes us.

Thank you to my parents, who have always insisted I follow my dreams, pushing me when needed and helping me rebuild so I could be where I am now.

Thank you to my best friend, Shaye, who has always been there for me. Your love and support have helped get me through everything.

Evan, who has helped me with all the nervousness of getting my first book published, thank you for listening to my panic repeatedly. Thanks to Donna and Trisha for always being encouraging and inspiring my creativity, grandmothers who always showed me love.

My editors, Angie and Amanda, were amazing to work with. My agent, Erica, was a vital step to realizing this dream, the first professional to believe in me. And thank you, Lynn, for taking a chance on a new author and providing the resources needed to make this book a reality.

There are so many others who have helped me throughout this venture. I'm so lucky for every family member and friend who has given me all their love and support. I appreciate every single one of you. Thank you.

About the Author

Natasha Simmons was born and raised in New Hampshire with her two sisters, whom she adores (most of the time). After enjoying a wonderful life with her husband, Tyler, she took the plunge and moved to Phoenix, trading in mountains and blizzards for ceaseless heat and desert sand.

These extremes suit her writing style well, as she likes to explore how the most chaotic events can shape characters, thinking deeply about the impact unexpected explosions can have on our lives. She enjoys writing about the morally gray areas that can be found in any person, in any story.

When Natasha is not writing or reading, she loves traveling, exploring new places, and spending time with her pets.

Read more at https://natashawriting.wordpress.com/.

About the Publisher

Dear Reader,

We hope you enjoyed this book. Please consider leaving a review on your favorite book site.

Visit https://RedAdeptPublishing.com to see our entire catalogue.

Don't forget to subscribe to our monthly newsletter to be notified of future releases and special sales.

CPSIA information can be obtained
at www.ICGtesting.com
Printed in the USA
BVHW041317310522
638499BV00007B/151

9 781948 051934